C.J. BOX
STORM WATCH

HEAD
of ZEUS

An Aries Book

First published in the UK in 2023 by Head of Zeus
This paperback edition first published in 2023 by Head of Zeus,
part of Bloomsbury Publishing Plc

Published by arrangement with G. P. Putnam's Sons, an imprint of
Penguin Publishing, a division of Penguin Random House LLC

Book design by Katy Riegel

9 7 5 3 1 2 4 6 8

A catalogue record for this book is available from the British Library.

ISBN (PB): 9781803283999
ISBN (E): 9781803283951

Printed and bound by CPI Group (UK) Ltd, Croydon, CR0 4YY

MIX
Paper | Supporting
responsible forestry
FSC® C171272

Head of Zeus
5–8 Hardwick Street
London EC1R 4RG

WWW.HEADOFZEUS.COM

Crime   OCT 23

ONE
REN

The library is always open at
renfrewshirelibraries.co.uk

Visit now for library news and
information,
 to **renew and
reserve** online, and
to download
free eBooks.

Phone: 0300 300 1188
Email: libraries@renfrewshire.gov.uk

STORM WATCH

In memory of Toby, our first horse,

and for Laurie, always

Wednesday, March 29

Doctor, doctor, I'm going mad
This is the worst day I've ever had
I can't remember ever feeling this bad
Under fifteen feet of pure white snow

—NICK CAVE AND THE BAD SEEDS,

"Fifteen Feet of Pure White Snow"

CHAPTER ONE

LATE MARCH IN the foothills of the Bighorn Mountains wasn't yet spring by any means, but there were a growing number of days when spring could be dreamt of.

For Wyoming game warden Joe Pickett, this wasn't one of those days. This was a day that would both start and end with blood on the snow.

At midday, he climbed out of the cab of his replacement green Ford F-150 pickup and pulled on coveralls and a winter parka over his red uniform shirt and wool Filson vest. He'd had the foresight to layer up that morning before leaving his house, and he was also wearing merino wool long johns and thick wool socks. He buckled knee-high nylon gaiters over his lace-up Sorel pack boots, then placed his hat crown-down on the dashboard and replaced it with a thick wool rancher's cap with the earflaps down.

On the open tailgate of his vehicle, he filled a light

daypack with gear: water, snowshoes, camera, necropsy kit, extra ammo, ticket book, binoculars, sat phone. While he did so, he shot a glance at the storm cloud shrouding the mountains and muting the sun. A significant "weather event" had been predicted by the National Weather Service for southern Montana and northern Wyoming. Joe didn't question it. It *felt* like snow was coming, maybe a lot of it, and he needed to find an injured elk cow and put her out of her misery before the storm roared down from those mountains and engulfed him.

The interstate highway had closed an hour before, as it so often did because of heavy snowfall, high winds, and vehicle crashes. The winter, thus far, had been brutal. Storm after storm since Christmas, and very little melting. The snowpack in the mountains was one hundred and fifty percent of normal, which was a relief after several years of drought, but getting through it had been cruel. During his lifetime in the Rocky Mountains, Joe had rarely been bothered by long winters, but this year was different. He was getting tired of constant snow making everything he did more difficult.

He was located fifteen miles from Saddlestring on a paved but potholed county road that ran east to west, parallel to the foothills. It was on that road that morning that a young male driver en route to a Montana ski resort for spring break had taken a shortcut from the interstate highway. He'd apparently been looking at the navigation app on his smartphone screen when he plowed into a small herd of elk crossing the road.

The driver's car was totaled and had been towed away. The

driver himself was under observation at the Twelve Sleep County Medical Center for an injury sustained when he bounced his forehead off his steering wheel upon impact. Two elk had been killed in the collision. A third elk, the cow Joe was after, had been seen by a state trooper who had responded to the accident call. On three good legs, the elk had somehow leapt over the fence beside the road and had last been seen limping away toward the mountains.

Joe had heard about the incident over his radio while he'd been in another corner of his district looking for another problematic animal: a one-hundred-and-twenty-pound wolf that had gutted two yearling calves within sight of a rancher's home. By the time Joe had responded, the wolf had gone and the rancher was furious.

Joe had photographed the dead yearlings as well as the massive wolf tracks in the snow, and he'd opened up an official incident report that would be forwarded to his agency, who would forward it to the U.S. Fish and Wildlife Service. The two yearlings had had their throats ripped out and they'd been disemboweled. The scene looked as if someone had dropped balloons filled with blood from a great height and they'd exploded on the hard-packed snow.

It was the fifth verified wolf kill of the current winter, and that was becoming a problem. Especially since there weren't *supposed* to be wolves in the area at all.

Joe knew that assumption was incorrect. He'd personally seen a big black alpha male and other wolves in the pack during the last decade. He usually saw them at times of danger or stress—so out of concern for the pack, he rarely mentioned seeing anything at all.

The rancher had crossed his arms across his chest and blamed Joe personally for the the wolves, since Joe worked for the state, which is to say the government, and it was the government that had introduced wolves back into Wyoming in the first place.

Joe had stood there and let the rancher blow off steam before speaking.

"You know that was the feds, right?" he'd asked the rancher. "Not us?"

"You're all the same," the rancher had said. "Bureaucrats paid with my tax money trying to ruin my way of life."

"Actually, we aren't. The feds reintroduced the wolves into Yellowstone Park. We're doing our best to deal with them now as they spread across the state."

The rancher pointed at his dead cattle. "And I must say you're doing a hell of a job." Then he chinned toward Joe and asked, "New truck?"

"Yup. My last one was totaled. I'm getting used to this one."

"You have to get used to a lot of new vehicles, don't you?" the rancher asked.

"Yup."

"Maybe if you wouldn't crash so many, it wouldn't be such a big deal."

"Maybe," Joe conceded. "You sound like my supervisor."

"I'm glad the state is rich enough to keep you in new trucks."

Joe was grateful when dispatch in Cheyenne called him

away from the ranch to try to put the wounded elk out of her misery.

IT HADN'T BEEN difficult to find the crash site. There were tiny squares of broken glass glittering like sequins on the roadbed, as well as a few bloody hunks of elk hair. The two dead elk had been rolled off the pavement into the ditch and large ravens had already found them. Joe wondered if any enterprising locals would take advantage of a new law allowing the harvesting of road-killed meat, but no one had arrived as of yet. Maybe the coming snow and the winter storm watch had discouraged them.

Joe dug his cell phone out of his breast pocket and speed-dialed a man named Clay Hutmacher, who was the foreman of the Double Diamond Ranch on the other side of the barbed-wire fence. The "Double D," as it was called by locals, stretched out over twenty thousand acres and was adjoined by Bureau of Land Management and U.S. Forest Service holdings. Hutmacher was a longtime local who guided fly-fishers in the summer and hunters in the fall. His twenty-five-year-old son, Clay Junior, had recently been spending time with Joe and Marybeth's twenty-four-year-old daughter, Sheridan. Too *much* time, in Joe's opinion, even though Clay Junior had done nothing untoward. Yet.

Joe looked at every potential suitor of his three daughters with suspicion. It was up to the interloper to prove himself trustworthy. Several had not. One had physically abused his middle girl, April, and had turned out to be rotten to the core, confirming Joe's first impressions.

"It's Joe Pickett," he said when Clay Senior answered his phone. "I'm out on the state highway just west of the ranch. I wanted to get permission to cross over onto your property and kill a wounded cow elk that got hit by a car."

Technically, all of the wild animals in the state were the property of the people of Wyoming. Nevertheless, it was required to obtain permission from local landowners to access private property.

"I heard about that," Hutmacher said. "Some guy from Florida looking at his phone. I hope he's in critical condition."

"Nope," Joe said. "I think he's okay."

"We ought to charge him for killing two elk and injuring a third one," Hutmacher said. Joe knew the man to be quite protective of the herd on the ranch, especially cows who could birth more animals to hunt.

"Hey, you know who I'm looking at right now?" Hutmacher asked.

"No."

"Sheridan Pickett. Clay Junior invited her out. She's a sweetie, Joe. You should be proud of her."

"We are," Joe said. But he was tight-lipped.

"Do you need to say anything to her while I've got you on the line?" Hutmacher asked.

"Not really."

"They're watching falconry videos on YouTube," the foreman said. "It's kind of cute," he sighed.

Joe rolled his eyes and was glad Hutmacher couldn't see him do it.

Sheridan worked for Nate Romanowski's bird abatement company and was close to becoming a master falconer herself. Joe knew Clay Junior had done a stint in the army and had been scheduled to graduate from an Ivy League university before the pandemic delayed all of his plans. As far as Joe knew, Clay Junior was unemployed at the moment, but he certainly had promise: local man, strong values, high school athlete, University of Wyoming graduate, military background. Still, Joe wanted to see more than promise before he softened his stance. Marybeth knew more about Clay Junior than Joe did, which was typical.

"Anyway, about that cow elk . . ." Joe said.

"Yeah, sorry. Go get her, Joe. Don't let her suffer even a minute longer than necessary."

"Thanks."

"Good luck. Shoot straight. And let me know if you can't find her."

"Will do."

"And for God's sake, Joe, get off the mountain before this storm hits."

"COME ON, GIRL," he said to Daisy, his yellow Labrador. Daisy bounded out of the cab and immediately walked away stiff-legged to check out the smells that came from the dead elk in the ditch. As she did so, she started to tremble with excitement. Daisy was getting old and chunky, but she delighted in being given a job to do—and when she got one, she became like a puppy again.

"You need to help me find one of those," he said to her. She was eager to go.

Joe slid a scoped Browning .338 Winchester Magnum rifle out from its case behind the seat of his pickup and checked the loads. It was a powerful cartridge, and he chose it because of its profound stopping power on big game. The trooper had said the wounded elk was a large female, which meant she could weigh four hundred to six hundred pounds. The last thing he wanted to do—ever—was to compound an already bad situation by further wounding an injured animal that might then elude him and die alone in misery. Or be finished off by a wolf.

He braced the rifle against a barbed-wire fence and then climbed over strand by strand. He didn't bolt a cartridge into the receiver until he was on the other side. Then he slung the weapon over his shoulder and started out.

Daisy's snout was already glued to the elk tracks in the loose snow.

MARCH WAS ALSO a very tough time to travel on foot in the mountains. Although some of the snow was frozen and crusted over well enough to walk on top of—especially if one possessed big Labrador paws—there were also huge soft piles of it stacked into the arroyos and draws that he'd have to cross. That would require wading up to his thighs or putting on snowshoes. In the deep winter or higher up in elevation, it was much easier to progress because Joe could use his snowmobile.

Unfortunately in March and April, there were too many bare, wide patches of dirt and sagebrush where the snow had melted away or been blown clear by wind, so a snowmobile wouldn't work. Over these patches on foot, Joe could make decent progress. But it was hard work and he wasn't as young as he used to be. After thirty minutes of hiking over, through, and around snowdrifts, Joe could feel all of his fifty-one years.

As he trailed Daisy through snow and bare ground, Joe continuously glanced up to monitor the progress of the storm coming down from the mountain. Snow was falling hard up there in billowing waves and the front was moving fast. He gave himself an hour before it hit. He hoped the wounded elk was near.

JOE LOST THE elk tracks in the hard dirt as he climbed and summited a bald, boulder-strewn knob, but Daisy had not. He followed her and her metronome-like tail over the top, where he stopped to catch his breath. Daisy looked back at him over her shoulder with disappointment.

"Give me a second," he said to her. She looked away as if embarrassed by his lack of stamina.

The swale sloped below him was choked with snow for what looked like half a mile, and it stretched all the way until it reached a thick grove of aspen on the opposite hillside. The elk couldn't be seen. He hoped the creature had stopped to rest in the grove, so he could locate her.

"Okay," he said.

Daisy's tail started up again and she turned toward the swale. He followed and was pleased that the condition of the snow was similar to concrete. Only the top few inches of it were loose and grainy.

The tracks of the elk were obvious again on the surface, and he read them as he walked. A single print on the left, followed by two others behind it. Meaning the elk had lost the use of its right front leg. When he noticed small droplets of blood in the snow, he guessed that the creature's leg had sustained a compound fracture where the broken bone had pierced through the skin.

Although he knew of instances where a three-legged elk had survived the winter and even produced a calf in the spring, it was rare. An injury like that usually resulted in a long and painful death.

Joe paused again and dug out his binoculars. He could clearly see the snowy hillside up beyond the aspen grove all the way to the top of the next rise. Up through the middle of the snow a deep track was cut in. It looked more substantial than the elk track they were following, as if the animal had plowed through the snow instead of high-stepping across it. Why had it changed its gait? Maybe the snow conditions were different going up the next rise? Maybe the pitch and angle of the light simply made it look bigger?

He sighed loudly. Tracking the elk would take more time than he had. Trekking into the teeth of a coming storm was the kind of thing he'd promised Marybeth he would no longer do.

Still . . .

If the wounded elk had bedded down on the other side of the hill just out of his sight he could be on her in five or ten minutes. That would be cutting it close. Beyond the next hill, the rise of the Bighorns truly began, and with it came heavy, dark timber that climbed all the way up the mountainside. If the elk went into the timber she'd be lost to him. Despite that, the thought of leaving her behind while he hightailed it back to his vehicle filled him with shame.

Joe glanced at his watch, then at the advancing storm.

If he picked up his pace, he figured, it should work out. And if the elk wasn't visible on the far side of the slope, well, he'd know that he'd done his best—even though it would leave him with a bad taste in his mouth.

As HE APPROACHED the aspen grove, Joe noticed for the first time an old two-track road leading to it from the north across the face of the rise. The two straight lines of white through the sagebrush gave it away. The old road appeared to end at the aspen grove itself. What surprised him was the fresh tire tracks on the road. He wondered who had been driving on the ranch that morning, and why Clay Hutmacher hadn't mentioned it to him.

Then he saw the glint of chrome within the trees. A vehicle was parked there, its engine shut off. He got closer and could see the outline of a late-model SUV. Tree branches blocked his view from seeing inside.

Joe knew from experience that things could sometimes get dicey out in the field if you walked up on a stranger unannounced. Especially when it was likely they were both armed.

He called out, "Hello? It's the game warden."

The result was one he hadn't expected. The cow elk he'd been tracking huffed from where she lay in the snow about twenty yards to his right. He'd nearly walked right past her. His shout had obviously roused her. Daisy tore after the elk out of instinct, but stopped when Joe shouted at her to come back.

The elk lurched to her three good legs and turned away from him, showing Joe her tawny-colored rump. Before he could get the rifle off his shoulder, she was running away, her front right leg flopping around. Blood from the compound fracture sprayed across the surface of the snow.

He thumbed the safety off and raised the rifle. Although she was moving away quickly, she was still so close that all he could see through the scope was dark brown hide.

Joe paused for a few seconds to let the injured elk get farther away, then trained the crosshairs at a spot just behind her
front shoulder.

BOOM.

The cow took two more steps and lurched forward to a
stop. Joe knew she was fatally hit. As he worked the bolt to
load a fresh cartridge, the elk shuddered and pitched to the
side. A last puff of condensation rose from her black snout.
He was glad it had been a clean kill.

Although Joe knew he'd done the humane thing, he also
felt instant regret. Normally, in better conditions, he'd set
about field dressing and quartering the elk so he could deliver
the meat to the senior center in town or the school district
for lunches. He hated the idea of leaving it. But there was no
way he could pack the meat out on foot—probably four trips
back and forth—given the fury of the oncoming weather.
More than a hundred pounds of elk meat would be left to
scavengers.

Daisy loped over to the carcass to confirm that the animal
she'd been tracking was dead. Then she held her head high
and her tail went stiff to salute herself for a job well done.

HIS EARS STILL ringing from the shot, Joe turned back to the
SUV in the trees. He wondered if the people inside had witnessed this and been frightened. The echo of the gunshot
washed over him.

He slung his weapon back on his shoulder and approached the vehicle. It was a maroon Toyota Land Cruiser and it appeared that no one was inside. Either that, or they'd dropped out of sight for cover because of the shot.

It wasn't a ranch vehicle, for sure. Ranchers and their hands drove pickups, usually battered ones. The SUV looked clean and new.

He neared it and squinted, looking for movement. There was none.

Joe circled the vehicle and peered inside. It was clean and neat and the only things out of place were a crumpled fast-food bag on the rear floor mat and an open topographical map on the front passenger seat. The Wyoming license plates revealed that the SUV was from county five: Albany County in southern Wyoming. A sticker in the left front corner of the windshield allowed access to a designated parking lot on the University of Wyoming campus in Laramie. UW was the only four-year college in the state.

He found the driver's-side door unlocked, then swung it open and leaned in. It was warmer inside, which meant the motor and heater had been turned off recently, probably within the hour. An electronic key fob poked out from a cup holder in the console.

While he didn't retrieve the topo map or even move it, he could see that someone had marked it with four X's with a black marker. The map itself encompassed the area where they were, so it suggested that the driver hadn't gotten lost, which had been Joe's first thought.

"No," Joe said to Daisy. "This guy didn't get lost. He planned to come here."

He stepped back and carefully surveyed the aspen grove. Deep boot tracks led from the SUV through the trees and in the direction of the next summit. Those were the tracks Joe had noticed as he walked down over the swale of snow. And because they were human and not elk tracks, they'd looked different.

Joe scratched Daisy's head and asked aloud, "What is going on? Who would drive out to the middle of nowhere and walk away into a snowstorm?"

He said, "Let's go find this fool before he dies out here."

Daisy looked back and sighed.

LARGE FLAKES WERE falling as Joe climbed up the hill toward the top. He stayed in the tracks made by the missing driver so he wouldn't have to cut his own. He called out several times, hoping for a response. Nothing.

As he climbed, he noticed that his ears were still ringing. He wondered if the loud concussion of the .338 Win Mag had damaged his eardrums. Then, as he neared the top of the rise, the whining got louder. It was high-pitched, and it wasn't coming from his ears. It sounded like the pitch you'd hear near high-capacity power lines.

Only, there weren't any power lines within view. And as far as Joe knew, there weren't any structures on this part of the Double D except crude open shelters for cattle to get out of the wind.

He was out of breath again when he got to the top. Daisy stayed on his heels. She was tired, too.

As he reached the summit, it was as if he'd walked into the beating heart of a snow cloud. Snowflakes swirled in a maelstrom of white. They clung to his parka and stuck to his face. The deep tracks he was following were already starting to fill up. He was eye level with the storm as it swept down the mountain.

The whine was louder now that he was on top, and he peered through the falling snow at the valley floor a half mile away. There was something down there—some kind of small metal building. It was the source of the sound. And it had been the destination of the SUV driver, because his tracks led right to it.

Joe raised his binoculars from around his neck and blew snowflakes from the lenses. He found the structure and sharpened the focus of his glasses.

The metal structure was about nine feet high and approximately thirty feet long. There was a closed door on the side of it, but no windows. On the back of the box, three long horizontal steel louvers opened out like rectangular wings. The openings below the metal awnings stretched across the width of the building. The whining sound was coming from inside.

Then he noticed a dark form protruding from the opening of the middle louver, like a black tongue hanging out of a grimacing mouth.

"Found him," Joe said aloud. "What are you doing down there?"

He tightened his elbows to his side so he could steady the binoculars.

The dark tongue turned out to be the lower half of a man. His top half was wedged into the opening of the louver.

The body was still.

He said, "Oh no."

CHAPTER TWO

FOR JOE, THE dilemma was obvious, and one he'd faced before. The longer he stayed out in the field with the storm blowing in, the more risk he took of being stranded, injured, or freezing to death. But he had no choice. This was his district and there was a human being down there. The conditions were such that he couldn't request backup or simply wait out the storm. And he couldn't just walk away.

First, he checked his cell phone. He wasn't surprised to find he had no service.

Joe shrugged his pack off and unlashed the top to locate his agency-issued satellite phone. He powered it on and watched the screen as it searched for a satellite. He hoped that the storm wouldn't impede the signal. The sat phone took a few seconds longer than usual to lock in, but it went live.

He shouldered the pack and rifle back on and started down the hill toward the metal building, staying in the tracks cut by the man he assumed was now stuck into it.

Clay Hutmacher picked up and said, "Double Diamond Ranch, Clay here."

"It's me again," Joe said. Hutmacher obviously hadn't recognized the number of the sat phone.

"Did you find that elk?" Hutmacher asked.

"Yup. But that's not what I'm calling about. Are any of your guys out here on this part of the ranch? Or was anybody over here this morning?"

Hutmacher said, "Joe, we haven't been over there since we moved the cattle off the mountain this fall. No, my guys are all at home watching the storm roll in. Just like I am. Just like *you* should be."

"Gotcha," Joe said. "I hear you. So here's the thing: I just located a Toyota Land Cruiser with Albany County plates parked in an aspen grove. It drove in today. I'm guessing the owner is a student at UW, but I don't know because he wandered off."

"*What?* Somebody trespassed on our place and went for a hike? If there wasn't a blizzard going on I'd send the cavalry out right now to run him off. A student, you say?"

"That's what it looks like, Clay. He hiked down to a metal building on the valley floor and it looks to me like he's stuck in it. I'm on my way to check it out."

"Stuck in it how?"

"His legs are hanging out of the opening on the front."

"This is crazy, Joe. I have no idea who this trespasser could be. But it pisses me off. No one except you has permission to be on that part of the Double D. I'm going to press charges, for sure. You tell him that, okay? Will you tell him?"

"Yup," Joe said, thinking, *If he's still alive, that is.*

Before Joe could go on, Hutmacher's voice rose and he said, "Hold it. Hold it. Are you saying you're out there now? You're not calling from your truck?"

"Nope. I'm using a satellite phone. That's why you didn't recognize the number."

"You're out there now in this storm? On foot?"

"Yup."

"Joe, I don't care about this idiot. He's not that important. It's a whiteout right now at our place, and it's headed your way. I can't even see the barn outside the window. You need to get off the mountain as soon as you can."

"That's my plan," Joe said. "But first I need to check it out. If he's hurt, I can't leave him out here. I'm not sure he could find his vehicle again in this snow."

"Fuck him, is what I say," Hutmacher said. "He got himself into this and he can get himself out."

"That's not how I operate, Clay," Joe said. Then: "What is this building for, anyway? I've never seen anything quite like it. And it's *loud*."

The foreman paused for a long time and Joe wondered if the call had dropped. Then Hutmacher said, "I'm not supposed to talk about that thing, Joe. It's a secret. I promised Thompson I'd keep it on the down-low."

Joe had once ticketed the man for fishing without a state conservation stamp. Thompson had cursed at him and promised to have his job. Nothing ever came of it.

"Clay, you've got to help me out here," Joe said. "If this turns out like I think it will, you won't be able to keep this metal building a secret."

"I ain't supposed to talk about it, Joe. You're putting me in a tough spot."

"I don't mean to, but I've got a job to do."

Hutmacher moaned. Joe waited.

"Joe, let me talk to the boss. I need his okay. Then I'll call you right back. Will you be at this number?"

"Yup."

"He doesn't like you, Joe."

"I know that. I don't much like him, either."

Clay was unusually tight-lipped about his employer, which Joe interpreted as a means to keep his job. Being foreman of a ranch as large as the Double D meant good free housing, vehicles on demand, and a decent income and benefits.

Hutmacher said, "Get off the mountain, Joe. Promise me you'll do that."

"As soon as I can, I will."

"Good. I'll call Thompson now."

"Clay?" Joe asked.

"Yes?"

"Don't mention this to Sheridan, please. She'll get worried and call Marybeth, and then they'll both be mad at me."

"Your secret is safe with me," Hutmacher said. "Just get off the mountain."

"Gotcha."

Joe dropped the sat phone into the breast pocket of his parka and continued down the slope toward the mystery building. Daisy was on his heel.

THREE MINUTES LATER, Joe felt the sat phone vibrate. He pulled off his right glove and retrieved the device.

"Clay?"

"Yeah. The boss says do what you have to do, but don't tell anyone what we built down there."

Joe shook his head. "That depends, Clay. If the guy is just looking inside the building and I walk him out, well, maybe not much has to be said about it. But if he's injured or dead, there'll have to be a lot of people involved."

Hutmacher said, "Shit, Joe, I get it. Sometimes these multimillionaires think they can just order everybody around. They get used to it. I'm just the middleman here."

"What is it about this building that's so top secret, anyway?"

"I told you I can't talk about it, Joe."

After a beat, Hutmacher sighed and said, "I guess you'll find out soon enough."

"I'll let you know how it goes," Joe said, punching off.

To avert later consequences, Joe called Marybeth next. She was the director of the Twelve Sleep County Library and she answered on the third ring.

"Where are you?" she asked. "It's a blizzard here and we're about to shoo all our patrons out and close for the day."

He explained the situation and told her he'd hike back to his truck and get off the mountain as soon as he could.

"Is it bad up there? I can't even see the mountains."

"It's not so bad," Joe said. It was kind of a lie.

"Wherever you're at, put a pin in it," she said.

"A pin?"

"You know: mark your location."

"So you can find the frozen body later?" he asked.

"Stop that. So you won't get lost on your way back."

"Did you know Sheridan is with Clay Junior? They seem to be spending a lot of time together."

"Joe, she doesn't tell me where she's going from day to day anymore. But I like Clay Junior. She could do a lot worse, you know. You need to give him a chance."

"I suppose."

"But first you need to put a pin in your location. Then come home. I hope this guy you found is okay."

"Yeah, me too."

————

THE WHINE FROM the building became almost unbearable as Joe got nearer to it. He was grateful that the flaps on his cap were pulled down and partially muted the sound.

He noted that the snow around the facility had been trampled fairly heavily. There were lots of prints. It looked like several people had been down there, or the man stuck in the building had circled it many times. Looking for what?

Then he saw two sets of tracks leading away from the building up the next slope to the east. He lost sight of them in the thick falling snow as they continued to the top. Those tracks, like the tracks around the building, were filling rapidly with fresh snowfall. They'd be gone within the hour.

Joe neared the figure and shouted to him. "Hey—are you all right?"

The man was slight and small, with his hands pinned to his sides and his back to the outside. His heavy boots grazed the concrete pad the building sat on. The man gave no indication that he'd heard Joe's shout.

Through the openings on the front of the building, Joe could see the source of the sound. Fast-spinning fans were sucking the outside air and forcing it inside the structure. He couldn't see what was behind them, but he now could make an educated guess: powerful computers.

Several years before, Joe had received a crash course on how terrorists planned to take down a U.S. Defense Department supercomputer by disabling the cooling system. Without constant cooling, computers overheated and went down.

But what these computers were doing in the middle of nowhere, on a ranch without an obvious source of power, was a question he couldn't answer. Nor the reason why a man was stuck inside. And then he saw it.

It looked like the man had hurled himself headfirst into the industrial fans. Or, he'd been forced into it. The top of the man's head had been sheared off. Blood, hair, and brain matter had spattered the inside walls of the opening.

Joe turned and gagged and closed his eyes for a moment. He sucked in cold air and snowflakes. They had a metallic taste.

He drew out his cell phone and took photo after photo of the victim, the building, the tracks in the snow around it, and the two sets of tracks going up the mountain. He did it almost frantically, because he knew the entire scene except for the body would be obscured within the hour. His photos would be the only documentation of the crime scene before it was completely covered with white.

After scores of camera shots, Joe approached the body. He didn't want to move it, but it disturbed him how close the blades of the fan were to the man's open skull. If the victim sagged forward, more of his head would be sliced off.

Joe eased the body back an inch or two, but didn't pull it out. He removed his right glove and shoved his hand in between the man's torso and pinned right arm. The inside of the armpit was still warm, meaning the death had occurred very recently.

"Poor guy," Joe said to himself and Daisy. "I can't carry him out. We're going to have to leave him like this."

He recalled what Marybeth had told him. Joe pulled his handheld GPS device from his bag, called up the topographical screen of his location, and put a pin on it. That way, investigators could find the body as quickly as possible once the storm eased up.

Then he patted down the body. The man wore an ill-fitting parka, insulated ski pants, and Sorel pack boots that were so new the leather was still shiny. Joe located the man's wallet in his front pants pocket and slid the wallet into his pack for later. He didn't want to spend one minute longer than necessary at the crime scene.

As he turned, he heard a sharp *ting* sound. At first, he thought it came from inside the building itself. The second *ting* came from right over his head, above the first opening to the fan.

Joe certainly knew what a bullet hole looked like, and now there were two of them pierced through the metal skin of the building. He shouted for Daisy and they ducked around the corner of the building and hunkered down.

He stripped off his pack again and worked the bolt of his rifle. His heart whumped in his chest and his mouth had gone dry. Whoever had shot at him had done it from the east—the same direction where the two sets of tracks had gone up the mountain. Now that he was on the other side of the building out of sight of them, he allowed himself to feel scared. The shiver that coursed down his spine had nothing to do with the cold.

Joe crab-walked down the length of the building and cautiously peered around the corner and up to the top of the eastern slope. He could barely make out the outline of the hilltop. He glimpsed the boxy front of an off-road vehicle of some kind back away from the top of the ridge. It was too far away and too obscured to see a license plate or even the color or make of the vehicle.

He gave it another three minutes to see if they'd come back. They didn't, and he rose to full height and peered through the scope and swept it across the top of the ridge. His hands trembled and he breathed in deeply to try and calm down.

There was nothing on the ridge. The shooter was gone.

As HE CLIMBED back in his tracks toward his truck, Joe was grateful for the fury of the snow. If he hadn't been able to see the top of the hill where the shooter had been, that meant the shooter hadn't been able to see him.

He paused and looked back in the valley. It was snowing so hard now that the computer facility—whatever it was—was lost in a world of white.

IT TOOK TWENTY-FIVE minutes to reach his pickup. There was six inches of wet snow on it. Daisy bounded into the cab and Joe placed his rifle muzzle-down in the passenger seat. He wanted it handy, just in case, for the drive back.

As the motor revved and the heater kicked up, he slowly removed each layer of clothing until he was down to his uniform shirt and Wranglers. Daisy was already curled up and sleeping on the seat. She, like him, was exhausted. His parka and coveralls were pooled on the passenger-seat floor and they steamed as it warmed up inside.

Joe wiped melted snow off the screen of his phone and called dispatch in Cheyenne. The wallet of the victim was open on his lap.

"The name on his Wyoming driver's license is Zhang Wei," Joe said. He spelled it out.

"It says he lives at 712 Garfield Street. There's also a laminated UW faculty card."

"He's a professor at the university?" the dispatcher asked.

"Yup," Joe said. Then: "*Was* a professor."

CHAPTER THREE

J OE DROVE BACK toward Saddlestring with his heater on high and his wipers on full as the wind picked up and the blizzard increased in intensity. It was a whiteout. His pickup was the only vehicle on the state highway and he couldn't see the pavement. Trees closed in on both sides and he stayed on the road by driving into the space between the trees and hoping for the best. He tracked each delineator post as he passed it to make sure he was going in the right direction.

This was a big one, he thought. It was impossible to see how much snow had fallen because the wind was moving it around in buffeting waves.

He used his Bluetooth feature to call Twelve Sleep County sheriff Scott Tibbs. Tibbs had declared April 15 to be his last day in office and he already had short-timer's syndrome. As Joe had expected, Tibbs was at his home instead of the county offices.

He answered by asking, "What now, Joe?"

"There's a dead body stuck in an industrial fan on the Double D Ranch," Joe said. "The victim is named Zhang Wei and he was a professor at UW."

Tibbs moaned as if in pain. Joe almost felt guilty for handing the case over during Tibbs's last weeks on the job. Almost.

"What exactly do you expect me to do about it?" Tibbs asked. "Have you looked outside?"

"I *am* outside," Joe said.

"Did you bring the body down with you?"

"No."

"You *left* it?"

"It couldn't be helped," Joe said. "I was on foot and I didn't want to disturb the scene. I'll send you the coordinates so you can get your team up there as soon as this storm blows through. You'll need a chopper, maybe, and for sure some guys on snowmobiles."

Another moan. "It might be days," Tibbs said.

"When I get home, I'll email you everything," Joe said. "Photos, his driver's license, everything I've got. Oh, and somebody took a shot at me while I was on the scene. Judging by the tracks, there were at least two of them."

"Someone *shot* at you?"

"Twice. You'll find the bullet holes."

"Did the shooters kill the guy?"

"I don't know yet, but I suspect they had something to do with it."

"Did you get eyes on them?"

"No. Too much snowfall."

"Jesus Christ in a handbasket," Tibbs said. "What a mess. Is this victim Chinese-Chinese or Chinese-American?"

"No idea," Joe said. "Does it matter?"

"I hate Chi-Coms. My dad fought 'em in Korea."

Joe winced.

"I told you he works for the university," Joe said. "But other than that, I don't know anything about him."

"What was he doing up there in the middle of this storm?"

"I don't know," Joe said. "That sounds like a job for the sheriff's department to figure out."

Tibbs had been vocal in the past about Joe sticking to game warden business and staying out of his world. As much as Joe had tried to do exactly that, Tibbs's laziness and ineptitude had forced Joe to get more involved in specific cases anyway. This time, Joe thought, he was making a good-faith effort to turn everything over to county law enforcement. He hoped Tibbs would conduct a proper by-the-book investigation and call in outside experts for help if he needed it. A dead college professor could certainly raise the profile of the situation, he thought.

Tibbs asked, "What do you think, Joe? Is this a suspicious death, an accident, or suicide?"

"Based on the fact that people were shooting at me," Joe said dryly, "I'd say it's a suspicious death. I don't know if our victim was meeting with the shooters, but I'd speculate that noting the position of his body, it's very possible a couple of guys might have muscled him into the fans. It's hard to believe anyone would do that to himself."

"That's a hell of a lot of guessing," Tibbs grumbled.

Joe said, "You're gonna need good tech guys up there, Scott. There were a bunch of boot prints around the victim and they might have left evidence of who they were. I couldn't get to any of that at the time. There might be shell casings up on the east ridge from the guy who shot at me. But honestly, everything is under a foot of snow right now and it looks like more is on the way."

Tibbs grunted. "Sometimes I think you exist on this planet to be a pain in my ass, Joe."

"Oh well."

"What kind of building is it that you're talking about, anyway? Commercial fans? What in the hell are you talking about?"

"We're talking about a steel building with a bunch of computers running inside it," Joe said. "I don't know what it's for or who built it there, although I suspect it was the owner of the ranch. I found the whole thing pretty strange."

"That's one word for it," Tibbs said.

"Dispatch in Cheyenne is fully up to speed," Joe said. "You might be hearing from them. And when it breaks that this was a UW professor, you might get press calls."

"Thanks for the warning."

"My pleasure."

As Joe terminated the call, he saw that he had a message on his voicemail. He assumed it would be Marybeth wondering where he was and when he'd be home, but it was from Rick Ewig, the director of the Wyoming Game and Fish Department.

Ewig was an old acquaintance and a former game warden himself, and it was odd to Joe that his boss had called him directly. Ewig usually texted when he wanted Joe's personal attention.

In Joe's opinion, Ewig was an excellent director and a pleasure to work for. He was less political than Joe's previous bosses, and he knew the unique challenges of working in the field from personal experience. Ewig had also restored Joe's seniority and badge number after he'd been wrongly fired, and he'd arranged for a new state-owned home on the bank of the Twelve Sleep River that was comfortable and roomy.

As Joe reached up to tap his screen to return the call, he noted what looked like a collection of white blobs floating in the roadway in front of him. It was snowing too hard to make out what they were at first.

That's when he saw the tracks plowed into the fresh snow, and the blobs turned out to be the rear haunches of pronghorn antelope proceeding in a huge caravan. They'd obviously chosen the road because the snow was drifting and piling up in the trees.

They were mesmerizing to watch. There were hundreds of them, tan and white forms, undulating like waves on the ocean. Occasionally, one of them turned its goatlike head back toward him and he could make out a single black eye.

He cut his speed so as not to panic them. They were moving fast enough to keep well ahead, but taxing them further was anathema to Joe. The herd had obviously been displaced by the heavy snowfall from the windswept ridges and hills where they'd been grazing.

He trailed the massive herd for two full miles until they turned to the left onto a sagebrush flat and left the roadway. Then he punched up Ewig's cell phone number.

"Joe!" Ewig shouted. "How in the hell are you doing?"

"Fine. We've got a big blizzard going on."

"I heard about that. Is your family safe and warm?"

"Yup. I'm on the way home now."

Ewig took a deep breath that Joe could hear over the speaker. Something significant was coming and Joe guessed it would pertain to Zhang Wei's death.

He was wrong.

"Joe," Ewig asked, "have you given a lot of thought to where you might want to end up in the department?"

"Am I in trouble?" Joe asked.

"Oh, hell no. Not at all. That's not what I meant."

"So what did you mean?"

"Well, correct me if I'm wrong, but that big windfall you were expecting didn't exactly turn out like you thought it would, right?"

"Correct," Joe said.

In fact, it had been a debacle. The fall before, Joe had been tasked with guiding the CEO of a high-tech firm on an elk hunt in the Bighorns. What they hadn't known at the time was that a family of locals were hunting *them*. Joe had managed to save the life of the tech mogul, known as Steve-2 Price, and Price had rewarded him with a handwritten IOU for one hundred thousand shares of first-class stock in ConFab, a subsidiary of Aloft Corporation. At the time, the shares had been worth approximately four and a half million dollars. Joe and Marybeth could scarcely believe their luck.

But that was before a ten-year-old tranche of emails surfaced, in which Steve-2 had made alleged racist, homophobic, and misogynistic comments on his rise to the top of the company he founded. The emails had been seized upon by Silicon Valley activists and the Hollywood elite, and within a matter of days, Steve-2 had been removed from the board of Aloft and was effectively canceled. The stock price had plummeted like a rock shortly after.

Because the IOU he'd handed to Joe had never been formalized, the attorneys for the remaining board members decided to offer three hundred thousand dollars to Joe and Marybeth to make the issue go away. Marybeth had consulted with lawyers, but they'd told her that battling the company would take years of litigation and legal fees and that by the time they finally "won," Aloft Corporation might not even exist any longer.

Joe had taken the situation in stride, since to him it had all seemed like Monopoly money in the first place. So they'd accepted the offer. The money knocked out a lot of bills and ensured that Marybeth's van was paid off, Lucy's college tuition was covered, and there was a decent nest egg of money left over for retirement. But it wasn't $4.5 million.

"So," Ewig said to Joe, "I'll come right out and say it. I'm looking to move on. I want to hunt and fish and play around with my grandkids. But I've put my life into this agency, and I want to leave it in good hands."

Joe made a face. He could see where this was headed.

"There's only one guy I can think of who could lead this agency into the future, Joe. Only one guy who could step up and keep it on the straight and narrow."

"Yes?" Joe said.

Then Ewig said, "Oh, shit. The governor is calling me. He never calls me at home, so I need to take this."

"I have a feeling I know what it's about," Joe said.

"I'll get right back to you as soon as I can," Ewig said as he punched off.

THE LATE AFTERNOON was morphing into dusk when Joe turned off the county road toward his home. If anything, the snow was falling harder than before and the wind was blowing with ferocity. The path to his house was a mile and a half through thick lodgepole pine trees. Drifts were forming at every opening between tree trunks and it was hard to see how much it was piling up in the half-light. For once, the cow moose that derived some kind of pleasure in blocking his return home every evening was nowhere to be seen.

He was close enough to his house to see the squares of lighted windows through the blizzard when his truck lurched to a stop. He'd driven straight into a three-foot snowdrift that had high-centered his pickup.

Joe slammed the vehicle into reverse and all it did was to dig it farther down into the snow. He was stuck fast. He tried four-wheel-drive low, to no avail. He regretted not putting on chains earlier.

Joe sighed and looked at Daisy. She looked back with what seemed like sympathy.

"Don't worry," he said to her. "We're not going to try and dig out tonight in the dark. We'll save that until tomorrow."

Joe was glad he was close to his house and that there weren't any witnesses to document his predicament. For reasons Joe always found kind of perplexing, game wardens loved to laugh at photos of other game wardens getting stuck in the mud or snow. Every year at the Wyoming Game Warden Foundation dinner, the session with the most attendance was a PowerPoint collection of stuck vehicles, accompanied by lots of laughter. The worse the truck was stuck, the funnier it was to everyone there. Joe had been featured at least four times, and he'd prefer it didn't turn into five.

There had also been a collection of photographs on display of the many pickups Joe had wrecked over the years. He held the record by far for racking up the most damage to state property. When the governor's office had heard about the presentation of Joe's wrecked vehicles, they'd sent an angry memo to Director Ewig to knock that off in the future.

Joe wasn't amused to find out that his truck was buried so deeply that he couldn't open his front door at first. He had to throw his shoulder into it several times to push the snow back far enough so he could squeeze out. Daisy followed.

He high-stepped through the snowdrift, but he could feel snow fill the top of his boots. Daisy bounded in his tracks behind him. It was thigh-high when he got out, but trailed off to ankle height as he neared his house. As he approached his home, he saw Marybeth looking out the front-room window. She was peering toward the road and she was obviously worried.

He waved at her to get her attention and she finally looked over and saw him coming through the front yard on foot. She shook her head with amused relief as if to say, *Can you believe this storm?*

JOE SAT ON a bench in the mudroom and unlaced his boots and brushed the snow off his socks. It was warm inside and although he could hear the wind buffeting the north side of the house, he was happy to be home.

Daisy padded off to find her dog bed and she was trailed by Tube, their half-Lab, half-Corgi, and their newest acquisition, a crazy-eyed Catahoula-like creature they still referred to as "Bert's Dog." Bert's Dog had been rescued a few months before from the property of a deceased local fishing guide.

Joe stood and peeled off his remaining layers until he was solely in long johns and socks. He put on an ancient bathrobe and stepped into a pair of oversized slippers and found Marybeth still at the living room window. She assessed his outfit with a smile and said, "It looks like romance is off the table."

"It doesn't have to be."

"Oh, yes it does."

"What a day I had," he said.

"I'm glad you made it. I was getting pretty worried," she said. "I nearly got stuck in that drift on our road."

"I *did* get stuck."

She turned and gave him a quick hug. "It's nice that we don't need to worry about the girls getting home anymore."

"Yup."

After more than twenty years, Joe and Marybeth were empty nesters and they were still getting used to it. Sheridan, twenty-four, was working for their friends Nate and Liv Romanowski in Nate's bird abatement business and apparently going out with Clay Junior. April, twenty-two, was interning for a private investigator in Bozeman, Montana. And their youngest, Lucy, was a sophomore at the University of Wyoming in Laramie.

"Come here," Marybeth said, grasping Joe's hand and pulling him toward the utility room. "I need to show you something."

He dutifully followed.

She reached down and grasped the handle for the clothes dryer and pulled it open. The inside was packed with snow.

Apparently, the wind had forced it into the aluminum vent on the wall outside and into the machine itself.

"That hasn't happened for a while," she said.

Joe smiled. He recalled another house and another storm years before when the dryer had filled up that way. Sheridan and Lucy had been in grade school, and April had been living with them for barely two years at that point.

She said, "I didn't want to stop at the store on the way home because it looked like a madhouse. You know how it gets when everyone decides to empty the shelves in a panic. So I thought I'd thaw out some of your elk chili for dinner. Does that work for you?"

"Chili sounds perfect," he said.

"So tell me about your day."

He said, "Let's get a drink first and sit down."

She arched her eyebrows.

"It was bloody," he said. "First there were two heifers torn apart by a wolf, then an injured cow elk from a car wreck, and then a dead man stuck in a building. Oh, and then I got shot at."

"*What?*"

AFTER FILLING HER in, he sat back in the dining room chair.

Her eyes were large. "You got shot at?" she repeated with incredulity.

"He missed."

"Still . . . Who do you think it was?"

"I have no idea," Joe said. "But I'd bet they were local. Navigating around the Double D in a snowstorm isn't an easy thing to do. They had to know how to get in and avoid the gates that were locked."

"Was it an inside job?" she asked.

Joe shrugged. "Clay told me none of his guys were on that part of the ranch this morning. I believe him."

"I'm just glad you're safe," she said. "And I'm glad I didn't know what was going on when it was happening."

"It was all pretty fast," he said.

"When do you suppose they'll be able to go back up there and retrieve the body?"

"Day or two, maybe. Whenever this storm eases up."

"I bet Sheriff Tibbs was thrilled to hear your news."

Joe said, "He was as thrilled as you can imagine."

"I looked at the weather report and it's supposed to stop snowing during the night," she said. "I'm guessing it'll take at least a day to dig out, so I'll probably keep the library closed tomorrow. Maybe we can have a snow day here."

"I've got to get my truck dug out," he said. "That'll be fun."

"I'll take pictures," she said with a wink.

"You'll do no such thing."

"I'll go heat up the chili."

"Great—I need to send those evidence photos to the sheriff's department."

As Marybeth got up, she looked over her shoulder at him.

"And that will be that, right?" she asked. "You'll send the photos and give your statement and then you'll be done with it."

He paused too long before he said, "Sure."

"Joe . . ."

"I wish I wasn't so curious to find out what happened," he said. "I'll bet you are, too. Admit it."

"I am," she said. "What's a UW professor doing up here on his own sticking his nose into where it doesn't belong?"

Joe snorted at that.

"I didn't mean it the way it sounded," she said defensively. Her face flushed red.

"I know what you meant," he said.

JOE'S SMALL OFFICE was in a spare bedroom off the living room. It consisted of a desk, a computer, file cabinets that still needed to be organized, and piles of clothing and gear he needed for his job. There was also a growing collection of antlers, moose paddles, old guns he'd found in the field, and a rusted bear trap the circumference of a truck tire. He usually kept the door closed so the dogs or unexpected visitors couldn't wander inside.

He downloaded the shots he'd taken from his phone and the coordinates of the crime scene from his GPS and forwarded the collection to the Twelve Sleep County Sheriff's Department.

Before starting his incident report, he looked up what information he could find on Zhang Wei. He hoped the man hadn't left a wife and family behind, and when he thought about it he got a pit in his stomach. How many people had lost a father, a husband, a colleague today and didn't even know it yet?

He hoped Tibbs would act quickly on the investigation and inform Wei's loved ones. He wished he had confidence in the sheriff's investigation.

It took only a few clicks on the University of Wyoming website to find Professor Zhang Wei.

Professor Wei was an associate dean and professor within the College of Engineering and Applied Science (CEAS). His photo showed him to be in his late forties or early fifties. He was unsmiling and looked serious and formidable. Joe knew he would not have been able to identify him from a lineup because he hadn't gotten a good look at the victim's face.

According to the website, CEAS students:

Build a wide variety of products and work in almost all industries. They design control and communication systems, sensors, displays, learning machines, robots, instruments, voice recognition, computer vision, electronics, motors, power systems, the internet of things—the list goes on and on . . . For instance, some of our graduates develop complex new mathematical algorithms to achieve the highest possible system performance; others work with basic physics to develop better circuits and devices; others work outside in the field to improve the generation and transmission of electric power; some become high-level executives at companies like Google . . . After graduating, our students have gone on to the world's best graduate programs: Stanford, MIT, Johns Hopkins, etc.

Joe concluded quite quickly that the subjects Professor Wei taught were well above his pay grade.

So again, he wondered, what was this man, with these kinds of credentials, doing on the Double D Ranch hundreds of miles away from Laramie during a snowstorm?

As Marybeth called out to let him know the chili was ready, Joe's cell phone lit up next to his keyboard on his desk. It was Director Ewig calling back.

"Hey, Rick," Joe said.

Ewig said, "I just got off the phone with the governor and I think my ear is bleeding."

"Uh-oh."

"I heard about what you found today."

"News travels fast," Joe said. "I didn't get an opening to tell you about it when you called earlier."

"Joe," Ewig said, "what have you gotten into now? The gov is furious. He wants you to back off from the investigation and show up for a meeting in his office as soon as you can get your 'game warden ass down here.' And that's a direct quote."

Joe sat back and sighed. "You know we've got a blizzard going on right now, don't you?"

"Joe, you've got to work with me here."

"That's the first bureaucratic thing I've ever heard you say, Rick. My truck is stuck in a snowdrift and all of the roads are closed to Cheyenne."

Ewig moaned. "I'll put him off as long as I can. But please, go through hell and high water to get down here."

"What's this all about?" Joe asked.

"I don't know," Ewig said. "All I know is that I've never heard him so worked up. He sounded desperate, if you want to know the truth. If I didn't know any better, I'd say he sounded scared."

"Of what?"

"Just get down here and we'll find out," Ewig said.

"You sound a little scared yourself, Rick."

Ewig hung up.

Joe gathered himself together to go have a nice dinner of elk chili with his wife. But his head was spinning.

Thursday, March 30

Announced by all the trumpets of the sky,
Arrives the snow, and, driving o'er the fields,
Seems nowhere to alight: the whited air
Hides hills and woods, the river, and the
   heaven,
And veils the farm-house at the garden's end.

—Ralph Waldo Emerson,

"The Snow-Storm"

CHAPTER FOUR

T HE NEXT MORNING, Joe left his house at six-thirty with a shovel on his shoulder and he didn't get his pickup free of the drift and the road clear until after eleven. By that time, the sun was high and warm and the snowscape was so dazzling it hurt his eyes.

The day after an epic blizzard in the Rockies was often like this, he thought—a hundred and eighty degrees from the day before. The sun was blazing in a cloudless sky and the pure white surface sparkled. It was almost a shame to mess it up. Despite the hard work of digging out, he was grateful for the increased snowpack. It meant future full rivers, healthy trout, irrigated fields, and satiated wildlife. Water meant everything in the arid West.

He also speculated that this might have been the last big storm of the year. No doubt there would be days with flurries and sleet, but he couldn't ever recall more than one massive snow dump per spring.

If it weren't for their new skid steer, digging the truck out would have been an all-day job. He was able to cut through the drifts to his pickup, attach a chain to it, and tug. But after he'd freed his pickup, he'd inadvertently backed the skid steer into a drift and got it stuck as well. So then he'd had to pull the machine out with his newly freed truck.

Sweaty and already exhausted, Joe found Marybeth baking bread in the kitchen. The library was indeed closed for the rest of the day because her staff couldn't get there, and she'd apparently decided to make the best of it. He couldn't remember the last time she'd baked, and the aroma made him swoon.

"The road's clear," he announced. "It took a while."

"I watched you through the window," she said. "What would have happened if you'd gotten your truck and the skid steer stuck at the same time?"

"I would stay right here and eat bread and wait for spring."

"Good thing we had that machine," she said. Then she looked heavenward and said, "Thanks, Steve-2."

Joe smiled.

"Too bad you can't stay home today with me," she said.

"Nope. Instead, I've got to go to Cheyenne. The interstate should be melted off by the time I get out. The governor is really worked up about something."

"Isn't he always?"

Joe nodded. Governor Colter Allen was in the last year of his first term and his administration had been a disaster, as had Allen himself. Although he *appeared* to be a formidable presence with his movie-star looks, high cheekbones, and swept-back, longish hair, his campaign biography as a hardworking rancher and entrepreneur had been shot full of holes.

Since he'd been elected, the governor had lurched from crisis to crisis. His response to the pandemic had been panic-driven, followed by the crash of energy prices and therefore the economy of the state, and then allegations had emerged of sexual impropriety with babysitters long before he'd run, *plus* a long-ago role in a soft-core porn movie called *Bunk House* had been laid, uh, bare. While all of this was happening, there was no apparent new economic development, and now there were claims of alleged mismanagement of federal funds. All of this had made him the most unpopular governor in Joe's lifetime.

It was said that Allen had lost his base as well as his donors.

The last time Joe had seen the governor, he'd noticed a striking physical change in the man. He'd aged, grown jowls that trembled when he spoke, and his dark hair was streaked with gray. Joe had felt sorry for him at the time and was grateful that he himself had never had to share the mental burden of running a state unsuccessfully.

It was even rumored that the first lady, a blue blood from Boston known as Poppy, had moved out of the governor's mansion.

Governor Allen was certainly no Spencer Rulon, who had come before him. Joe had once had a very special relationship with Rulon, who had given Joe special assignments and referred to him as his "range rider." Joe had had a good, if at times contentious, relationship with the man. But he'd certainly been better than Allen in the job.

Allen, though, had wanted Joe to take on a more political role, and it was one Joe had refused. Their interactions over the last three years had been rocky at best.

There had been some recent rumors that Rulon was considering another run for governor, but nothing official had been announced. Joe was in favor of the idea.

Although Wyoming was usually the most Republican of all the U.S. states, the population had elected a surprising number of Democratic governors like Rulon over the years. Rulon liked to call himself the "last conservative Democrat" in the nation, and he'd been wildly popular over his previous two terms. Rulon liked nothing more than taking it to the feds as well as his own party if he thought their agenda was too anti-energy, anti-gun, and anti–state independence.

Joe wasn't persuaded that Rulon would run again. The man seemed content to head up his law firm and he was no doubt making more money in the private sector than he ever did as head of the state.

Still . . .

JOE HAD MADE the four-and-a-half-hour journey to Cheyenne more times than he could count. But he knew he'd need to get going in order to arrive before dark and the closure of state offices.

"Oh," he said to Marybeth, "when I talked to Rick yesterday, I think he was working up to something. I think he wants to recommend me to be the new director."

Marybeth paused and looked him over closely. She had a smudge of flour on her cheek that he found oddly attractive.

"Do you want it?" she asked.

"What—to live in Cheyenne? To become a political animal?"

"If you want it, I'll support you," she said. "You know that."

"I don't want it," he said. Then: "Do you?"

She shook her head no.

"Good," he said. "But it might be off the table anyway. I can't see Rick talking the governor into it. Especially now that it seems he's mad at me."

"Why is that, exactly?"

"I guess I'm going to find out," Joe said.

Marybeth said, "Well, if you have to go down south, can I prevail upon you to deliver a couple of boxes of summer clothes to Lucy? She texted me about it this morning."

"Summer clothes? Has she looked outside?"

"Spring break is coming," Marybeth said. "She said she needs outfits to wear on South Padre Island. She wants to go with a bunch of her friends."

Joe cringed. "And you said that was okay?"

"Sheridan went when she was in school," Marybeth said. "She survived."

"I sometimes wish Lucy wasn't so darned popular," Joe said.

"She's sweet, kind, and beautiful. Why wouldn't people want to be around her?"

Joe shrugged. Marybeth was right. Their youngest daughter had always been the most social, and one of her biggest dilemmas was managing invitations.

Laramie, the home of the University of Wyoming, was fifty miles west of Cheyenne. It wasn't exactly on the way, but in Wyoming a fifty-mile drive was like a two-block detour in other places.

"Sure," Joe said. "It'll be good to see her."

"The boxes are in her bedroom."

"Boxes? More than one?" he asked.

"She said she needs options."

CHAPTER FIVE

AT THE SAME time, twelve miles to the northwest of Joe Pickett's house, Nate Romanowski was digging out as well. He was behind the wheel of his vintage 1948 Dodge Power Wagon slowly driving up the access road, blowing a thick plume of snow to the side. He'd welded a rotary plow to the frame of the vehicle the summer before for exactly these conditions, and he was pleased with himself for how well the snowblower worked. The blades bit into the thirty-six inches of snow, broke it up within the spinning blades, then threw it to the right side of the roadway in a steady stream of smoky white.

His wife, Liv, and toddler, Kestrel, were warm and snug in their house a half mile behind him. When he'd left that morning, Kestrel had been ecstatic about the snow and begging to get on her snowsuit and out into it. Liv had promised their daughter that they would as soon as they could get organized after breakfast.

Since the Romanowski family lived on a two-hundred-acre compound in a vast sagebrush-covered swale west of Saddlestring, Nate had no choice but to clear the road himself. His nearest neighbor was two miles away to the east, and the man lived alone in a single-wide trailer and had no means of digging out. Nate thought it would be neighborly to cut a path across his land and past his neighbors to the county road. He hoped the county snowplows were out, as well as the state workers on the highway.

Nate was anxious to clear the route because he was expecting visitors later that day: Geronimo Jones, his wife, Jacinda, and their newborn baby girl. The baby was named Pearl after her grandmother, Nate was told. Geronimo was a fellow outlaw falconer and ex–special operator, and they'd driven halfway across Wyoming from their home outside Denver the day before the storm closed the roads.

Geronimo had told Nate he had a business idea and that Nate was the only person he wanted to share it with. Nate was intrigued, and he'd invited his new friend to visit and present it to Liv and him. Liv had the better business mind of the two because she'd been running their bird abatement business, Yarak, Inc., since it had been founded.

Nate hadn't seen Geronimo since the man returned with his stolen falcons a few months before. During the search for them that culminated in a violent shootout in the heart of downtown Portland, they'd bonded in a way that only fellow master falconers could, with a shared sense of purpose as well as an understanding about both the nature of man and man's relationship with wild creatures.

During the many hours they'd spent together on the road, Geronimo had asked Nate a lot of questions about Yarak, Inc. Nate had explained that the business suited him once he'd finally come back on the grid and he was no longer being constantly pursued by rogue federal operatives connected to his past as a covert special operator. Nate had married Liv, they'd had Kestrel, and Nate traveled the region and throughout the country with his band of falcons to clear facilities of problem birds and wildly propagated invasive species.

Winegrowers, golf courses, amusement parks, refineries— any location that was overrun with starlings or other invasive species of birds—could rid themselves of the issue once the sky was populated by predatory falcons. Often, simply the sight of raptors in the air caused the problem birds to depart en masse. It was a natural solution to a man-made problem.

Thanks to Liv's management of it, the company had turned out to be much more profitable than they'd imagined. Nate had hired Sheridan Pickett and mentored her to become a master falconer and assume a share of the load. Even with Sheridan on board, which enabled them to send two flights of falcons at once in two different locations, Yarak, Inc., was still turning down jobs.

An added potential benefit to the bird abatement business was the opportunity to hire out-of-work falconers. Falconers were a breed unto their own, as Nate and Geronimo well knew. Master falconers were often solitary and obsessed with their chosen avocation and unsuited to corporate or laptop jobs—or bosses of any kind. Setting them up with a franchise business opportunity where they could practice their skill *and* make a living at the same time was a good thing. Nate had contracted with five different falconers the year before, and based on the calls they'd received, he'd need to double that soon.

Geronimo had joked about establishing a Yarak, Inc., South franchise, and perhaps others around the region. Nate had entertained the idea as well. Expansion was good, right?

But Liv needed to be convinced it was feasible. It was important to her that she get along well with both Geronimo and Jacinda, and that their visions didn't clash.

When Geronimo had floated the idea of financing the expansion with cryptocurrency mining, Nate had been clueless what that meant and Liv had been skeptical. Geronimo had offered to travel north to Wyoming to show them his business plan, and Liv hadn't rejected the idea out of hand. Nate had agreed because he wanted to see Geronimo again, and he owed Jacinda for her hospitality a few months before when he was desperate.

So when Nate returned the Power Wagon to the out-building and strode outside, he assumed that the dark-colored SUV slowly approaching on the just-plowed road belonged to Geronimo and Jacinda.

He was surprised they'd arrived so early in the day, and thought that Geronimo must have started before the roads were officially reopened. Jumping the road closure checkpoints was illegal, of course, so that would be like Geronimo. Nate wondered if the man had also packed his triple-barrel shotgun.

Liv, cradling Kestrel, stepped out onto the front deck. Kestrel squirmed out of her grip and shrieked at the snow before plunging into it headfirst. She came up sputtering.

Liv gestured toward the oncoming car. "Is that them?"

"I think so," Nate said. "I don't recognize the vehicle, but who else could it be?"

Nonetheless, Nate returned to the cab of the Power Wagon for his weapon. He removed his parka and slipped on a shoulder holster and his .454 Casull revolver. Then he zipped the parka back over it and walked out into the compound yard.

When the SUV was close enough that Nate could make out Montana plates instead of the Colorado plates he'd been expecting, he turned to Liv.

"Give me a minute to check this out," he said. "Please take Kestrel back inside until I know who this is."

"She's not going to want to go," Liv said.

"Then take her out back."

"That's a good idea," Liv said, nodding. She scooped up their daughter and carried her under her arm around the side of the house. In her oversized snowsuit, Kestrel resembled a large loaf of bread. The toddler whooped because she assumed it was a game.

As the SUV neared the compound, Nate was grateful once again for the location in which they'd chosen to live. Because the bowl was treeless and wide open, no one could sneak up on them. When he saw that the driver was a single white man and not the Black fellow falconer and his wife, Nate narrowed his eyes and unzipped his parka a few inches so he'd have quick access to his weapon if necessary.

The SUV slowed to a stop and the driver eyed him and nodded a greeting through the side window. Nate couldn't recall ever seeing the man before.

The door opened and two thick insulated boots thumped to the snow. The driver held his arms out at his sides, as if to indicate he meant no threat.

The driver was younger than Nate, likely in his mid-thirties, and he had close-cropped red hair and a thick neck that strained at the collar of his shirt. He was wide-faced, with heavy-lidded eyes. Well over six feet and two hundred and twenty pounds, the man looked fit and lethal. Nate could tell from the man's presence and comportment that he had a military background.

"I assume you're the famous Nate Romanowski," the man said.

"I don't know about famous, but yes. This is my place and you're on it."

"That was my intent. Thank you for plowing the road for me."

"It wasn't for you. What do you want?"

"Just a few minutes of your time."

"Regarding what?"

The man paused and a slow grin crept across his face. "My name is Jason Demo," he said. "I'm here to try and recruit you to help us save our country."

Nate didn't move or respond. One of his falcons shrieked from the mews on the edge of the compound. The shrill cry knifed through the still morning air.

"That must be your Air Force," Demo said. "I've heard a lot about your abilities over the years. A bunch of us have looked up to you for a long time."

"Who were you with?"

"Army Rangers, then the Wolverines. I assume you've heard of them."

Nate nodded. The Wolverines were a hybrid special operations unit similar to the group Nate had once belonged to. Each branch of the military—and a half-dozen intelligence agencies—had lethal squads of special operators who were unknown to the public at large and sometimes even among themselves. They were unofficial and off the books, and like Nate's Peregrines, which were associated with the air force, the Wolverines didn't exist on paper. They were also even more shadowy than Nate's Peregrine unit, at least as far as Nate was concerned. He'd heard the Wolverines were under the NSA or an NSA-CIA joint secret squad.

Nate wanted no part of them.

He said, "Then you might not have heard I'm back on the

grid now. I'm done with all of that. I'd suggest you get in your SUV and go back to where you came from. I've got a busy day ahead."

Demo nodded his head in a reasonable way. "I'm not here to recruit you for the Wolverines. They're in my rearview mirror. I'm here for a much bigger purpose, and from what I've heard about you, I'm thinking you might want to join our effort. Do you want to hear more?"

Nate didn't respond.

"As I'm sure you noticed," Demo said, "there's a new war on the West going on. The coastal elites see us as a threat and they're attacking us from both coasts. They think they're on the right side of history and all of that crap."

Nate didn't stop him.

Demo noted that and said, "They want us to go away. They want to shut down our energy industry, our cattle ranches, our timber companies, and just about every part of our way of life. They've never owned a gun, gone to church, driven a pickup, or served in the military. They've never changed a tire in their lives. Hell, they've never stepped inside Walmart.

"All we have to do is look around us," Demo said while sweeping his arms to encompass all they could see. "Everybody we know is unemployed or underemployed. Our little towns are drying up and blowing away. Addiction is the highest it's ever been in the next generation."

Then he pointed toward his boots. "There's oil, natural gas, coal, and uranium beneath the surface that we stand on," he said. He then pointed at the hulking blue of the Bighorn

Mountains. "There's lumber everywhere you look. But we can't touch any of it because it's *federal* land. We beg foreign terrorist states to send us oil, but we refuse to let our own people get good jobs making us energy-independent again.

"It's gone too far and some of us feel that it's time to make a stand," Demo said.

Nate raised his eyebrows. "How?" he asked.

"We think we can beat them."

"There are a lot more of them than there are of us," Nate said. When he realized what he'd said, he corrected himself and said, "I mean of *you*." But he knew he'd made a tacit admission of sorts, even though he was keeping his own counsel about the rest of it.

"True," Demo said. "But you know as well as I do what a determined insurgency can accomplish. They have the high-tech companies," Demo said, "but we have other skills."

Demo chinned toward the outbuilding where Nate had recently parked after plowing. "Like that."

"A '48 Power Wagon?" Nate said.

"Exactly," Demo said. "You have a 1948 Power Wagon that you know how to adapt for your needs and you keep it running. You know how to weld a snowblower on the front of it with your own hands and your welding equipment. How many of them could do that? We know how to *do* things."

"How many of you are there?" Nate asked.

Demo nodded and said, "I'm from Montana. There are a bunch of us from there. We're growing in Wyoming, Idaho, Utah, North and South Dakota, Colorado, Texas, Arizona, and Florida. We've got folks from the rural parts of New Mexico, Nevada, Oregon, Washington, and all over the Deep South and Midwest. Even a few on the East Coast in places like Maine and Vermont.

"The thing is," he continued, "we all agree on principles. We provide their energy, their food, and most of the soldiers they send to foreign wars on their behalf. We fix their cars and remodel their apartments. We unclog their toilets. But they never thank us, do they? They exist in their little enclaves. They don't think about the fact that we have guns and we know how to use them, we know the terrain, we've learned counterinsurgency tactics, and we can survive outside of air-conditioned offices."

He paused. "I like our chances."

"How do you plan to go up against them?" Nate asked.

Demo's grin was long and slow. He shook his head. "Not yet," he said. "I don't want to talk about that yet. Not until I get your temperature and I know I can trust you."

Nate said, "I'm not a joiner. I'm a grown-ass man with a wife and a child and I want to be left alone."

"I think I may know who you are better than you do," Demo said. "You were one of the best special operators our country ever produced, but they took advantage of you and you quit on your own terms. You bought that big gun you have under your arm and you fought them off for years because they couldn't stand the idea of a freethinking American outlaw out in the world who knew all about them. They came after you time after time, but in the end you made them stand down."

Nate said nothing.

Demo said, "You're the kind of man we need on our side. But let's set that aside for now. I'm here to plant the seed, nothing more."

"I asked you how many of you are there?"

"More every day," Demo said. "We've got the Keystoners with us."

"Never heard of them."

"You will," Demo said. He nodded at Nate and moved toward his SUV.

"Are you talking about secession?" Nate asked.

"I'll be in touch," Demo said.

A FEW MOMENTS later, Liv came around the side of the house carrying Kestrel. The little girl was covered with snow and loving it.

"Who was that?" she asked Nate, who had not moved since Demo drove away.

"Says his name is Demo."

"What did he want?"

Nate shook his head. "That's what I'm trying to figure out," he said. Then: "I'm going to ask you, Marybeth, and Sheridan for some help."

"Doing what?" Liv asked.

"Researching the hell out of Jason Demo. I need to know if he's real. I also need to know about some group called the Keystoners."

CHAPTER SIX

JASON DEMO KEPT his eyes on his rearview mirrors as he drove away from the Romanowski compound. He saw Nate's wife and child emerge from the back of the house and the exchange between Liv and her husband. He wished he could hear what they were saying.

Demo was proud of the positions he had laid out, and he strongly suspected that Romanowski had found them persuasive. Demo had certainly convinced *himself* of his righteousness.

There was no danger of driving off the road, even as his eyes were glued to the mirrors. Romanowski had plowed a ditch of sorts with high walls through the deep snow and Demo proceeded as if he were clattering down a bobsled run, bouncing off the walls back into the middle.

Soon, the home and outbuildings receded into the background as Demo took a long slow turn through tall reddish willows, and then onto a long flat. For the second time that morning, he passed a single-wide trailer tucked into an open pocket of aspen trees on a hillside. Steam rose from a single pipe on the top of the trailer and an old man wearing a parka and overalls was outside shoving heavy snow off his vehicle with a push broom. The man waved a greeting at Demo and Demo waved back.

He probably wanted some help getting unstuck, Demo thought. Then, *Oh, well . . .*

At that moment, Demo felt his cell phone vibrate in his breast pocket. He ignored it until it stopped. After thirty seconds, it vibrated again. The man calling was impatient and willful. He would not be denied.

THERE WAS A carved-out clearing in the snow about a mile from the state highway, and Demo pulled over into it. He kept his SUV running and the heater on while he unzipped his jacket and retrieved the phone. He'd hoped that there wouldn't be a signal this far out of town, but no such luck.

The phone was a cheap off-brand flip phone with less than a hundred prepaid minutes. The burner had only one number programmed into it.

"How'd it go?" the man asked without saying hello. Demo knew the man only by his code name: the Big Fish.

"I told you I'd call you afterward," Demo said. "What if I was talking with him and my phone rang? That wouldn't have been a good look because I'd have to scramble and make something up."

"But that didn't happen."

"No, but it *could* have. I said I'd call you afterward."

"But you didn't."

"*Because I literally just drove away,*" Demo said, raising his voice.

"Enough of that. How'd it go?"

"He heard me out," Demo said with a sigh.

"Is he interested?"

Demo shrugged, even though he knew the man on the other end couldn't see him. "He didn't kick me off his property. He didn't shoot me. So yeah, I'd say he was intrigued."

"Was Joe Pickett with him?"

"No," Demo said. "His wife was there and so was his daughter. Nobody else."

"Did he ask you any questions?"

"A couple," Demo said. "But in no way can I say he committed to us. He's a hard man to read. He declared at one point that he just wanted to be left alone."

"That cuts both ways," the Big Fish said. "Was he referring to the elites or to us?"

"Unsure."

"But like you said, he didn't kick you out and he didn't blow your head off. I'd consider that a fairly successful first encounter."

Demo grunted, then said, "I can tell you I'd rather have him with us than against us. He's . . . formidable."

"I told you he was."

"Yeah. You did."

What a know-it-all this man was, Demo thought. It was just one of the growing number of things about the Big Fish that annoyed him. The man was so sure of himself and his cause. It was tiring just to be around him.

"Tell me what he asked you," the Big Fish said.

"Well, he asked me how we think we can beat them."

"And what did you tell him?"

"Not much, as we discussed. I withheld any details of our operation. I didn't even give him a hint."

"Good, good. You left him wanting to find out more, as we discussed."

"Roger that," Demo said.

"It'll be a process," the Big Fish said. "We need to be patient. We don't really know where his sympathies lie, or how far he'll be willing to go with us. He may need a little nudge in the right direction."

"What kind of nudge?" Demo asked.

"Don't worry. I'll handle it."

The Big Fish asked, "Did you mention the gathering? Or who is coming?"

"No."

"That's probably best left for the next time you talk with him."

"I agree," Demo said. "I'd rather he asked me more questions. It needs to come from him. He made a point of saying he isn't a joiner, and I believe him. This will only work if he expresses interest. It won't work if I push him."

"That's exactly as I anticipated," the Big Fish said. Once

again, taking the credit for outthinking everyone around him.

"I'll tell you one thing," Demo said. "I'm concerned about this nudge you mentioned. We could lose him if you nudge too hard, is what I'm saying."

"Leave it to me," the Big Fish said. "I know what I'm doing."

Demo let out another sigh. "I'm going to head back to town now."

"Keep your phone on," the man said.

"Always."

"We'll need to get together soon to work out our next step," the man said. "Maybe tomorrow night if I can get ahold of the others."

"Fine."

"I'm encouraged," the Big Fish said. "Things are working out like I hoped they would."

"Whatever," Demo said, and punched off. He was tired of talking to this man, tired of his pomposity.

As DEMO SLID the burner back into his breast pocket, he saw a glint of sun on chrome wink through the trees on the road ahead. Since Nate had plowed a narrow path through the snow, there was only room on the road for one vehicle at a time. Demo stayed put in the pullout.

A three-quarter-ton four-door pickup nosed around a turn

ahead of him and proceeded his way. The truck pulled a long trailer with a metal structure on top of it. Both the grille of the pickup and the metal building glinted in the midday sun.

Demo noted green Colorado plates. The truck slowed as it approached and pulled to a stop parallel to his SUV.

The driver's-side window slid down. At the wheel was the burly form of a Black man with a mop of braided dreads that fell to his shoulders. He had a wide, expansive face. He was alone.

In the passenger area behind the driver, Demo could see the silhouetted heads of three tall birds of prey of some kind. Their heads were covered with leather hoods topped by tassels. They stared straight ahead. It was a bizarre sight. *See no evil, hear no evil,* he thought.

"Are you stuck in the snow, brother?" the man asked.

"No," Demo said. "I'm just waiting for you to pass by."

"Gotcha. Is this the road to Nate Romanowski's place?"

Demo nodded.

"Cool," the man said. "Take care."

"What's that you're hauling?" Demo asked.

The man behind the wheel grinned. "Our future," he said.

"So what's with the birds?" Demo asked.

"They're falcons, brother. And they're ready to eat."

A woman's voice joined in with a groan from a phone mounted on the dashboard next to the driver. Apparently, Demo realized, he had interrupted a conversation. The woman laughed and said, "Let's get *going*, Geronimo."

"You heard the lady," the man said to Demo. "Mama's at home and she wants to move things along." He said it as his window rose up into place.

The pickup and trailer lurched and drove away. Demo eased his SUV out of the turnout and continued to the state highway.

The future of what? he asked himself. And who was this interloper?

CHAPTER SEVEN

A N HOUR LATER, Sheridan Pickett turned her GMC Yukon into the entrance of the alleyway behind her apartment and suddenly hit the brakes. Although the paved streets through downtown Saddlestring had been plowed and the excess snow stood as high as hedgerows against the curbs, the town plow drivers had yet to get to the alleys. Her designated parking spot was behind the building. The snow looked to be two and a half feet deep and no one had yet attempted to bull their way through it.

She backed away, drove around the block, and found an open space on the street between the old storefronts of the Saddlestring *Roundup* newspaper office and the Stockman's Bar. Her new two-bedroom apartment was up a set of outside stairs above the Stockman's. Sheridan liked the location of her new place, and enjoyed being in the middle of town, where she could walk to get coffee and food. The clientele of the

Stockman's was also an interesting glimpse into the social fabric of Twelve Sleep County.

She parked and climbed out and stretched. The drive into town from the Double Diamond had been long and slow. She'd been forced to follow a snowplow as it made its first pass-through on the county road and then the state highway. What should have been a forty-minute journey had taken three hours.

Plus, she was stiff and sore. The bunk bed she'd been assigned at the Double D headquarters by Clay's father was ancient and lumpy and she hadn't slept well. It was also down the hall from Clay Junior's room. Maybe twenty steps. She knew when she went to bed that he'd been thinking about that, too.

CLAY JUNIOR HAD spent his formative years actively ignoring Sheridan, she frequently reminded him. He'd been a year ahead of her in school, where he was the quarterback of the football team and a forward on the state championship basketball squad. Much to the chagrin of the more attractive and popular girls in Saddlestring High School, Clay Junior was off the market due to his longtime relationship with Amber McKenzie, who had ambitions to become an actress. If Clay Junior had even looked her way during those years, Sheridan couldn't recall it.

But in subsequent years, their paths kept crossing as if fate had stepped in.

After a stint in the army, and after Amber had broken things off and gone to Hollywood and never been heard from again, Clay Junior returned to the state and enrolled at the University of Wyoming. The house he'd lived in with his roommates was directly across the street from Sheridan's rental. Since they'd shared the same hometown and were in several classes together, they'd teamed up in a surprisingly natural way, she thought. There'd been nothing romantic about their relationship, but it'd seemed like they found each other at parties, and at football and basketball games, and at graduation, where Clay Junior had majored in range management.

Even after Sheridan had left Laramie for a two-year stint at an exclusive dude ranch, they'd met again when Clay Junior had delivered a half-dozen horses from the ranch his father managed outside of Saddlestring. Although Sheridan had been with Lance Ramsey at the time, she'd slipped away with Clay Junior for a night of beer (Clay Junior) and wine (Sheridan) at the Beartrap Cafe & Bar in Encampment. She'd never told Lance—or anyone—about it. But from that evening on, she'd thought about Clay Junior in a wholly different way.

It was obvious he was quite a catch. He was tall, with broad shoulders, a cleft chin, blue eyes, black hair, and a confident but humble manner. He could have easily been a model instead of a budding ranch manager if he'd chosen to go that direction, she reckoned.

Still, it wasn't until the two of them found themselves back in Saddlestring that they actually went on a real date. And it *was* a real date, she thought. Not like the "dates" she was used to with other males that seemed more like "beers with the bros."

It was the kind of date people used to have, she thought, where he picked her up at her place, opened his truck door for her, took her to dinner and paid for it without suggesting they split the check, followed by a two-hour stroll along the banks of the river, where they actually talked about their dreams.

Clay Junior was respectful, courteous, self-deprecating, and surprisingly funny when he wanted to be. And he didn't immediately press her into anything she didn't want to do.

Her mom seemed to like Clay, which made Sheridan kind of nervous. She almost preferred her dad's predictable reaction, which was to be instantly suspicious of any male who wanted to be around his daughters.

April certainly approved, but only because she told Sheridan she wanted to "steal him away and move to the Double D." Lucy's reaction was surprise that a local legend like Clay Junior would want to be with her oldest sister, which Sheridan found to be very annoying, especially since it was something she'd wondered about herself.

Sheridan's relationship with Clay Junior had just been so easy, so smooth, so inevitable-feeling, that she'd sometimes felt an urge to wish for roadblocks to slow it down and make it more difficult.

ACTUALLY, CLAY JUNIOR had provided just that kind of roadblock the night before when he'd visited her twice just "to talk," he'd claimed. Although nothing romantic had happened, since Mr. Hutmacher's bedroom was adjacent to Sheridan's room, it had been an uncomfortable night filled with impassioned whispers. When he reached under the covers and stroked her naked inner thigh, she'd shifted her weight so his hand dropped away.

For the first time since she'd been with Clay Junior, Sheridan had felt somewhat pressured by him.

It wasn't a good feeling.

During the night, Clay Junior had asked her, when they got more serious, if she thought they should live in town or take one of the houses located on the Double D. At one point he said they'd need room for their children. At least three of them, he'd said.

She'd sent him away, not exactly feigning a headache.

And that morning, despite the offer of a big ranch breakfast, she'd said she had to go. She had falcons to feed.

It was true. But what she really had needed was a break from Clay Junior. Which made her think that there must be something wrong with her.

SHERIDAN FISHED THE key out of her jacket pocket and entered her new place. There were still unopened boxes stacked high in the corners and the only thing on the walls was a poster she'd helped design advertising her employer. It read:

YARAK, INC.

Bird Abatement Specialists

Saddlestring, Wyoming

We Make Your Problems Go Away

Beneath the copy were stylized graphics of Nate Romanowski and Sheridan standing shoulder to shoulder beneath a cloudless Wyoming sky with falcons on their fists.

Sheridan had suggested to Nate that the tagline, "We Make Your Problems Go Away," could be improved by adding the word *birds*, as in "We Make Your Problem *Birds* Go Away." But after working for the master falconer for over a year, she'd come to find out that the tagline was extremely accurate as it stood. Nate was a specialist in making problems go away, as her dad and mom had learned years before.

As a greeting to her, one of two hooded prairie falcons perched on the wooden backrest of a kitchen chair called out in a shrill cry. It was especially loud in the closed apartment.

"Be patient," she said to the two birds. "We don't want to upset the bartender downstairs and get kicked out of this place."

The falcons were yearlings who had been captured from the same nest by a local amateur birder the fall before. The birder, a hipster known by the name of "Dash" who worked as a barista and participated in poetry slam events at the town park, had had ambitions to become a falconer himself. Dash had kept the birds in dog crates in his garage while he watched

YouTube videos of professional falconers hunting small deer and other game in the Middle East.

But like so many people who brought home high-energy puppies and had no idea what to do with them when the dogs behaved like dogs and chewed up all the rugs and furniture, Dash had recently discovered that the care, feeding, and training of falcons was akin to a full-time job. So he put the word out on social media that he'd *happily* donate the prairie falcons to a good home.

Sheridan had responded to the birder, and her plan was to take the falcons to Nate's compound and get them set up within the mews with the more experienced birds. Then the storm hit.

The angry one shrieked again as Sheridan opened the freezer compartment above the refrigerator and found several shrink-wrapped plastic bags of road-killed gophers. The packages existed among frozen bags of peas, corn, and hash browns.

She pierced the plastic with a fork and put the frozen carcasses into the microwave and set it to thaw them out. While the microwave oven hummed and the rock-hard bodies softened and oozed blood and fluids inside the plastic, she thought as she often did that she was glad she wasn't squeamish.

WHILE TAKING THE hoods off the prairie falcons and hand-feeding them the dead rodents one by one, she thought over another thing that had made her uncomfortable that morning before she left the Double D Ranch.

It was a phone call that Mr. Hutmacher had received while Clay Junior was in the shower. Sheridan was in the kitchen and the foreman had sat at the table with his morning coffee.

"What do you mean?" he'd asked into the receiver. "What do you mean, there are *people on the ranch*? How'd they get on us?"

Sheridan was familiar with ranchers referring to the property they owned or managed as "us."

"What did they use to get through the gate?" Mr. Hutmacher asked the caller. "Bolt cutters?"

Sheridan couldn't hear what was said on the other end, but she'd picked up on the urgency of the other man's tone.

"Are they cattle thieves?" Mr. Hutmacher asked. "Or poachers? Or what?"

Then: "How many are there?"

When Clay Senior had disconnected the call, he'd stared into a space somewhere over Sheridan's head. He'd looked worried, she thought. She'd never seen him in such a state before.

Clay Senior quickly made another call. "Burt, get the snowmobiles fired up and bring them up to the house. We need at least three guys, and I want everybody armed. We've got trespassers on snowmobiles and we need to find out why they're here and kick them off. Don't waste any time."

Sheridan had surmised Mr. Hutmacher was speaking to

Burt Reno, a grizzled old cowboy who had worked for decades on various ranches in the valley and who had found a permanent home on the Double D. Reno was a friend of her dad's and they occasionally floated the river together to fly-fish for trout.

After a few beats, Mr. Hutmacher said, "Burt, don't you think I know what it's like out there? It doesn't matter. Get those fucking machines up here."

Mr. Hutmacher had tossed the rest of his coffee into the sink like he was angry about doing so. It was then that he seemed to realize that Sheridan had witnessed his behavior.

"I'm sorry," he'd said to her. "I'm sorry about my language. I've got an emergency to take care of."

She'd nodded and told him she'd heard worse in her life.

"Please tell Clay Junior I had to go," Mr. Hutmacher said. "And by all means make yourself at home. There's coffee in the machine and food in the fridge. If you don't cook, you can ask Mrs. Wheatridge to make breakfast."

Mrs. Wheatridge was the full-time housekeeper. Clay Junior had told Sheridan that Mrs. Wheatridge sometimes slept with his father, who'd been widowed when Clay Junior's mother had died of cancer when he was fourteen. Mrs. Wheatridge had worked on the ranch for a decade.

"I can cook," Sheridan said.

"Of course you can. Of course you can. You're a good hand, Sheridan."

"Thank you."

"Stay around as long as you want," he said. He looked at her very sincerely when he said it. She wasn't sure what to make of the comment, or the situation he was in.

People on the ranch.

She'd left as soon as she could tell Clay Junior about the falcons she needed to feed. She'd done it quickly before he could point out that the house was theirs and they were finally alone in it.

SHERIDAN SAT BACK and wiped the blood and feathers off her hands with a dish towel. Both prairie falcons were sated, their gullets bulging and the size of hen's eggs. They'd consumed the gophers whole: hide, bone, sinew, head, torso.

The birds perched on the chairs like big plastic figurines. They were in the throes of a food coma that could last several hours.

She leaned forward and peered deeply into the eyes of the formerly angry one. His eyes were black, shiny, and without any hint of a soul or interior thought. Falcons' eyes had endless depth that went beyond what she could see, and she could imagine that it was like looking into the eyes of a *Tyrannosaurus rex*.

As she put their hoods back on, she thought about Clay Junior and the things he had said and hinted at and she asked the falcons:

"What are we going to do?"

CHAPTER EIGHT

THE SUN WAS so bright on the untrammeled sea of fresh snow all around him that Joe wished he had sunglasses for his sunglasses. Snowplows had scraped the surface of the highway clear on I-25 South and the direct rays of the high-altitude light were doing the rest. The road surface steamed as it heated and melted, and at times Joe got to behold an awesome and unusual sight: miles upon miles of fog-like steam rising both from the road and from the Middle Fork of the Twelve Sleep River as it coursed parallel to him through the snow-blanketed sagebrush.

Because the snow was so deep, Joe couldn't clearly see oncoming traffic in the northbound lane. All he could make out was the top half of cars and the cabs of pickups looking like the conning towers of partially submerged submarines.

It wasn't until he got to Kaycee that he started to observe the delayed movement of cattle and wildlife in the distance where the creatures high-stepped through the snowfall. As he shot by the little town, Joe, as he always did, tipped an imaginary glass to the memory of Wyoming legend Chris LeDoux.

The looming humpbacks of the Bighorns framed the western horizon, and there wasn't a cloud in the sky.

What there was, however, was billboard after billboard featuring the stoic profile of Governor Colter Allen wearing a battered cowboy hat as he stared steely-eyed at the distance.

The billboards read:

> REELECT GOV ALLEN.
> PROVEN FIGHTER.
> PROVEN MAVERICK.
> PROVEN VISIONARY.
> AND HE'S JUST GETTING STARTED.

Joe snorted at the last line and said aloud, "That's just what everybody is worried about—*that he's just getting started*."

As HE DROVE south, the depth of snow on the terrain decreased and he could see the tops of tall sagebrush poking through. The fury of the storm, he determined, had been largely concentrated on the eastern side of the Bighorns after all.

To confirm that it would be smooth sailing the rest of the way to Cheyenne, Joe turned on the radio and searched for Wyoming meteorologist Don Day's hourly forecast segment.

He found it sandwiched between political commercials touting the reelection of Governor Colter Allen.

Which told Joe two things: the huge spring storm had dumped over thirty inches of snow in some parts of north-central Wyoming, and that the Allen for Governor campaign was extremely well funded, even though there had been no official announcement to date. It was clearly doing everything it could to persuade any potential challengers to stay out of the race by buying up all the airtime and available billboards.

As far as Joe knew, no credible candidates had yet announced, only the usual assortment of house painters, one-issue cranks, and far-right and far-left political hacks. He couldn't recall such a one-sided media campaign ever before and he wondered what was going on.

He thought again about the rumors that Spencer Rulon might run. Could Allen actually keep Rulon out by buying a win?

JOE WAS AT Twenty Mile Hill north of Casper when his phone lit up. It was Sheriff Scott Tibbs.

"He's gone, Joe," Tibbs said between heavy breaths. "If he was ever there in the first place."

"What are you talking about?"

"This victim you claimed to find," Tibbs said. "The UW professor. He's not where you said he was."

Joe took the phone away from his face and looked at it with suspicion for a few seconds. Then: "Come again?"

Tibbs said, "I'm parked out on the highway right now, but I sent three of my guys up there on snowmobiles and they found that metal building you described. But when they found it, there was no body."

"Hold it," Joe said. "You saw the photos I sent you. The victim was very clearly where I said he was."

"I know what you said and I know what you sent," Tibbs said. "But he's not there now. Is it possible he was injured and he woke up and walked away?"

"Not a chance," Joe said. "The top of his head was missing. He was deader than dead when I found him. Did your guys see tracks in the snow around the building?"

Tibbs didn't respond immediately. Then he said, "I don't know. I didn't ask them."

Joe rolled his eyes. "Maybe you should do that, Sheriff. Because it might mean either a wolf or a mountain lion got to the body and dragged him off."

"What about a bear?" Tibbs speculated.

"They're still hibernating, so I doubt it."

"Oh."

"But it's even more likely that it was the same guys who shot at me," Joe said. "Whoever it was, somebody might have gotten there before your deputies and retrieved the body. I don't know why and I don't know when. Did you check with Clay Hutmacher? Maybe he sent some of his employees out there?"

"I'll give him a call," Tibbs said.

"Who did you send up there on snowmobiles?" Joe asked.

"Deputies Steck, Bass, and Holmes," Tibbs said a little defensively. He didn't like to be questioned, and especially by Joe.

Joe knew Ryan Steck quite well, and he knew that the deputy planned to run for sheriff when Tibbs officially announced his retirement in the coming weeks. Tom Bass had no ambitions to move up himself, and no real ambitions at all except to retire unhurt with his pension funded in full. Buck Holmes was the newest hire at the department, and he'd come with an impressive track record: U.S. Marines and three years at the Teton County Sheriff's Office. There were rumors that Holmes eyed the top job as well.

"Why didn't you send Gary Norwood?" Joe asked. Norwood was the forensic evidence tech who was shared by three counties.

"I figured he'd be snowed in," Tibbs said.

Joe shook his head. It wasn't that Norwood was snowed in, but that Tibbs *figured* he might be.

"Can I please talk to one of your guys who was at the scene?" Joe asked.

Tibbs sighed. Joe could hear the sheriff call out of his pickup window for "Buck."

"This is Buck Holmes," the deputy said.

"Joe Pickett. Can you please describe what you found at the scene? I was the one who discovered the body."

"Gotcha," Holmes said. "It was a modern metal building, just as you described. Right there in the middle of nowhere. But there was no body."

"Was the building operating?"

"Operating?"

"Were the fans on the outside wall turning? Was it making a lot of noise?"

"It was dead quiet," Holmes said. "If it weren't for the co-ordinates you sent us, we would have missed it."

"Were there recent tracks in the snow around it?"

"Yeah, there were. Some of them were covered with too much fresh snow to be any good to us. But it looked like somebody got there in a snow machine early this morning. Maybe pulling some kind of trailer. We could see the track marks and some long lines parallel to each other through the snow. You know, like a big kid's sled."

"Did you get photos?" Joe asked.

"Yeah, I did. Do you want me to send them to you?"

"Please," Joe said. "What about the opening where the fans were? Did you look inside?"

"I did."

"What did you see?"

"What did I see?"

"Yes," Joe said, trying to keep irritation out of his voice.

"Metal walls, I guess. Metal fan blades."

"So it was clean? You didn't see blood, or hair, or brains on the surfaces?"

"Nope."

"Did you take photos of that as well?"

"Ryan might have. I didn't see a reason."

"Can you please ask Deputy Steck to send along his images to me?"

"Sure, if it's okay with the boss."

"Gary Norwood would be helpful to get on the scene," Joe said. "He might be able to find traces of who or what took the body."

"Yeah, maybe," Holmes said. He sounded skeptical.

"Did you look inside the building?" Joe asked.

"The door was locked," Holmes said. "We didn't have any way to get in and we didn't want to break down the door. There wasn't any probable cause to do that."

Joe's mind was spinning. Someone had gotten to the building ahead of law enforcement, taken the body, shut off the power, and possibly absconded with whatever had been inside.

"Did you notice anything else at the scene?"

"Not really," Holmes said. "Clay Hutmacher showed up with a couple of his ranch hands. Clay is the manager of the place."

"Yes, I know him. Why was he there?"

"He said someone had cut the chain on a gate into the ranch on the west side of the property. Clay was looking for the trespassers. He was pretty pissed off, I'll tell you."

"Did he find them?"

"Not that I know of."

"I don't have any idea what's going on," Joe told Holmes. "Do you have any working theories?"

"My working theory is we spent half the day on a wild-goose chase on behalf of the local game warden," Holmes said. Joe could hear Tibbs guffaw in the background.

"It was no wild-goose chase," Joe said. "You saw the crime scene shots I took. I've got the professor's wallet in my office. It's not like he was never there."

"I suppose," Holmes said. "We've got some questions about those photos ourselves, but I think they can wait until we sit down with you and have a little conversation."

Joe shook his head. What questions? Did Deputy Holmes and the others think he set them up to be humiliated? It made no logical sense. Nothing he had heard in the last five minutes did.

"I'll be back tomorrow," Joe said. "Please send those photos to my phone."

"Yeah," Holmes responded. "You'll see a whole lot of nothing except tracks in the snow."

Joe punched off and tossed the phone onto the passenger seat as if it were infected by some kind of virus that made people stupid.

He retrieved the phone again as he passed through Casper, and he called Clay Hutmacher.

"Hey, Joe," the ranch manager said. "Did Sheridan make it back okay? She left this morning."

"As far as I know," Joe said. "But that's not why I'm calling." He made a mental note to make sure to confirm that Sheridan was safe in her new apartment.

"That girl is special, Joe," Hutmacher said. "You and Marybeth did a good job of raising her."

"Thank you. Marybeth gets all the credit. But like I said, that isn't why I called."

"Shoot."

Joe briefed Hutmacher on the missing body. Then:

"I talked to Deputy Holmes a while back. He said you were out this morning looking for some trespassers. Did you find them?"

"No, damn it," Hutmacher said. "We followed their tracks for a while, but then the snow drifted over and we never saw anyone."

"Did you see any mountain lions in the area? Any wolves?"

"If I did, I would have shot them," Hutmacher said. Then he chuckled and said, "I suppose I shouldn't say that to a game warden."

"You are correct."

"But no, we didn't see any predators about. And we didn't find a dead body of a professor, either."

"How'd they get on the ranch?"

"They must have brought along some bolt cutters. The bastards cut the locked chain on a gate and came right in."

"Could you tell when it happened?"

"My guess is early this morning," Hutmacher said. "It was hard to tell by the tracks, though. It could have been yesterday afternoon. I guess we'll never know. One thing I do know is that I need to buy heavier chains and locks."

"Do you have any idea who it was?"

"No clue, Joe. It could have been some snowmobilers looking for fresh powder, or elk poachers, or it could have been something else entirely. My boss rubs a lot of people the wrong way. He has lots of enemies."

Joe noted that fact as well.

Hutmacher's voice rose when he asked, "Do you think these trespassers had something to do with that professor's death? Is that why you're asking?"

"I don't know," Joe said. "But it's possible. Somebody did take a couple of shots at me. Maybe it was your trespassers."

"I wish we could figure out what they were doing on us," Hutmacher said. "All this snow covers everything up."

"Speaking of covering things up," Joe said, "it's time to come clean on what was in that building, Clay. The facts on the ground have changed since we last talked. I need to know."

Hutmacher moaned.

"Clay?"

"It was a bunch of computers, a few million dollars' worth," he said. "I was told by the owner never to talk about it because he didn't want the word to get out. He was afraid someone would get on the ranch and steal them, I think."

"What were the computers used for?" Joe asked.

"I honestly don't have a clue. He didn't tell me and I didn't ask."

"Who would have shut off the operation?" Joe asked.

"I don't know that, either. I figure it was run remotely. Like I told you, I have no idea what that building is for."

Joe believed him. "If you find out will you let me know?" he asked.

Hutmacher moaned again.

"Clay?"

"I've got to go, Joe."

"Clay?"

"I've got to run this by the boss."

"Thank you."

JOE USED HIS Bluetooth to dial Sheridan's phone. She answered on the third ring.

"Is everything okay?" he asked her.

"Sure. Is that why you're calling?"

"Yes. I wanted to make sure you made it home after the storm."

"Yes, Dad."

"Great."

After a beat, she said, "Is that all?"

"Yup."

"Where are you?"

"Nearly to Wheatland."

"Why?"

"I've been summoned to Cheyenne."

"Well, say hi to the governor for me," she laughed.

"Will do."

ALTHOUGH CHEYENNE WAS known for spectacular blizzards of its own, the storm Joe had just experienced hadn't made it this far south. The sky was darkening and a spectacular sunset was forming when Joe got to the northern outskirts of the city. He could see the gold dome of the capitol building lit up within a shaft of sunlight in the center of town.

He checked his watch to see that it was four forty-five. Fifteen minutes until all of the state offices shut down for the night.

A text flashed on his phone from his boss, Director Rick Ewig.

Where are you?

10 min., Joe texted back.

Hurry. I'll meet you in the lobby.

JOE PARKED ON the street in front of the capitol and climbed the stairs. The building had undergone a massive refurbishment recently when the state's economy was supercharged by mineral extraction wealth—before the bottom dropped out.

There were no visitors or employees inside, and except for the governor's office all the doors he could see were closed and the lights behind them were turned off. Apparently, everyone had gotten a jump on five o'clock.

He found Rick Ewig sitting by himself in the anteroom of the governor's office. Ewig looked to be immersed in his own thoughts: bent forward, head down, hands dangling between his knees.

"Made it," Joe said.

"Great," Ewig said.

Joe thought the director looked ten years older than the last time he'd seen him. Probably a combination of helming the agency through the COVID pandemic, budget cuts, personal issues, and dealing daily with Governor Allen.

A prim receptionist behind a desk picked up her handset and said, "They're here." Then, after replacing it, she said, "The governor will see you now."

Joe followed Ewig through a heavy door.

The governor had both a large public office for meetings and announcements, and a small windowless private office, which wasn't much wider than his desk. The walls were covered with framed photos of him with national politicians and celebrities, and the man himself was lit by the orange glow from two banker's lamps on his desk.

"Greetings, gentlemen. I'm *so* glad you could make it."

"We had a big storm up north," Joe said.

Allen ignored Joe and said, "Shut the door and have a seat." He was dressed in a tuxedo and he wore a black bow tie.

Ewig and Joe slid into two of three leather-covered chairs facing Governor Allen. Joe removed his Stetson and placed it crown-down in the third chair.

Joe had observed before that Allen reserved small talk and pleasantries for supporters, donors, and fellow politicos. State employees, *his* employees in the governor's mind, didn't rate the same consideration.

"I have to get to an important dinner," the governor said. "So I don't have much time."

Joe and Ewig nodded.

"I'll get right to it, then," Allen said. He then fixed his gaze directly on Joe. "You again," he said.

"Yes, sir."

"I'm starting to think you were put on this earth to be my nemesis. Is that why you were put here?"

Joe shook his head. "Is that really a question?"

He could feel Director Ewig squirm in the next chair.

Allen simply shook his head. "It didn't exactly work out very well when you were asked to guide Steve Price on that elk hunt last fall, did it? He was hunted down like a dog by your locals and the two of you made it off that mountain by the skin of your teeth. And it was such a harrowing experience that Price wouldn't even consider locating a server farm here, even though that was the whole point of the assignment. What a black eye that was."

"It didn't work out as hoped," Joe said.

Allen rolled his eyes. "I should have fired you then. I *could* have fired you then."

But you didn't because Price threatened to go public with information on you that would hurt your reelection chances, Joe thought but didn't say. There was no need.

What that information *was* had remained under wraps.

Joe could only speculate as to the contents. He was simply glad he hadn't lost his job.

Allen continued. "And now you stumble on a situation that is best described as extremely sensitive. A situation that could blow up into an international scandal. How is it that a guy like you keeps finding himself in the middle of every shitshow in the state?"

Joe shrugged. "I wish I knew, sir. Finding Professor Wei's body out there was a shock."

Allen turned to Ewig. "Rick, do you ask this guy to go out there every day and find a new way to embarrass my administration?"

"No, I do not, sir," Ewig said. His voice was strained.

"That's what it seems like to me," Allen said. "And it needs to stop right here and right now."

There was a long silent pause. Ewig finally said, "What is it you want us to do, sir?"

"It's very simple," Allen said. "I want you, your agency, and Mr. Pickett here to keep this situation under wraps. Put a lid on it right now and never speak of it again."

"Put a lid on it?"

Joe could sense Ewig's confusion because he shared it.

"You have no idea what you've stumbled into," Allen said. "And I have no intention of filling you in. Just know that the governor of the state of Wyoming has ordered you to stand down and not to pursue any aspect of the investigation. Pretend that this incident never took place."

"How can that work, sir?" Ewig asked. "From what I understand, he was a prominent professor—"

"*That's not of your concern, Director,*" Allen said sharply, cutting Ewig off. "We'll handle it on this end. You two should just return to your duties. Go hand out some tickets or something."

Joe said, "Local law enforcement in Twelve Sleep County is aware of the discovery of Mr. Wei's body. His car is still parked up there. I talked with the sheriff's department this afternoon and they've opened a case file."

Allen's eyes flashed and he spoke through clenched teeth. "Didn't you hear me just say we would handle it? Did I mumble?"

"No, sir," Joe said, feeling his face flush.

"I understand you took photos of the scene with your state-issued iPhone," Allen said.

"Yes, sir, I did. I forwarded them to local law enforcement."

"You need to delete them from your phone. We'll get the material from the sheriff's department and turn everything over to DCI."

The Division of Criminal Investigation was a state agency headquartered in Cheyenne. It was well known that Allen considered the agency to be his personal law enforcement arm even though the statutes governing it said otherwise.

"Delete them?" Joe asked.

"Do it now," Allen said firmly.

Reluctantly, Joe selected all of the photos on his phone and transferred them into the digital trash can. But not before surreptitiously sending them all to Marybeth. Then he held his screen up so Allen could see they were gone. "Good," Allen said.

"This goes well beyond what you could imagine," Allen said to both of them. "It involves extremely sensitive issues. It involves national security concerns, and potential accusations of racism and xenophobia that are well above your pay grade, gentlemen. Do I make myself clear?"

"You do, sir," Ewig said.

Allen glared at Joe.

Finally, Joe said, "I hear you. I don't get it, but I hear you."

"You don't need to *get* anything," Allen said. "You need to do what's best for this state and this country. And what's best for my administration. Is that clear?"

Ewig said he understood and Joe nodded.

"And," Allen said, pushing back from his desk, "since you've nearly made me late for my important event, this meeting is now over."

He stood up, shot out his hands to smooth the sleeves of his tuxedo jacket, and exited through the door behind his desk.

JOE TURNED TO Rick Ewig. "Did any of that make any sense to you?"

Ewig looked around before shaking his head. "None of it," he said softly so as not to be overheard. "But it didn't need to.

I understand an order when I hear one. We need to lay off of this case."

"Shouldn't we do our job?" Joe asked.

Ewig sat back, sighed, and rubbed his eyes with the tips of his fingers. "The governor has a point about you, Joe. You always seem to find yourself in the middle of every debacle. You could be described as a shit magnet. Maybe you can just sit this one out."

Joe didn't respond as he stood up and turned on his heel.

He said, "I didn't lie to the governor. I said I heard him. But that's all I said."

"Joe . . ."

"I don't want your job, Rick," Joe said. "I need to be able to look at myself in the mirror in the morning."

JOE WAS REACHING for the door handle to his truck when he realized he'd been so angry that he'd forgotten his hat in the governor's office. He quickly strode up the sidewalk and up the stairs and was grateful that the security guard hadn't yet locked the front door.

The governor's receptionist was sliding on her coat when Joe once again entered the office.

"Forgot my hat," he said.

She waved him on with impatience.

His hat was where he'd left it and he snatched it up, thanked the receptionist, and clamped it on his head as he walked to the exit.

As he did, he heard the trill of a woman's voice and the deep laugh of a man. He recognized the laugh as coming from Governor Allen at his most charming. The trill made his insides seize up.

The couple was in the hallway outside the governor's public office, and not in Joe's line of sight. So he backed up enough to see them.

The governor had his back to Joe as he ambled down the hallway to another exit. He was pulling on his coat and talking in an animated way to the small, well-dressed woman at his side. She was slim and slinky and she looked up to Allen with sparkling eyes and an expression that seemed to hang on every word that came out of his mouth.

Joe's jaw dropped and he felt a chill roll up his spine.

Missy, his mother-in-law who had multiple marriages behind her as well as a couple of felonies she'd never been charged for, looped her arm through the arm of the governor and leaned tightly into him as they pushed through the double doors.

"Are you ready to go?" came a voice to his right. A security guard held the door to the building open.

"I've never been more ready," Joe said.

CHAPTER NINE

WHILE HE WOUND his way through the canyon to Laramie on I-80, Joe replayed parts of the brief meeting in his head. *National security? Extremely sensitive issues? Xenophobia? Missy . . .*

None of this made sense to him. It had come off as hyperbole, he thought. A smoke screen to hide something else.

He tried to concentrate on his driving, but it was difficult. The Summit on I-80 between Cheyenne and Laramie was one of the most treacherous stretches in the state and it seemed to harbor a weather system all its own. No other interstate highway in the nation was closed as often for hazardous conditions, sometimes eighty or ninety days a year, and the Summit was usually the bottleneck that slowed down or stopped thousands of tractor trailers on their east-to-west or west-to-east routes.

This drive was no different. Although it hadn't been snowing in Cheyenne, and Laramie reported clear skies, it was sleeting in the canyon and the slush was piling up on the asphalt. Massive trucks were inching their way down the canyon and a couple had already slid off the road.

A jackknifed semi partially blocked the parallel eastbound lanes and Joe could see a line of vehicles stacking up behind it.

Joe waited until the snow eased up and he could see the twinkling lights of Laramie before calling Marybeth. She sounded relaxed when she answered, and Joe thought the day at home had been good for her and he envied it.

"Guess who I just saw in Cheyenne cozying up to Governor Allen?" he asked.

She waited a beat, then said, "No—not Missy."

"How'd you guess?"

"From your tone. There's a certain kind of pain in your voice when you talk about her. So am I right?"

"None other," Joe said. "Missy has a knack for being right there when I'm being humiliated. I'm pretty sure she was in the next room, probably listening through the door and enjoying every second of it."

"Why is she in Cheyenne?" Marybeth asked. "The last time I heard from her, she was tending to Marcus Hand. How could she leave him when he's in hospice care for pancreatic cancer?"

Marcus Hand had once been a celebrated Jackson Hole defense attorney who had achieved a national profile by winning huge judgments against corporations and appearing on cable television legal shows. He was famous for his full mane of silver hair, his fringed buckskin jackets, his in-home tele-vision studio so he could opine live on cable news shows, and his country-boy way of speaking. He had served as Missy's defense attorney before the two married. He was Missy's fifth or sixth husband—Joe couldn't keep track. Each husband had been wealthier than the previous one, and she'd amassed a fortune over the years by constantly trading up.

Joe said to Marybeth, "It appears she's reverting to form. She moves fast."

"Poor Marcus Hand . . ." Marybeth said.

"Allen may not be richer than Marcus, but he's certainly more powerful."

In fact, Joe knew, Missy had been one of Allen's biggest campaign contributors in his first-term election.

Joe said, "Maybe her checkbook is how Allen has bought every billboard in the state and every second of airtime."

"I wouldn't put it past her," Marybeth said. "I could see her spending Marcus's money while he's in a coma waiting to die. He probably doesn't even know she's gone—or that she has his checkbook.

"You know what I'm going to do?" Marybeth asked in a controlled fury. "I'm going to go online and find out how much she's contributed to the Allen for Governor campaign—and when."

"What good would that do?" Joe asked.

"Probably not much," Marybeth conceded. "It's public in-formation. But we'd at least know when she started scheming this time. The information might be of use to whoever runs against the governor."

"I think we should stay out of it," Joe said. "I'm already on thin ice with Allen."

"I'm still going to look," she said. "We can discuss it when you get home. Speaking of, when will that be?"

He shrugged. "I'll probably make it as far as Casper tonight. I'll be back early tomorrow."

"Have you looked at the weather report?"

"Not recently."

"Don Day says there's a high-wind warning for Central Wyoming starting at midnight," Marybeth said. "With all of this snow . . ."

Joe visualized two-to-three-foot drifts across the top half of the state, and closed roads everywhere.

"I'll get as far as I can tonight," he said. "Maybe I can outrun it."

"Kiss Lucy for me," she said.

"Will do."

SHE CALLED BACK a minute later. She said, "I knew there was something I wanted to tell you."

"What's that?"

"I got an interesting voicemail at the library today. A group wants to rent out the building for Monday, April 3."

"Yes?" Joe asked.

"The group is called 'He's Just Getting Started.'"

Joe shook his head. "I've never heard of it." And then he thought again. "You don't mean . . ."

"It's Governor Allen's campaign committee," she said. Marybeth paused to let that sink in. "I think he might be making his official announcement that day. If he does what he did last time, he'll barnstorm the state and make speeches in Jackson, Casper, Sheridan, and Cheyenne, all in the same day. I don't know why he's adding Saddlestring this time."

"Maybe he doesn't realize the locals don't exactly love him there."

"Or maybe he thinks he'll win them over," she said. "Anyway, it's interesting."

"Yup. I wonder why he didn't mention it to me when I was in his office."

"Good question," she said.

JOE SECURED A booth in the back of a restaurant downtown called the Altitude Chophouse & Brewery and he grinned when Lucy came through the front door, saw him, and beamed.

Although he'd been with her in person just a few months before at Thanksgiving, Lucy appeared to be older and more self-assured than he'd ever noticed before. She was in her element, it seemed, and she greeted several friends in the restaurant on the way to the table. Like her mother, Lucy was blond, willowy, and green-eyed. She had such an easy and approachable way about her, Joe thought.

"I was hoping we could meet at the Washakie Center for dinner," Joe said. That was the UW campus dining facility.

"Ha!" Lucy said. "Why would we go to Washakie when we can eat downtown like civilized people and you can pick up the check?"

It was an ongoing joke between Joe and his daughters when he came to Laramie. Neither Sheridan nor Lucy would invite him to the student dining hall. He knew it was because they were embarrassed to be seen with him—an older guy in a red uniform shirt with a sidearm and a cowboy hat—and he didn't blame them.

"Do you remember Fong?" Lucy asked him as her roommate shyly slid into the booth next to her.

"Of course," he said to her. "It's good to see you again."

Lucy had invited Fong Chan to Saddlestring for the Thanksgiving holiday as well. Fong was an exchange student from Hong Kong and she was sweet and as smart as a whip, Joe thought.

"It's good to see you again, Mr. Pickett," Fong said with what appeared to be a genuine smile. "I told my family all about going to your home and they said it sounded like being in a cowboy movie. My dad loves Westerns. He made us watch them growing up, and he was the one who urged me to go to school here."

Fong had a high girlish voice that tinkled like wind chimes, Joe noted.

He nodded. "When Lucy is there with her sisters it's a Wild West place, all right."

"Especially if April is there," Lucy added with an eye roll. "Things can get Western in a hurry."

Joe couldn't argue with that.

HE ORDERED A cheeseburger and coffee, while the girls opted for salads. They ate and talked about Laramie, the university, and the crazy Wyoming spring weather. Joe told them about getting stuck trying to drive to the house and digging out, and Fong said she wished she could be there to experience three feet of snow.

"No, you don't," Lucy said. "Trust me."

"But I do!" Fong insisted. "We get a lot of wind here, but not that much snow."

"It's still March," Joe said. "Hang around . . ."

JOE JOKED TO Lucy about all of the "cargo" he'd been tasked to deliver to her for spring break. "I didn't know swimsuits could take up that much room," he said.

"Mom said you'd give me a hard time about that," Lucy said. "But thank you. I need my summer clothes, so I should be set."

"You need to be careful down there in Texas," Joe said. "From what I hear, it can be a crazy place."

"I'm always careful," Lucy said between bites. Joe believed her. Lucy had learned from her sisters' missteps. She had nothing to prove to anyone, and she knew there were consequences for her actions. Joe wanted to give her a bear hug, but he didn't want to embarrass her in front of her friend by doing it.

Joe told Lucy he'd seen her grandmother that evening, but didn't detail the circumstances of why he'd been in Cheyenne.

"Missy was there?" Lucy asked, wide-eyed. "Isn't she supposed to be in Jackson?"

Joe shrugged and the two exchanged a long glance that confirmed what they both suspected: Missy was at it again.

"Wow," Lucy said. Then to Fong: "Missy is the grandmother I told you about. The one who doesn't want to be called 'Grandma.'"

"She always liked Lucy the best," Joe explained to Fong. "Because Lucy indulged her."

"I just liked the clothes she bought me," Lucy said with a shrug. "I've always been onto her."

While they traded Missy stories, Joe caught Fong looking at the time on her phone beneath the table. She was either bored or had someplace to be, he decided.

"Should I ask for the check?" he said. He made it a point not to reference Fong when he asked.

But Lucy intuited what had happened. She leaned over and hugged her roommate. "Fong studies every night, starting at eight. I don't know when she even sleeps. I'm trying to break her of that bad habit." Then: "Let's order dessert!"

Fong giggled and agreed that they should look at the dessert menu. Joe thought Lucy had handled things well, even though he didn't want to keep the girls out too late and because he had a long drive ahead of him as well.

"I know you told me," he said to Fong, "but I forgot what you're studying."

"It's very boring and uninteresting," she replied with a blush.

"No it isn't," Lucy answered for her. "She's studying to be an engineer. She goes to CEAS. Fong is brilliant."

"CEAS," Joe said, recalling his research from last night. "The College of Engineering and Applied Science?"

Fong nodded in a shy way. But Joe could tell she was pleased that he knew what the acronym stood for.

"That's interesting," Joe said, knowing he needed to be very cautious about what he would say to her next. "Do you know a professor named Zhang Wei?"

Fong's head jerked up and she looked stricken.

"What's wrong?" Lucy asked. She shot an accusatory glance at Joe.

"I'm sorry," Joe said. "I didn't mean to—"

Fong said, "Thank you for dinner," as she slid out of the booth with her coat.

"Fong!" Lucy called after her. But Fong didn't slow down until she was through the front doors onto Second Street.

"Dad," Lucy said as she glared at him, "what did you just do?"

"I'm not really sure," he said.

"I've never seen her react like that before. Who is this professor?"

"He's the only professor I know of from CEAS," Joe said.

Lucy narrowed her eyes and looked at him with suspicion. Joe knew the look because he'd seen it from Marybeth many, many times. Lucy knew he was withholding something.

He said, "If I tell you something, can you keep it confidential between us?"

"You know I can," she said.

JOE BRIEFED LUCY on everything over the last two days, including the meeting with the governor. He said that he suspected the murder victim was Professor Wei, but there was no confirmation without a body.

"I'm sure you'll hear it on the news at some point," Joe said, "I just don't know when that will happen. For reasons I can't explain, it's all supposed to be very hush-hush for the time being.

"I have no idea what I did to Fong," Joe said. "Is she close to this guy?"

"No clue," Lucy said. "She's never mentioned his name around me and I doubt she knows what happened to him. If she did, she never mentioned it. I don't really hang out with the engineering students, except for Fong. I have no idea what goes on over there at CEAS, or why she reacted the way she did."

"I'm really sorry," Joe said. "I hit a nerve without realizing it."

Lucy waved him off. "Now I'm a little concerned," she

said. "I hate to see her so worked up. I'm going to worry about her. She's a long way from home. I hope she'll talk to me."

Joe nodded. "Please tell her I didn't mean to upset her."

"I will, because you didn't," Lucy said.

"I'll GIVE YOU a ride back to your place and carry in your cargo," Joe said after handing the waitress his credit card.

"It was great to see you, Dad. And thank you."

"It was my pleasure," he said. "Mom told me to give you a kiss."

She leaned across the table and turned her cheek to him. He kissed her twice.

CHAPTER TEN

DEMO SLOWLY WEAVED his SUV through the curved roads of the lodgepole pine forest in the dark. His beams illuminated the bronzed trunks of the trees and low-hanging branches. He switched between four-wheel-drive high and four-wheel-drive low to navigate the deep snow. He was grateful the crust of snow on the road had been broken by several vehicles that had been there before him.

He knew he was a few minutes late, which was something the Big Fish didn't like. But it couldn't be helped. His progress out of Saddlestring to the remote campground had been delayed by the highway patrol, who had blocked the highway while a tow truck winched a sedan out of the bank of snow into which the driver had plunged.

The massive thirty-nine-foot Entegra Reatta motor home was tucked into the last space of the campground and the aluminum skin of it lit up in his headlights. The vehicle was literally a snooty house on wheels, with satellite TV and Wi-Fi, a king bed, a fireplace, a washer/dryer—all powered by a propane generator. Supposedly, it slept eight people, although the Big Fish was alone.

Demo had looked up what the 2019 vehicle was worth and he was astounded to find out: three hundred and twenty-eight thousand dollars. Where the Big Fish had come into that kind of fortune was unclear to him. Something about a big settlement because the Big Fish had been injured on the job. That's all Demo knew.

There were two vehicles parked on the side of the motor home, a jacked-up Chevy Silverado and a Jeep. Both had local plates. The Big Fish's Bronco, which he towed behind the motor home, was also there.

The shades of the RV were pulled down on the many windows, but they glowed yellow from the lights inside.

Demo parked next to the Silverado and climbed out of his rig. The pickup was an older model and it had been through the wringer. The sides were scratched by branches, there were dents in the doors and cracks in the windshield. On the back window was a decal loosely based on the bad boy comic character Calvin peeing with his pants down.

A snowmobile was tilted into the bed of the truck, its back end resting on the closed tailgate. Demo noted packed snow in the tracks of the machine, indicating that it had been recently used.

Meaning Leland Christensen and Ogden Driskill were already inside.

The Jeep had a window decal as well: the stick figures of a mother, father, and three children. A bumper sticker read: MY DAUGHTER IS AN HONOR STUDENT AT SADDLESTRING MIDDLE SCHOOL.

Meaning Avery Sue White was there as well.

Which was *just* about everybody.

As DEMO RAISED his hand to knock on the door of the motor home, he was hit by an intense red beam that temporarily blinded him. He clenched his eyes shut and turned toward the source of the light.

"Get that goddam laser out of my face," he growled.

"Sorry, man," Leland Christensen said. "I had to make sure it was you."

Demo cautiously opened his eyes as the red-dot laser sight slid down his parka and finally rested on the snow near his feet. Christensen stepped from around the back of the motor home, cradling an AR-15.

"You're late," Christensen said.

"You're an idiot," Demo responded.

Christensen *was* an idiot. He was a local toothless reprobate meth head who lived in the basement of an auto-parts store on Main Street in Saddlestring. Christensen did odd jobs for contractors and outfitters, but his primary income was from dealing weed and meth. Christensen was dark and skeletal and he had long limbs and a pinched face. The man had no business holding a weapon, and no training on how to use it. No professional would *ever* point a red dot at a target's face. Instead, he'd point it at the target's heart.

"It's okay," Christensen shouted as he thumped the side of the motor home with the heel of his left hand. "It's Demo."

The door opened and Demo stepped aside so it wouldn't hit him. The doorway was filled with Ogden Driskill, Christensen's cohort. Also in his mid-thirties, Driskill was a pudgy ginger with tiny eyes who had grown up as the son of the local car dealer, but had recently lost his job as janitor at the Catholic church for spying on parishioners in the restroom. He was a three-time loser who'd spent as much of his adult life in the Wyoming State Penitentiary in Rawlins as he had on the streets in Saddlestring.

Driskill, like Christensen, was a well-known tweaker.

"You're late," Driskill said.

"So I've been told," Demo said.

"Let him in," the Big Fish commanded from inside the motor home. "Let's get this thing started."

Demo rubbed his eyes as he climbed the steps to enter. All he could see through his left eye was the lingering afterimage of the red dot.

"You need to train these meth heads on how to handle a weapon," he said to the Big Fish.

"Hey—we don't do that no more," Driskill said. He sounded hurt by the accusation. "We quit that shit."

"Sure you did," Demo said.

"We fucking did," Christensen said as he entered the RV

behind Demo and closed the door. "Didn't we, sir?" he asked the Big Fish.

As Demo's eyes adjusted, he noted Avery Sue White sitting primly at the head of the table with pursed lips and her hands in her lap. She wore a powder-blue pantsuit and Ugg boots. She seemed to disapprove of the situation—and the language—that was taking place in front of her.

Also in attendance was Cade Molvar, who sat quietly in a camp chair in the hallway that went to the master bedroom in the back of the motor home. Demo was surprised to see him there since his vehicle hadn't been outside.

Molvar was a bear of a man with a full white beard and mitt-sized hands that were folded on his lap. He had intense eyes that poked out from his round face like twin black pinpricks. Molvar nodded to Demo, and Demo nodded back.

Molvar was the ringleader of a group of five or six locals known as the Keystoners. They were rough-hewn, blue-collar types who wore heavy outerwear and boots best suited for the oil fields they no longer worked in, although there was a whiff of petroleum that clung to their clothing.

They'd adopted the name the Keystoners for two reasons, Demo knew. The first was that all of them were pipe fitters or welders who had once made very good money working on pipelines across the country. They'd lost their jobs when a massive interstate pipeline from Canada to refineries in the Southwest had been abruptly killed by the U.S. government because it had become a symbol for increased reliance on fossil fuels. The second reason for the name was that the un-employed men had recently grouped together to corner the market on weed distribution in the tri-county area.

The Keystoners were tough, ruthless, and ideological. They shared their views with other informal chapters throughout the west and south of the country. They all hated the Washington, D.C., elites that had eliminated their legitimate liveli-hoods and had labeled them as troglodyte throwbacks. They openly carried firearms, supported legalized marijuana use, and considered any politician who disagreed with them a mortal enemy.

Demo was not surprised by the fact that Molvar was in attendance, but he was by how he had gotten there. The Key-stoner must have gotten a ride from the tweakers, he determined. That was one alliance he would not have predicted, and it bothered him.

The Big Fish cleared his throat and said, "Let's bring this meeting of the Sovereign Nation to order. One of our team members is coming later, but I don't want to wait for him."

Demo sat down at the table in the dining alcove across from the Big Fish. Christensen and Driskill sprawled on a built-in sofa. A propane fire crackled in the fireplace. A large yellow Gadsden DON'T TREAD ON ME flag hung on the wall behind the Big Fish, its coiled snake ready to strike.

"Jason," the Big Fish said, "please play the pertinent part of your recording."

Demo nodded and fished his phone out of his pocket. He placed it on the table and opened the app.

Demo: "You're the kind of man we need on our side. But let's set that aside for now. I'm here to plant the seed, nothing more."

Nate: "Are you talking about secession?"

Demo: "I'll be in touch."

"The first voice you heard was Jason, of course," the Big Fish said. "The second belonged to Nate Romanowski. I think we've made progress."

Christensen and Driskill exchanged glances, then Christensen said, "Nate Romanowski? Are we trying to recruit him? Are you shitting me?"

"I am not," the Big Fish said. "He'd be an extremely valuable addition to our movement."

Demo observed the Big Fish as he talked. He was so sure of himself. The Big Fish had short-cropped brown hair, rimless glasses, a thin face, and he had trouble walking without bracing himself against objects. Probably late fifties, early sixties. He seemed to be a physical contradiction, Demo thought. There was a way a man came across when he'd been weak all his life, a certain way he carried himself. The Big Fish wasn't like that. He seemed to possess confidence that came from a previous time in his life when he wasn't a spent force.

Something had happened to the Big Fish, Demo surmised. Something that now drove him. Demo assumed it had to do with his injury, and his mysterious settlement.

Christensen pleaded to the group not to recruit Nate Romanowski. He became more animated as he spoke. "You want to know the first time I ever saw the guy?" he said. "I was floating on the river trying to catch a fish and this weird feeling came over me, like I was being watched. Then I look up and there he was, that son of a bitch Nate Romanowski. Sitting on the branch of a tree watching me float under him. *Naked*. He was naked. Is that just crazy, or what?"

The Big Fish smiled at the story, which wasn't the reaction Christensen wanted to elicit.

Christensen continued. "I thought for a minute he was going to take a dump on me or something. I asked him what the hell he was doing up there and he told me to *move along*. And he fixed those eyes on me when he said it . . ."

Christensen mimicked an involuntary chill.

Driskill said, "I've heard things about him, too. That he twists people's ears off or pulls them apart with his hands. And that big gun of his—he's fuckin' scary."

"*Language*," White admonished, a scowl on her face.

"Not only that," Christensen said, "but Romanowski is pals with Joe Pickett. Pickett is the local game warden—"

"A real Boy Scout," Driskill interjected. "He's been a pain in our ass for years."

The Big Fish waved both objections away. "I know of Joe Pickett, but none of your reasons are relevant. What is relevant is that Romanowski soured on our government many years ago. He thinks like we do. He's a natural leader of men, and he'd quickly become the face of our movement. He'll bring others along with him. We need capable men like him."

White said, "Nate Romanowski has an infant daughter, right?"

Demo nodded. "His wife and daughter were there."

"I think that's a good thing," White said. "He'll be concerned about his daughter, so he'll be more sympathetic to our cause."

Demo wasn't surprised that she'd keyed upon that aspect of Romanowski's life. Avery Sue White had joined the group because of her fear that her children were being indoctrinated and corrupted in their schools by unscrupulous teachers and administrators who preached gender fluidity and taught critical race theory. White and her husband had recently moved to Wyoming from California, primarily to get their children away from all of that.

White had declared that she'd like to see the entire school system go down in flames. And that was just one of the benefits that the Big Fish's secession movement had offered her.

White claimed she knew dozens of parents who felt the same way who were eager to join up with the uprising the Big Fish was fomenting. All she needed, she said, was the word on when to reach out to them.

"I think Mr. Romanowski could be one of us," she said to Demo. Then: "What do you think, Mr. Molvar?"

"The more the merrier," Molvar said. "We need numbers."

As he said it, a low-grade buzz emitted from a computer monitor on the Big Fish's desk. Everyone inside the motor home looked over to see a pair of headlights sweep across the screen. The motion detector and camera were hidden among the trees on the first turn toward the interior of the campground.

The Big Fish motioned to Christensen and Driskill.

"Go see who it is," he said. "Get yourselves into position."

Both men leapt to their feet. Christensen retrieved the rifle with the laser-dot site on it. Driskill unsnapped the security strap on the shoulder holster he wore under his parka. Molvar rose and patted the grip of his weapon and followed them.

When they were out the door, Demo turned to the Big Fish. What he was about to say probably shouldn't be overheard by Avery Sue White, he thought, but he couldn't help himself.

"You've got to get rid of those two," Demo said. "Christensen and Driskill. They're idiots and loose cannons. I don't believe for a second they're clean and sober. Even if they were, they're still lowlifes. I don't think they believe in what you want them to believe, sir. Their only ideology is how to get away with the next scam so they can afford to buy more meth."

The Big Fish said, "They're both patriots. Like Molvar said, we need numbers. I think you're too hard on them."

Demo shook his head. "I'm not. They can't be trusted. They've always got something going and it usually goes wrong. We don't need the attention they bring. And I don't like the fact that the Keystoners are palling around with them."

The Big Fish looked skeptical. "We need all kinds," he said. "Let me worry about what's best for the movement."

"I assume they're on your payroll," Demo said.

"Of course. I can't expect them to donate all of their time for free. I also need them to recruit more locals."

"What about the Keystoners?"

"They're on retainer," the Big Fish said. "They've got outside income and don't really need the money, but who can't use more?"

Demo was flummoxed by the Big Fish's philosophy and tactics. Literally paying lowlifes to be part of the cause didn't buy long-term loyalty. To Demo, the quality of personnel mattered, especially in an insurgency. Why the Big Fish didn't cull miscreants was baffling to Demo.

"You don't want this kind around," Demo said. "Believe me—they're working something now right under your nose. They have a snowmobile in the back of their pickup that's been out recently. I know from the snow in the tracks. They're up to something."

The Big Fish shrugged. "Christensen said something about gathering sheds earlier today."

Sheds were elk antlers that annually dropped to the ground. There was substantial money in gathering sheds and selling them to traveling dealers.

"That's exactly what I'm saying," Demo said, lowering his voice to make it sound more urgent. "Shed season isn't open for more than a month. Those guys are breaking the law, which is what they do. If they're caught, it could lead to us. It could lead to *you*."

The rumble of a truck motor vibrated through the interior

of the motor home, and bright headlights from outside penetrated the blinds.

The front door opened and Driskill poked his head inside. "He's here," he said.

Demo folded his arms across his chest. He had every intention of continuing his argument about purging Christensen and Driskill with the Big Fish at the next opportunity he had to do so.

Driskill stepped to the side and Deputy Buck Holmes climbed the steps and entered the motor home. He was wearing his uniform and he looked formidable, Demo thought.

"Sorry I'm late," Holmes said to the Big Fish. "There's a lot going on."

Holmes sat down on the couch formerly used by Christensen and Driskill. He looked over at Demo as the two tweakers filed in behind him and stood there uncomfortably.

Demo and Holmes nodded their acknowledgment of the other.

They had an understanding in regard to why they were both there. At least, Demo thought they did.

Holmes, like Demo, had been carefully recruited by the Big Fish. Demo knew why he'd been targeted, and he wondered what the Big Fish had on Holmes to make him cooperate.

Or maybe, Demo thought, Buck Holmes was a true believer in the Sovereign Nation. The movement did have appeal to rural law enforcement personnel, since one of the tenets of the ideology purported that the county sheriff was the sole authority in charge and that he wasn't required to listen to state or federal authorities. Not only that, but county sheriffs could interpret the law as they wished. Sovereign citizens pledged to obey county sheriffs and no one else.

The Keystoners had made it clear they accepted the convention.

And there was no doubt in Demo's mind that having someone inside the local law enforcement entity would be extremely useful to the Big Fish, and therefore his efforts. Especially now since the operation the Big Fish had hinted at previously was being planned at this meeting.

The Big Fish paused, then said, "We now have a date and a time. We can proceed."

Holmes cleared his throat to get everyone's attention, and said, "I think we have a problem."

"What's that?" the Big Fish asked.

"His name is Joe Pickett," Holmes said.

"Him again," the Big Fish said with a snarl. Then: "We don't want him around messing with our operation. He has a knack for screwing things up."

Friday, March 31

One must have a mind of winter
To regard the frost and the boughs
Of the pine-trees crusted with snow;

And have been cold a long time
To behold the junipers shagged with ice,
The spruces rough in the distant glitter.

—WALLACE STEVENS,

"The Snow Man"

CHAPTER ELEVEN

IN THE MORNING, after a big breakfast of tamales at Eggington's in Casper, Joe cruised through downtown and jumped onto I-25 North to go home. He checked in with Marybeth, who was on her way to the library to open it back up, and he put in a call to Sheriff Tibbs to get an update on the investigation.

Tibbs didn't pick up and Joe's call went straight to voicemail.

Joe knew that the sheriff was *never* without his phone in his hand, especially in the last year or so. That way, his wife wouldn't notice the many calls and texts he received each day from Ruthanne Hubbard, the dispatcher Tibbs was sneaking around with. So, Joe speculated, Tibbs had seen Joe's name on the screen and had chosen to ignore it.

"So that's how it's going to be, is it?" Joe grumbled to himself. He guessed that the governor's office had already contacted Tibbs and informed him of their takeover of the Zhang Wei investigation.

Knowing Tibbs and his short-timer's attitude toward his duties, Joe guessed that the sheriff had welcomed the call.

It also occurred to Joe that Buck Holmes hadn't yet forwarded the crime scene photos he'd promised to send.

BEFORE GOING TO his house to pick up Daisy, Joe diverted en route to Nate's compound. The road was plowed and there seemed to be an unusual increase of tire tracks previous to his arrival, he thought.

Yarak, Inc., clients didn't normally show up in person. Business was conducted primarily over the phone and online. So who was visiting?

As the trees cleared and the vast sagebrush bowl opened up, Joe noted a puff of dark smoke in the sky to the west of Nate's outbuildings. It looked almost like a small exploded rocket. But he heard no report.

That's when he noticed that the "smoke" was drifting down to the snow-covered clearing. And that a falcon rose from the center of the explosion and climbed toward the lone cumulus cloud in the sky.

As he drove closer, Joe could see three figures in the clearing wading through knee-high snow. They wore low-slung gear bags and their heads were tilted upward. He identified the three falconers as Nate, Sheridan, and Geronimo Jones.

In the sky above them, at least three raptors soared at different altitudes.

Joe pulled to the side of the road and watched them. Sheridan swung a weighted pigeon-feather lure around her head like a lasso until it attracted the attention of the falcon she was flying. The prairie falcon banked from a turn and shot down through the air. Its talons descended in time to smack the lure and send it flopping to the surface. Then, after a tight turn, it flew back and landed on Sheridan's gloved fist.

Joe found that quite impressive.

The "smoke" he had seen wasn't smoke at all, of course. It was feathers from a pigeon Nate had released that had been hit so hard in midflight by a screaming-fast peregrine falcon that the target bird had exploded. Nate's peregrine, which could reach speeds of up to two hundred miles per hour, now returned to the scene of the kill and to Nate's fist. His friend walked the bird over to the remains of the pigeon, lowered it to the ground, and let it eat.

With Nate's and Sheridan's birds out of the sky, Geronimo dug into his gear bag and produced a duck. Joe smiled, because the actions of falconers always surprised and amused him. Who *else* would have a duck within reach?

Geronimo held the mallard drake tight with both hands, then tossed it into the air like an offering to the gods. The drake quickly found its wings and shot away—flying low toward the trees Joe had just emerged from. It seemed to know what was coming.

Geronimo's gyrfalcon dropped from nowhere and hit the duck hard enough that Joe could hear a *pock* sound inside the cab. The duck tumbled and landed dead less than twenty feet from the front of his truck. Right in the road. Errant feathers floated down and lit on the surface of the snow.

The gyrfalcon, the largest of all falcons, seemed to revel in the conditions, for it was a bird of the arctic coasts and tundra. Mottled brown and white, it blended with the terrain so perfectly that when it landed on the duck and began to rip it apart, Joe could only track its movement against the snowy background by its black, piercing eyes.

He carefully steered around it and made his way to the compound. Liv and Kestrel, who was bundled up in an oversized snowsuit, had also been observing the falconers in the field.

"Good morning," Joe said to Liv as he climbed out of his truck. "What's going on out here?"

Liv smiled. "Nate calls it spring training."

"Seems more like winter," Joe said.

"It always does," she said. "But we have so many jobs scheduled ahead of us we need to get the birds tuned up."

Kestrel waddled over to Joe and held her arms out and he picked her up. She called him "Unka Joe," which thrilled him.

"Geronimo wanted to show off his gyrfalcon for Nate and Sheridan," Liv said. "His wife, Jacinda, told me to tell you not to be impressed by his falcons," Liv said. "She said his head is big enough as it is."

Joe chuckled at that. Then: "I thought Jacinda and the baby would be with him?"

"Me too," Liv said. "I wanted to meet them both. But apparently Jacinda's mother is visiting for a few weeks to help out with baby Pearl. And with the roads the way they are, Geronimo didn't want to chance it. I don't blame him."

THE THREE FALCONERS in the field waited until their raptors had eaten their fill—feathers and bones included. Then they hooded the birds with leather head coverings and walked them back to the mews at the edge of the compound. Each bird's gullet was swollen from their meal.

While Liv had retreated back into the house for Kestrel's morning snack, Joe went to meet up with the falconers as they secured their birds. On the way, he noticed the snout of a big blue pickup parked on the side of one of Nate's outbuildings. He guessed from the green and white Colorado plates that Geronimo and Jacinda had driven it north. As he rounded the corner of the building he noted the flatbed trailer attached behind it with a metal structure secured to the platform.

The sight of it stopped him cold.

The structure was twelve feet long, nine feet high, and about eight feet wide. It had a single metal door on the side and three louvered hoods on the front of it. The hoods shaded the large inert fan blades that were attached to motors mounted inside.

As Nate and Geronimo appeared, Joe gestured toward the structure and said, "I've seen one of these before. Just a couple of days ago, in fact. *What is it?*"

Nate and Geronimo exchanged glances, as if deciding who would take the lead.

Geronimo said, "It's called a minipod building. They make them in Casper and I picked it up on my way through."

"What does it do?" Joe asked.

Geronimo paused and grinned. "This, my friend, is how we grow Yarak, Inc. The financing for expanding the company across the country will come from this minipod—and others like it."

Joe didn't understand and he looked to Nate for an explanation.

"This is Geronimo's scheme," Nate said. "He talked me into it once he found out where we live."

"I'm happy to explain," Geronimo said.

"Get ready," Nate said to Joe. "He can go on for hours. He literally wore me down to the point where I said, 'Okay, just bring it up here. Quit talking about it and bring it up here.'"

Geronimo chuckled at that, and his eyes sparkled. He was obviously excited and he wanted Joe to share in his enthusiasm.

"First, how much do you know about Bitcoin?" Geronimo asked.

"Very little," Joe said.

"I'd say absolutely nothing," Sheridan chimed in as she

was cleaning blood from her hands with a wet wipe. She'd fed the birds in the mews who hadn't yet participated in spring training. "Technology has never been my dad's strong suit."

Joe nodded a sarcastic *Thanks* to her and she grinned back and winked.

"This minipod, my friend, will not only help change the world for the better, but it'll help make Yarak, Inc., financially secure," Geronimo said. "Once we get it up and running, nobody can mess with us. Not the banks, not the feds—nobody. We'll literally be minting money right here in the middle of nowhere. This structure you see before you is a Bitcoin miner."

"If it works," Nate added cautiously.

"Oh, it'll work," Geronimo said to him. "I did my homework. You *know* that."

Nate shrugged as if to say, *Go on*.

"So you don't know anything about Bitcoin," Geronimo said to Joe. "That's okay, that's okay. A lot of people don't get it. Some people own it and they still don't understand it. I'll make it real simple, okay?"

"You'll have to," Sheridan said with a snort.

"Enough from you," Joe said to her.

"Okay," Geronimo said, stepping to the side of Nate so he could gesture wildly with his hands. "Bitcoin is not a physical coin at all. Bitcoin is a digital currency for the whole world and the uses are mainly to own it or send it."

He said, "Start with knowing there is a finite amount of Bitcoin to be mined—twenty-one million, to be exact. That's where the value comes from, because it's *finite*. As it's traded, the value goes up. It's volatile for sure, but those who were on the ground floor of it are very rich folks now."

Nate said to Joe, "I'm just learning all of this stuff myself. One thing I really like about it is that the government doesn't control it. Unlike dollars, they can't just print more of it whenever they feel like it."

"So how can you mine it?" Joe asked. "That doesn't make much sense to me."

"It's not like you go out there and pluck it out of the network," Geronimo said. "What you can do, what *we* will do"—he glanced at Nate as he said it—"is provide super-high-speed computing power to help process the transactions that are going on right now. For that, we get a commission for the transaction paid to us in Bitcoin. The more computing power we bring online, the more we can make in profit from transaction fees.

"What we will do," Geronimo said, "is fill this minipod with two hundred and twenty ASIC supercomputers. The computers will be linked up to create a much bigger and more powerful computer that will 'mine' the internet to assist in transactions. If it all goes well, we'll add more minipods. We've got the space and power for at least twenty."

Joe whistled and said, "This sounds very expensive."

"Oh, it is," Geronimo agreed. "It is. Each ASIC computer costs up to ten thousand dollars when the market is hot. We've got over two hundred arriving this month. That's over two million in computers alone, and they'll only last twelve to eighteen months before they burn out and we have to buy faster equipment to keep up. So the sooner we get this online, the better."

Joe looked to Nate. "Yarak, Inc., must be doing better than I thought."

"We're doing okay," Nate said. "But not *that* good. No, Geronimo is putting up the front money. We've got a deal that if it works like his business plan shows, he becomes a full partner in Yarak and oversees our expansion."

"Actually," Geronimo said, "we can thank Jacinda. She may act otherwise, but she believes in me."

"Fool that she is," Nate chided.

Joe recalled that Jacinda was heir to a massive fashion and cosmetics fortune. So apparently she could afford it.

"If you think Nate was hard to convince about investing in this," Geronimo said, "you should have overheard my negotiations with my wife. She's a tough customer, and she's not foolish with money. My plan had to be solid."

Joe asked, "Why here? Why put this minipod in the middle of nowhere, as you put it?"

"Three good reasons," Geronimo said. "The first is that we're off the grid, so to speak. The remote location is a benefit to us because the fewer people who know about the minipod, the better. Those computers inside, as I said, are damned valuable pieces of technology. Anyone who knew about it could back their truck up and strip this building clean and resell the hardware. So remote is good.

"Second, the Rocky Mountain climate is the best for

keeping computers cool. They get insanely hot and degrade when they're operating at full capacity. The cool nights and cool mornings help keep the minipod in operation longer."

"I know something about that," Joe said. "Go on."

"The third reason is the most important of all," Geronimo continued. "Mining Bitcoin uses an *insane* amount of energy. That's why some people hate it. I saw recently that Bitcoin mining uses over a hundred terawatt hours per year globally. That compares to the energy used by all the clothes dryers in America. That's *a lot* of energy, and the greenies really hate that."

"Wow," Sheridan said. "I had no idea." She seemed alarmed.

"Yeah," Geronimo said, "but here's where it gets interesting. Wyoming and other western states have thousands of oil and gas wells that aren't producing, for one reason or another. Usually, it's because there isn't enough oil coming out of the well to make it worthwhile to the operator. But there's still oil down there and plenty of natural gas that would have been flared off otherwise."

Joe knew that "flaring" was the term for the burning off of excess natural gas. It was controversial. Some states had banned it.

"So instead of flaring off the gas, which is wasteful and bad for the environment," Geronimo said, "we put a generator on top of the capped well and use the gas to power the minipod! We don't have to pull electricity from the grid, or run a bunch of power lines across the country to our site.

We're self-sufficient, and we're making money from resources that would have gone to waste. It all works, from where I sit."

"I didn't know you had old gas wells on your place," Joe said to Nate.

"I inherited them when I bought the land," Nate said with a shrug. "I always knew they were there, but I didn't know what to do with them. Now maybe I do."

Joe rubbed his chin. It sounded complicated and too good to be true at the same time.

"You're a good salesman," Joe said to Geronimo. "You've almost got me convinced this is a good idea. I really have to think about it."

"Me too," Sheridan said. "I didn't know about how much energy was involved in mining Bitcoin. I always thought it was eco-friendly, you know?"

"Life is about trade-offs," Geronimo countered. "Would you rather the gas just burns off with no benefit to anyone— or the planet? At least this way it gets used.

"It's not like I'm inventing something that isn't in operation in other places in the West," Geronimo said. "These minipods are going in all over the place. Most of them are owned by the landowners or the energy companies as a way to use resources that aren't economical on their own."

Geronimo narrowed his eyes at Joe. "Didn't you say you've seen one of these?" Geronimo asked.

"Two days ago," Joe responded. "It was on the Double D Ranch about fifteen miles from here."

Geronimo shook his head. "I figured we'd be the first in the area. It pisses me off that someone beat us to it."

"They did," Joe said. He glanced at Sheridan, who had obviously picked up something in his tone. "And now I know what Michael Thompson is up to on his ranch and why he is keeping it a big secret.

"But that's not all . . ."

JOE BRIEFED THE falconers on what had happened since he discovered the body of Professor Wei.

"I remember him," Sheridan said in awe. "I took a class of his. It wasn't my thing, but he was brilliant."

Geronimo crossed his arms over his barrel chest. "It's interesting that he was Chinese."

Joe looked at him for more.

"It's just that since we've been talking about Bitcoin, it reminds me that the Chinese Communist Party threw out all their Bitcoin miners a few years ago because they couldn't control them. It was called 'Chexit.' That killed off fifty percent of the computing power in the network for a while and it took months to recover the value of each Bitcoin. I wonder if this incident with the professor is related in any way."

"No clue," Joe said. He'd never heard of Chexit until that moment.

"So who is responsible?" Sheridan asked Joe. "Any ideas?"

Joe said, "Nope. And it's all officially out of my hands."

"Why isn't this in the news?" Sheridan asked.

"The powers that be don't want it out there," Joe said with a shrug.

Geronimo said, "You say the building was shut down after you found this Chinese professor? That it was no longer operating?"

"That's what I was told."

"So the computers were either turned off, stolen, or removed by the owner," Geronimo said. "I hope we don't have thieves around here. If that's the case, we'll need more security around our system."

Nate patted his shoulder holster under his arm and said, "Here's your security."

Geronimo laughed and said, "I've got three barrels of security myself. Ain't that so, Joe?"

"Yup."

On the walk back to his truck, Joe noticed that Nate was right behind him. Geronimo and Sheridan had headed back to the house. Joe looked over his shoulder and arched his eyebrows expectantly.

"What can you tell me about a man named Jason Demo?" Nate asked. Nate wasn't much for preambles.

"I don't believe I've heard of him," Joe said. "Why?"

"He came to me with a proposition. I need to find out more about him."

"What kind of proposition?"

"You don't want to know," Nate said.

Joe took him at his word. "I'll ask Marybeth to do some research."

"I already did." Then: "What about the Keystoners?" Nate asked.

"You don't want to get mixed up with them," Joe said. "They're led by a hard case named Cade Molvar, and the word on them is they've taken over weed distribution in the area. They're bitter and they're well armed and they hate the feds."

"They sound like my kind of guys," Nate said.

"I hope you're kidding," Joe responded. He'd encountered several of them recently because they liked to hang out and drink beer at the Wet Fly Bar on the outskirts of town.

Joe knew them from their nicknames. Adam "Ant" had a mop of black hair, a beard streaked with silver, and hollow eyes. When he opened his mouth, he resembled a jack-o'-lantern with all of his missing teeth.

Brandon was known as "Weedy" for obvious reasons. Weedy was in his early sixties and was the oldest of the group. He liked to brag that he'd been doing weed nonstop for fifty years without a break. He had tawny long hair that was going thin, severely scarred forearms and hands from some kind of oil field accident, and a low, mumbling way of talking that you could barely understand.

Daniel "the Bear" was the youngest of the Keystoners. The Bear got his name because he'd wrestled one in a bar outside of Green River, Wyoming. He was tall and rangy with a shaved head and a beard that hid his neck and flowed over his sternum. His neck tattoos were of serpents and swordsmen, and he wore the same clothes he always did: extra-thick chamois work shirt, baggy carpenter jeans, and unlaced Sorel pack boots.

Barry, known as "Buddy," was a tiny man with bug eyes and protruding ears who dressed exclusively in Harley-Davidson paraphernalia. Black T-shirts and caps, leather riding trousers, and heavy motorcycle boots. Buddy got his name because he reminded the others of an elf and the only elf any of them had ever heard of was Buddy the Elf from the movie. He also had the quick temper of a tiny man with a chip on his shoulder for being tiny.

Nate grinned slyly, then turned and walked toward his home.

JOE CALLED CLAY Hutmacher as soon as he got a cell signal on the way out from Nate's compound.

He said, "I now know what you've been up to. My question is whether the computers inside the building were shut off, removed, or stolen."

Hutmacher paused a long time before saying, "How did you find out?"

"That's not important. So which was it?"

Hutmacher sighed. "Don't tell Thompson we discussed this."

"I won't."

"The computers are all packed up and sitting in our hay

barn. I assume he's going to fire them up again at some point, but right now I think he's figuring out where the next location of the pod will be. We've got a bunch of potential sites."

"Meaning you've got a lot of capped gas wells out there," Joe said.

"Yes, we do."

"Was Professor Wei connected to you guys in some way?" Joe asked. "Was he a consultant or an engineer?"

"Honestly, Joe, I'd never heard of him until you told me his name. I swear."

"Then why was he up there?"

"I have no idea."

"Where is his body?"

"Seriously, I don't know, Joe," Hutmacher said. "Please don't think I know anything about what happened, because I don't. I'm being square with you."

"What about Thompson?"

"You'll have to ask him yourself, I guess. That's all I can tell you."

Joe terminated the call and nodded his head as he drove, trying to make some sense of it all.

Saturday, April 1

The man turns and there—
his solitary track stretched out
upon the world.

—WILLIAM CARLOS WILLIAMS,

"Blizzard"

CHAPTER TWELVE

THE NEXT MORNING, Joe chose to place aside solving the dilemma because he wasn't getting anywhere. Instead, he checked messages on the agency landline number in his home office. It was early, barely light out, and he could hear Marybeth upstairs in the shower. Daisy was curled up at his feet and there was a cup of strong coffee on his desk.

After reviewing the messages, he determined he could deal with nearly all of the calls later on a bad-weather day when he was office-bound. Some were from out-of-state hunters asking for advice and recommendations, and two were from local landowners complaining about changes in hunting regulations that would go into effect in July. One anonymous call, though, made an hour before, got his attention.

The reporting party identified herself as a cross-country skier. She sounded young, maybe in her early twenties. She

also had the annoying affectation known as "uptalking," or
ending every sentence in a higher tone so that it sounded like
her message was a series of questions.

"I'm calling to report something that's just really bad? I've
been skiing the trails around Hazelton Road, you know? Yesterday afternoon I saw snowmobilers up here harassing elk?
They were chasing them around in the deep snow? It's just
really disturbing and it makes me want to cry for the poor
elk? You really need to do something about it? Like I said, I'm
parked at the pullout on Hazelton Road and their trucks are
right here? *I don't know what they're doing, but I really hope you
get these assholes?*"

Joe thought: *I think I* do *know what they're doing.*

WITH A SNOWMOBILE trailer hitched to his pickup, Joe drove
up Bighorn Road into the timbered national forest. He welcomed the diversion to do real Game and Fish work that
morning.

Over the years, Joe had found that often he came up with
theories and solutions to problems like the death of Professor
Wei and its aftermath when he *wasn't* focused on it exclusively. Some of his most revelatory discoveries came while he
showered, or drove, or engaged in other duties. It was as if
he'd given permission to his subconscious to roam freely and
make connections on its own.

He hoped that would happen again.

———

THE SNOW WAS deep on top of the mountains, although the two-lane had been cleared the day before. Sheets of melted runoff coursed across the blacktop and his tires hissed through it.

A turnoff to a snowmobile parking area was also plowed, and he took it and drove a mile and a half down a forest service access road. The parking area was heavily used in deep winter by recreational snowmobilers from across the country, but there were only three vehicles in it when Joe arrived, two rough-looking pickups with empty trailers, and a green Subaru Outback with Colorado plates and a c*o*e*x*i*s*t bumper sticker.

A fit-looking young woman in high-tech winter wear was loading a pair of cross-country skis into the open hatchback of the Subaru when she heard him drive up.

She had a pale open face and her red hair flowed over her shoulders from beneath a headband.

He parked, got out, and said, "Good morning. I'm Joe Pickett. Are you the one who called me about the snowmobilers?"

She hesitated and a worried look passed over her face. She checked out the pronghorn logo on the door of his pickup and the small badge pinned to his green vest. It was obvious that she wished to remain anonymous, but his arrival had changed the equation.

Finally: "Yes—that was me. But I need to get going."

"You can," he said.

She gestured toward the two parked vehicles in the lot. "As you can see, they're back."

"How many of them are there?"

"Three or four? Maybe five? I'm not sure. But I saw them literally chasing hundreds of elk yesterday? It made me sick, you know?" She was back to her uptalk now.

"Why didn't you call last night?" Joe asked.

"I *did*," she said with anger. "I called the sheriff's department? They said they were busy and to leave my name and number. They did absolutely nothing, you know?"

Joe nodded to indicate that he heard her and sympathized with her frustration. It annoyed him that the sheriff's department hadn't even made the effort to refer the call to him.

"I found your number this morning and called," she said. "But as I said, I can't stick around. And the last thing I want to do is share this mountain with those rednecks, you know?"

"Gotcha," Joe said. "Thanks for letting me know."

"I hope you arrest them all," she said.

"It's a little more complicated than that," he said. "I've got to catch them in the act of harassing wildlife. Riding snowmobiles around in a national forest is perfectly legal."

"I wish it *were* illegal," she said with a sniff. "You don't want to know what I have to say about snowmobiles invading cross-country ski trails."

Joe said, "I think I know. Too bad you can't just *coexist* with them."

Her eyes flashed. "Is that supposed to be funny?"

"Nope," he said.

AFTER SHE DROVE away, Joe circled the two empty vehicles and looked them over. He recognized one of them, a beat-up Chevy Silverado with a peeing Calvin decal in the back window. He'd seen it outside the Stockman's Bar and the Wet Fly Bar, but he didn't know its owner. The other big unit was an aging Suburban with a winch on the front bumper and a Gadsden DON'T TREAD ON ME sticker on the back door. It also had bumper stickers that read KEYSTONE PIPELINE: ECO-NOMIC PROSPERITY AND ENERGY INDEPENDENCE and GREEN IS THE NEW RED.

Locals.

Cell service was nonexistent where he was located, as it was throughout fifty percent of his district, so Joe keyed the mic in his pickup and used the State Agency Law Enforce-ment Communications System (SALECS) to call dispatch in Cheyenne for a license plate check. In less than a minute, he learned that the Silverado was registered to Ogden Driskill and the Suburban was registered to Irving "Cade" Molvar.

He jotted the plates and names down in his notebook and took phone camera photos of the outfits.

Molvar, he'd heard, was associated with the Keystoners. Driskill and his buddy Leland Christensen were local tweak-ers who were often in trouble for one thing or another. He'd not talked to any of them before.

IT WAS EASY enough to track them in the snow. Joe ran his Polaris on their well-worn route from the lot, across the side of a treeless mountainside, and over a ridge into the forest. As the reporting party had said, there were three to five tracked machines. Occasionally, one of the riders had diverged from the trail to go into the deep snow in the timber on their own and then return to the convoy.

He observed that when one of the machines had left the trail for a while, he could see a pair of thin cargo sled tracks in the path. The sled tracks vanished again when the errant rider returned to the pack and rode over them.

The question was why the riders needed to take a cargo sled in the first place.

Although he thought he had a pretty good theory.

JOE WORE HIS snowmobile suit, boots, and helmet and he'd loaded his saddlebags with optics, a spare radio, a long-lens camera, and a small winter survival kit containing flares, blankets, canned food, and a folded-up shovel that could be used to dig a shelter. He'd strapped his personal twelve-gauge Remington Wingmaster shotgun to the back of his machine and his service-issue .40 Glock was zipped inside his suit, as was his canister of bear spray.

The trail took him through dark heavy timber for a while before it lightened and he felt the presence of a big opening up ahead of him. He knew this part of the mountains held a series of huge meadows bordered by thick trees on all sides. They were perfect cover for the herds of elk that lived there.

The trees thinned as he climbed a ridge, and the top of the summit was bare. Instead of following the trail and plunging over the top into a meadow, Joe slowed his machine and turned off the engine. He knew that if there was anyone over in the meadow he wouldn't be able to hear them over the buzz of his own sled.

Joe removed his helmet and sat there, listening. His limbs tingled from the vibration of his machine and it took a couple of minutes to feel overcome by the quiet.

Then he heard it: the high-pitched whining of several snowmobiles in the distance. They sounded like large electric razors and their noise cut through the stillness. He couldn't determine how many were over there.

Dismounting, he fished his binoculars from the saddlebag and waded up the slope through knee-deep powder. When he sank to his upper thighs and found it hard going, Joe climbed back on the packed-down snowmobile trail and crab-walked to the top.

He flattened to his belly and wriggled on his knees and elbows the rest of the way, careful not to show his profile on the bald ridge to those below.

The meadow before him was vast and partially windswept of snow. It was that reason, he knew, that the elk hung out there. There was both food on the mountainside and shelter in the trees. The bare ground of the slope was covered with elk pellets in the dried grass.

AT LEAST TWO hundred elk were tightly packed on the bottom of the swale about three hundred yards away. Sun glinted off the massive antlers of bulls, and the cows and calves within the herd milled nervously. Elk shed their antlers in March and April, much later than any other member of the deer family. The elk below him had obviously seen or heard interlopers, and they were nervous.

As he observed, the sound of snowmobiles got louder and higher pitched.

Suddenly, two machines broke out from the heavy timber on the eastern flank of the meadow. Then a third and a fourth. The snowmobilers looked as if they were conducting a military operation, attacking the entire herd in a four-pronged ground assault.

Within seconds, the herd panicked and broke for the trees to the west. This big patch of timber looked blacker and more gnarled than the timber to the east where the snowmobilers had come from.

Joe raised the binoculars to try and identify the men on the machines, but it was impossible. The riders were a considerable distance away and they all wore bulky black snowmobile suits like he did. Their helmets and visors were dark. The only distinctive feature he observed was a set of gold lightning bolts on the side of one snowmobiler's helmet.

The animals plunged into the woods, with the men on machines in pursuit. The woods were so dense Joe couldn't see a single animal once they were inside. But he could hear branches cracking and small trees snapping off. It was surprisingly loud, and it sounded like chaos inside the timber. The tops of some of the pine trees rocked and threw off clouds of snow as elk bodies pounded into and around their trunks.

The snowmobilers didn't follow them into the dark timber. Instead, they buzzed back and forth along the tree line to prevent any of the animals from escaping.

Within a minute or so, several elk leaked out of the top of the woods onto a bare ridge on its western side. Soon, the bulk of the herd followed and the elk flowed over the top looking like brown and tawny liquid until they were gone into the next drainage.

Joe noted that it seemed like a lot fewer big bulls emerged from the timber than had been driven into it. Then he saw why: scores of magnificent antlered bull elk had entered the timber, and dozens of them came out bareheaded with red hollows on their skulls where their antlers had been just moments before.

THE ONLY SOUND that remained was the whining of the snowmobiles, and, one by one, the drivers gathered in a knot in the meadow and shut off their machines.

Joe focused in on the group, trying to see their faces. Unfortunately, he was too far away to get a good look at them when they raised their visors. One of them let out a hoarse whoop and another raised his arms over his head to celebrate what they'd done.

And what had they done?

Joe had heard of the underhanded technique, but had never observed it before in person. His neck got hot with anger. Shed hunting was fine and many people did it as a hobby. But the commercialization of wildlife was illegal. So was harassing them on their winter range.

Bull elk had roughly forty pounds of antlers. The price of them grew every year in value, and they were used as furniture, jewelry, or knife handles, or ground into powder and sold in Asia as an aphrodisiac. Buyers who arrived in trailers and set themselves up on corners in little mountain towns like Saddlestring were paying up to twenty-five dollars a pound. Meaning a single bull elk produced eight hundred dollars' worth of antlers.

Although the season for gathering sheds was still a month away, unscrupulous shed hunters liked to jump the gun. Joe had caught only a few of them in his career, and it was because someone had turned them in or called in a tip.

This time, he'd seen them in action. The snowmobilers had forced the herd into the thick timber for one reason—to create the panic and chaos that resulted. Inside the tangle of timber, bull elk caught their loosened antlers on branches and trunks and many of the sheds fell to the ground right there on the forest floor.

Later, the shed hunters would enter the timber and gather the antlers that had been clubbed loose. They'd make thousands, and stressed big-game animals could burn up their energy reserves and die before spring finally came.

Joe also noticed something distinctive about the snowmobilers. All were armed. The snowmobiles had saddle scabbards with the butts of rifles poking out, and two of the four riders wore shoulder holsters outside their suits for easy access to their handguns.

This was the second time in three days that Joe faced armed outlaw snowmobilers in the mountains. He didn't believe it was a coincidence.

He was in a situation.

THERE WAS NO way he could ride down the slope in full view of the four riders without alerting them to his presence. They'd have plenty of time to escape if they chose, or plenty of time to unsheathe their weapons and take him on.

As much as he wanted to swoop down and arrest the law-breaking shed hunters, Joe knew how dangerous and unwise it could be. He'd learned a lot from observing people in the field over the years, and these four exuded menace. They could overwhelm him easily if they chose to. They could beat him, shoot him, or take his machine away and leave him stranded in the deep snow. Joe was miles away from the parking lot and no one knew his precise location.

To arrest a party of four armed men on-site, Joe would need backup. Since the sheriff no longer answered his calls, Joe would have to find help elsewhere.

He made a decision.

Instead of confronting them, he decided to get as much documentation and evidence as he could of the crimes the shed hunters were committing and methodically build the case. He'd already identified the owners of the two vehicles, and he had to assume that Driskill and Molvar were among the four riders. He couldn't prove it yet, but the odds were with him.

Once he confirmed their involvement with the crimes, the two others shouldn't be hard to find.

He'd arrest them one by one, and maybe with a game warden from another district or a departmental investigator to back him up. As with poachers, there was no honor among shed hunters.

Joe knew the snowmobilers could gather up hundreds of pounds of antlers, but they'd need a place to cache them for a month until the antler merchants arrived in town. Elk antlers were large and bulky and hard to hide. Once he located their cache, tying the antlers to the crime would be fairly easy.

If he had the evidence and confronted each man with it, he could expect them to turn on each other.

Joe planned to employ a tactic he had used many times before to surprising success. He'd knock on each of their doors and simply say, "I guess you know why I'm here," and see where it went.

Men who committed wildlife crimes tended to commit crimes against humans as well. It would be a good thing for his district to put these four miscreants away for a while. It would also help discourage illegal shed hunting.

Joe nodded to himself. He was getting wiser.

AFTER TAKING DOZENS of photos of the shed hunters with his long lens, and after the group retrieved their cargo sled to gather antlers and go in on foot into the woods, Joe backed off the ridge.

To cover his exit, he waited until he heard one of the machines from down below start up. Then he fired up his Polaris and raced away on the track he'd used to get there.

JOE RAN HIS snowmobile up the fold-down ramps onto the trailer and strapped the machine down tight. He kept alert for the sound of snowmobiles returning. If so, he'd need to make a quick exit. But all was still.

For a moment, he considered leaving his card with a note that said *Call me* beneath the windshield wipers of both vehicles in the lot. He could only imagine what consternation that would cause. He decided against it because he didn't want to tip his hand.

Joe wanted to know more about Molvar and Driskill. He could look up their criminal records on his own, but it would be helpful to get more background on them. Had they jumped the legal shed season before? Were they engaged in other criminal activity together?

Until that morning, Joe hadn't been aware that the two ran together. But there were four snowmobilers in all, and the other two were unknown.

HIS PHONE VIBRATED when he reached an area on the mountain where he could receive a decent phone signal.

It was a text from Marybeth:

> Nate and Liv invited us to dinner tonight with
> Geronimo and Jacinda. 7 at the Ramshorn.
> You in?

Rather than sending a thumbs-up emoji or any of the other graphics with which his daughters were so enamored, Joe wrote out Yes. He refused to use emojis.

ALTHOUGH HE WASN'T sure he would be able to accomplish much, he called the sheriff's department and asked for Tibbs. The receptionist said the man was on a conference call at the moment and couldn't be disturbed. Joe asked for Deputy Buck Holmes, instead.

"He's not available, either," the receptionist said. "Buck called in sick today."

"Can you please leave a message for both of them to give me a call back?" Joe said.

"Certainly" was the quick reply.

"Please mention to the sheriff that I made an attempt to keep him informed of a new situation in the mountains. He has told me time and time again that he wants to be in the loop. So tell him to consider this my attempt to do that."

She said, "Will do."

Joe hung up. He wondered if he'd ever hear from either of them.

ON THE WAY down the mountain, Joe realized that his subconscious had been at work and several items had thrust their way to the front of his brain.

The sled tracks he'd seen on the snowmobile trail were similar to those he'd seen around the Bitcoin minipod on the Double D Ranch, although snowmobile sleds like it were extremely common in the Bighorns. Still, it was a notable coincidence.

Then there were the shots taken at him while he huddled behind the remote building. They'd been rifle shots fired by individuals who didn't care that he was a member of law enforcement. That in itself revealed something about the mindset of the shooters.

All four shed hunters had been armed with rifles.

Additionally, they had brazenly broken the law right in

front of him. People who didn't respect wildlife and put the animals in unnecessary danger tended not to respect law enforcement officers, either.

Was it possible, Joe wondered, that the yahoos he'd observed that morning had been shed hunting on the Double D? That they'd somehow encountered Professor Wei along the way? That maybe they'd found his body before Joe got there?

Or maybe they had something to do with the murder itself?

Was it possible that they'd gone back and retrieved the body before anyone else could get there?

His mind filled with contingencies and possibilities.

Joe knew he needed to locate the cache of antlers so he could put pressure on the shed hunters. Without that pressure, they might not break.

He'd also need help, especially since he couldn't count on the sheriff, his director, or the governor's administration.

Joe needed both intelligence assistance and muscle.

He knew where to find both. They'd be at dinner later that night.

CHAPTER THIRTEEN

THE RAMSHORN RESTAURANT and Lounge was located on a downtown corner inside a historic hotel that had gone through a half-dozen iterations through the years, including an extensive renovation supervised by Marybeth herself. The federal Bureau of Land Management had taken it over for five years before the agency relocated to a massive new brick palace on the outskirts of town, and since then it had been occupied by three consecutive restaurants that had failed: a barbecue joint, a wine bar, and a nightclub. After the pandemic had killed the business of the nightclub, the new owners had launched the Ramshorn, and in Joe's view, it might just stick.

The place served local beef and bison, vegetables from a greenhouse located on a local ranch, and strong drinks.

Marybeth drove her minivan and Joe helped to try and find a parking place.

Joe had changed into Wranglers, a Cinch shirt, and a pair of butter-soft Ariat boots that he refused to part with. Marybeth looked alluring in a gray sweater dress and pearls.

"Nate and Geronimo found a place," Joe said, nodding toward a big SUV with green Colorado plates. "I can't believe this. We might need to park a few blocks away."

"Walking is good," Marybeth said.

AN UNEXPECTED BY-PRODUCT of the pandemic and the resulting COVID-19 restrictions in other states was that in the last two years it had created a mini-boom of new residents and new money to the valley. People had fled cities and state regulations to seek refuge in small mountain towns like Saddlestring that had largely shrugged its shoulders at the virus and gone on with life. There had been no school closures, no mask mandates, and no proof-of-vaccination requirements for anything.

Realtors said that they had sold available houses over the phone sight unseen to buyers, and that many of the properties—some of which had sat empty for years—had been sold for tens of thousands above the asking price.

For the first time since Joe and Marybeth had moved to the area to manage the district, new foundations were being poured and houses were being built. It was a totally unexpected development, Joe thought. When they'd moved there twenty years before, the town had been depressed and the end had seemed near.

The influx had also created a worker shortage in the Twelve Sleep Valley. HELP WANTED signs were posted in the front windows of nearly every retail establishment in town, including the Ramshorn, which was perennially understaffed.

"There," Joe said, pointing out a space along the street where a car was pulling out.

NATE, LIV, GERONIMO, and Sheridan had secured an elevated table in the corner of the restaurant that would allow them all a measure of privacy. They waved at Joe and Marybeth to join them.

As they sat down, Geronimo gestured toward his phone, which was placed faceup in the middle of the table. "Jacinda is on the line from home," he said. "If we're talking business, she needs to be included in the discussion."

"Hello, Jacinda," Marybeth said. "Welcome."

"Thank you," Jacinda said. "I'll stay on as long as I can, but if Pearl starts to fuss I'll need to beg off. I'm sure you know how that goes."

"We do," Liv and Marybeth said in unison.

"When that girl wants to eat, she wants to *eat*," Jacinda said. "Just like her daddy."

"Oh, man," Geronimo said, rolling his eyes.

"This is the important table," Marybeth said with a smile as she unfurled her napkin and spread it on her lap. "I feel privileged just to be here."

Geronimo was obviously puzzled.

"The big shots in town all have lunch here every day," Marybeth explained to him. "They used to hang out at the Burg-O-Pardner, but now they've relocated here. Don't even *try* to sit at this table from eleven to one on a workday."

"Gotcha," Geronimo said. "I forgot what it was like to live in a small town."

"I grew up in Chicago," Jacinda said. "It isn't all that different. All the big decisions were made at special tables in special restaurants by special big shots. Not that I or anyone I knew were ever included."

GERONIMO SIPPED A large Manhattan and studied the menu. "This looks like civilized food. I thought you people only ate what you killed." To Jacinda on the phone, he said, "Since I've been at Nate's, I've had antelope backstrap, elk steaks, pine grouse, and roast duck."

"Sometimes we go out to see how the other half lives," Nate said.

"He *loved* the duck," Jacinda said with a laugh. "He texted me that. And don't pay any attention to Geronimo when he complains. He's a city boy and he *loves* to eat."

A stout, harried waitress showed up blowing a strand of errant hair out of her face.

"Sorry," she said. "We're short-staffed." To Marybeth and Joe, she asked, "Can I take your drink orders?"

"You sure can," Joe said.

———

AFTER THEIR DRINKS arrived and their orders were in, Mary-beth paused until the waitress was gone. "Jason Demo checks out," she said to Nate.

"There wasn't much in the public records about him, but just enough to confirm that he's the real deal," she said. "He was born in Livingston, Montana, he's in his early thirties, he was an all-state athlete, and he joined the military right out of high school. There were a couple of items in the Livingston newspaper citing his graduation from boot camp and his acceptance into special operations. The items were glowing, and my guess is they were written and submitted by his parents. That's how it works around here, too," she said.

"Then, for twelve years—nothing. He vanished from the internet. If he had social media accounts at all, he kept them well hidden."

"Is that unusual?" Jacinda asked.

"Not for special operators," Marybeth said. "Ask Nate. He was off the grid most of his life."

"I wish I still was at times," Nate said as Liv shot a look at him. Then: "Officers in special ops pounded into our heads that we had to be ghosts. Even innocent things you might post, like a selfie or a reference to the weather, can give away your location. Some guys had anonymous accounts, but I stayed away from it entirely. Plus, I didn't grow up online like Sheridan here."

He looked at her with a smile as he said it.

Sheridan had been quiet since her parents arrived, and Joe guessed she was both a little thrilled to be at dinner with them all and at the same time a little embarrassed to be included. She sipped at a glass of wine and tried to act nonchalant, he thought, but at the same time he could tell that she was listening closely to every word.

"There was a story from two years ago announcing Demo's honorable discharge," Marybeth continued. "It said he served in Iraq, Afghanistan, Yemen, and other countries not specified. I confirmed that information on a DoD site as well."

"Sounds about right," Nate said. "And since then?"

"Very little. He pretty much stays off the grid, although he has made contributions to libertarian candidates in Montana and across the country."

"Maybe that's why I liked him," Nate said.

Geronimo shook his head, obviously disagreeing with Nate. "You need to stay clear of those nuts. I keep telling you that."

Nate didn't respond.

"What about the Sovereign Nation?" Nate asked Marybeth. "Could you find anything on them?"

Marybeth rolled her eyes. "Plenty. They have a couple of crude websites of their own, where they lay out their philosophy and outlook. They also ask for donations to help them save the country. There's no list of members, though.

"Their name pops up on some lists of domestic terrorism organizations," she said. "I did a deep dive and I couldn't find any instances where members of the Sovereign Nation committed crimes or carried out any of the actions they purport to want to do. At least not any incidents where they claim credit."

"So you couldn't find any link between Demo and them?" Nate asked.

"No, but I didn't really expect to. That's not the kind of thing you put online. Especially when the U.S. Department of Justice says 'domestic terrorists' are the greatest threat facing our nation."

"That's bullshit," Nate said. "They want to paint everyone who disagrees with them as criminals. It's what they do."

"Here we go," Geronimo said to Nate. "Here comes the anti-government rant."

"No rant from me," Nate said. "I think you've heard it enough."

"Bless your soul," Geronimo said with a sly grin.

"What about the Keystoners?" Joe asked Marybeth. "Did you find much on them?"

"Not much more than what we already know," she said. "They're not a big movement of any kind that I could tell. They're fairly local and concentrated in places where the pipeline was supposed to be built. So Montana, North and South Dakota, Wyoming, Nebraska, Kansas, Oklahoma, and Texas. Wherever these guys lost their jobs.

"I don't think they're very organized," she said. "And I don't think they have an overall leadership structure. In a few states they hold rallies and lobby the legislature, and a couple of them don't seem to do much at all except get together and complain and hate on the politicians and environmentalists who they blame for what happened to them."

"So our local Keystoners are unique," Joe said.

"They are," she agreed. "Ours seem like the most radical. Especially if they're involved in drug trafficking. Ours seems more like a gang than an activist group. They're led by Cade Molvar."

Joe nodded. "Have you met him?" he asked her.

"In the library a couple of times," she said. "He refused to get a library card because he said he didn't want to be on any kind of database that could be accessed by the feds. I told him we don't share that information, but he didn't believe me. So he sat at a table and read stuff without ever checking anything out. Mainly, he creeped out other patrons."

"What was he reading?" Sheridan asked.

Marybeth said, "I didn't ask and I didn't spy on him. If I did, I'd be making his point for him, wouldn't I?"

"It would just be interesting to know," Sheridan said. "I mean, if he's reading bomb-making manuals, that would be of interest, right?"

"We're not the content police," Marybeth said.

"Good for you," Nate added.

The waitress jogged over and unfolded a stand next to the table, then followed it up with everyone's food.

They could all clearly hear a baby cry in the background from Geronimo's phone. "Uh-oh," Jacinda said. "I have to go now."

"I'll fill you in later," Geronimo said. "Kiss Pearl for me."

All conversation ceased for a few minutes as they ate.

———

"THIS SECESSION THING is just crazy," Geronimo said to the table. "I mean, why do they want even to talk about it? What is it with these bizarro states?"

"We're tired of being colonies," Nate said. "Did you know that half of Wyoming is owned by the federal government? That most of the West is run out of agencies in Washington, D.C.?"

"Seriously?" Geronimo said.

"Look it up," Nate said. "Our president is not the guy in the White House—it's the secretary of the interior. We have very little say in how we're governed by those bureaucrats. Doesn't that seem unfair?"

Geronimo looked around the table with a puzzled look on his face. "How did I not know this?" he said.

"You came from the eastern half of the country," Nate said. "It's not the same there."

"You're not going to get involved with this Demo guy, are you?" Geronimo asked. "We've got work to do. We've got a *plan*."

Nate didn't answer. Joe watched the exchange with interest.

As did Sheridan, who hadn't noticed that Clay Hutmacher Jr. had sneaked up behind her. He had a big smile on his face and his finger to his lips to indicate they should remain quiet.

Clay Junior placed his hands on Sheridan's shoulders and bent over and kissed her on the cheek. Sheridan recoiled and Joe did, too.

Sheridan turned to see who had touched her and her face softened.

"Clay, what are you doing here?"

"I saw your car out front," he said to her. "I thought I'd surprise you."

"Well, you did," she said. Then to Nate, Geronimo, and Liv: "This is Clay. He's a friend of mine."

"Looks like it," Geronimo said, arching his eyebrows. Clay Junior smiled at that.

Sheridan introduced the rest of the table to Clay Junior, and he politely said that it was a pleasure to meet them all.

Joe observed his daughter. She didn't seem thrilled. He was both a little surprised—and heartened—by her reaction.

"What are you up to after dinner?" Clay Junior asked her. "Do you want to meet me at the Stockman's?"

"This may go on for a while," she told him.

"I don't mind. You're worth the wait," he said with a wink to Joe and Marybeth.

"I'll text you," Sheridan said. It was obvious to Joe that she wanted to disengage with Clay Junior at the moment.

Clay Junior lifted his hands off her shoulders, as if withdrawing his attention would punish her a little and send her a message of its own.

"It was nice to meet all of you," he said with a wave and a bright smile. To Sheridan, he raised his hand next to his face and pantomimed taking a call from her later.

Joe nodded goodbye.

———

"I ALSO CHECKED on the status of Professor Zhang Wei on the UW website," Marybeth said as desserts arrived.

"All of his classes are canceled until further notice," Marybeth continued. "But there's no indication that anyone there knows what happened to him."

"That's bizarre," Sheridan said.

"Either they don't know or they're covering it up," Marybeth said. "What do you think, Joe?"

He said, "It's only been a few days. They might think he's ill or something."

Marybeth placed her napkin on the table. "Are you saying that the only people who know he was killed are sitting at this table?"

"The sheriff's department knows," Joe said. "Clay Hutmacher knows. The governor knows."

"Do you think the governor asked the university to keep things quiet?" Marybeth asked. "Why would he do that?"

"Why are *we* supposed to keep it quiet?" Joe asked. "I don't like the sound of that."

Geronimo looked from Joe to Nate to Marybeth. "You-all are going to get involved in this, aren't you?"

"I'm already there," Joe said. "I found his body."

Geronimo shook his head and his long dreads brushed the top of his shoulders. "Nate told me you were always getting yourself in the middle of bad situations."

"I'm a game warden," Joe said. "I swore an oath. And I'm going to need help from everybody at this table to figure this out and see it through."

"And that's why I call him Dudley Do-Right," Nate said to Geronimo, who laughed. Then: "What can we do, Joe?"

Joe turned to Sheridan. "Sherry, can I ask you to dig deep on social media for posts and networks? Can you find out what you can on Demo, Molvar, the Keystoners, even Professor Wei? Maybe you can find some type of connection in there."

She said, "I assume you want me to access socials beyond Facebook, Twitter, and Instagram?"

Joe nodded and said, "Absolutely. Whatever is out there. I know there are plenty of obscure sites I don't know a thing about."

"There are," Sheridan assured him. To Nate and Liv, she said, "Are you okay if I spend some time on this?"

"Absolutely," Liv said. "Take as much time as you need."

Joe asked Marybeth to continue doing what she was already doing in regard to mining public information and accessing law enforcement and other official databases. She said she planned to proceed.

"What about me?" Geronimo asked. "What can I do?"

Joe took a moment to answer. "You can sit this one out," he said. "You're new to the area and you've got a new little baby at home. Plus, don't you need to set up that minipod?"

"I guess I do," Geronimo said. "But I'm willing to do my part."

"I'll keep you posted," Joe said. "Everybody please keep me in the loop and I'll do the same. I'm starting with those shed poachers. I think they're involved somehow."

AFTER SETTLING THE bill for the evening, Joe and Marybeth started on their walk to her minivan. Within half a block, Joe felt a familiar presence and glanced over his shoulder to see that Nate was ten feet behind them.

"I'll meet you at the car," he said to Marybeth. She nodded.

"You forgot someone when you were handing out assignments," Nate said to Joe.

"I didn't forget."

Nate glared at Joe a long time. They'd been around each other so long and knew each other so well that things didn't always need to be said.

"You want me to reach out to Jason Demo and the Sovereign Nation people, don't you?"

"I'd never ask that," Joe said.

"You want me to spy on them."

"I want you to do the right thing," Joe said.

"What if I decide to join up?" Nate asked. "Then what?"

"Then it would probably be the end of a beautiful friendship," Joe said.

Nate nodded and looked hard at Joe. Then he turned and walked away.

CHAPTER FOURTEEN

THREE HOURS LATER, Jason Demo and Cade Molvar returned to Demo's SUV, which was parked in the shadow of a downtown bank building. The Big Fish waited for them in the back seat in the dark. He rolled his window down as they approached.

"What's the verdict?"

"Like I told you before," Molvar said, "there's an alarm system on the front door and the keypad for it is just inside the vestibule. There's a closed-circuit camera there and one over the front desk. I could see the red light in the dark."

"Any more cameras that you could see?"

"No."

"Demo?" the Big Fish asked.

"Going through the front is a losing proposition," Demo said. "Too much exposure. But there's a back entrance in the alley. There's a metal door where it looks like they get shipments or packages. It's locked, but really old. I doubt it's connected to the alarm system."

The Big Fish nodded, then turned his head away from the two men to think. While he did, Molvar fired up a lighter and lit the end of a blunt he had clamped in his mouth. The flame revealed his features for a moment.

"Put that out," the Big Fish ordered.

"In a minute," Molvar said, inhaling like he was sucking oxygen after being submerged. After holding the smoke in, he exhaled a massive cloud of it. Demo grimaced against the waft of weed smoke that washed over him.

Demo was getting more and more concerned about the direction in which the Big Fish was taking them. Recruiting the tweakers was bad enough, but literally doubling the numbers of the group by bringing in the Keystoners? It was all getting unwieldy, he thought. He knew why he was there—he didn't have a choice. And he knew that the tweakers were in it for the money the Big Fish paid them.

The Keystoners hated the federal government, that was for sure. But they were a wild card and Demo didn't trust them. Especially Molvar. The man was oily and duplicitous and he seemed to be in it for himself. Why the Big Fish found it necessary to include Molvar in the planning and execution of their operation was beyond Demo.

He wished he could wash his hands of all of them and go home. But he knew he couldn't. Not until the deed was done.

———

"So the alley," the Big Fish said. "Are there lights back there?"

"No," Demo said. "It's darker than hell."

"Good. Get in and we can drive there."

Demo nodded and opened the driver's-side door. The interior lighting had been toggled off before they left the Big Fish's RV in the woods.

"No smoking in my rig," he said to Molvar.

"Fuck off," Molvar responded. "I'll roll down the window."

"Please," the Big Fish said to them. "Let's just get to work."

The building was one of the few original Andrew Carnegie–funded facilities still in operation in the Mountain West. The country had once had over sixteen thousand of them. It was built of stone and had a pitched roof and ancient slate shingles. The inside had been renovated several times, but the original hardwood floors and tin ceiling remained. When the building had been constructed in 1920 in Saddlestring, the conventional wisdom had been that it was simply too large for the community. Now it was too small.

Demo checked the street before pulling out. There was no traffic in either direction. He eased away from the lot with his headlights off and drove a half block before turning into the entrance of the alleyway. It was narrow and dark and there was only room for one vehicle. He clicked on his parking lights so he could avoid clipping a dumpster and a stack of empty boxes behind a hardware store.

"That's it," he said as he pulled up beside the back door of the target building. TWELVE SLEEP COUNTY LIBRARY was stenciled on the metal of the door.

Demo killed the engine and Molvar climbed out with the leather satchel he had brought along. Demo could hear the tinkling of metal as Molvar opened the bag and fished his paw into it. All he could see of the man was the cherry of his joint bobbing up and down in the dark.

In a moment, the beam of a penlight flashed on the door. Molvar choked down the light into a saucer-sized orb. Then he tossed away his smoke and replaced it in his mouth with the butt end of the flashlight. The beam illuminated the doorknob and lock plate next to the doorframe.

"This shouldn't be too hard," Molvar said. "It's an old lock. It's not the original, but it isn't very sophisticated."

"I'm not surprised," Demo said. "Who breaks into a library?"

"We do," the Big Fish said from the back.

"COME OUT HERE and hold the flashlight for me," Molvar said to Demo. "Make yourself useful."

"Fuck off," Demo said, echoing the sentiment expressed earlier by Molvar. But he got out and joined the man by the door. He trained the light on the keyhole.

Molvar found a bundled set of lockpicks in his satchel as well as a small silver tension wrench. He untied the bundle and selected two thin metal picks tipped with smooth rounded teeth spaced at different lengths.

"Are you sure you know what you're doing?" Demo asked.

"Watch me," Molvar replied. "I used to practice for hours at night on the job site. The guys would bring me padlocks and other locks and bet each other how long it would take me to get them open. An old lock like the one on this door should be fucking easy."

Demo snorted, but didn't respond further. He kept trying to find reasons to warm up to Molvar, but so far he'd been unsuccessful. The guy was an arrogant blowhard, and except for bringing the rest of the Keystoners along for the Big Fish's cause, Demo didn't think Molvar had any redeeming qualities.

As Molvar inserted one and then the other pick into the door lock, Demo smiled to himself. He enjoyed being there in person when Molvar screwed up.

The thin picks looked ludicrous in Molvar's sausage fingers, Demo thought. Like a slide rule in a bear cub's paw.

"Harder than I thought," Molvar grumbled to himself.

"How is it going?" the Big Fish asked from the open window of the SUV.

"About as well as I expected," Demo replied.

"Fuck off," Molvar said. "I'm getting close."

SUDDENLY, THEY WERE bathed in bright light that lit up the entire alley. Demo stepped back and squinted at the source. A vehicle rolled slowly toward them with its headlights on bright and a mounted spotlight swiveling from the dirt alley floor to eye level. Demo turned away when it hit him in the eyes.

"Shit," Molvar said. "I almost had that lock figured out."

The Big Fish turned in his seat and looked out the back window. Demo could tell that the man was surprised and shaken, even though he could barely see beyond the lingering aftereffect of the spotlight.

"Cops," Molvar spat. He said it as if it were a curse word. "Fuckin' town cops."

Molvar stood up and faced the oncoming vehicle and hid the bundle of lockpicks behind his back.

"What the hell should we say to him?" Demo asked the Big Fish.

"I don't know," the Big Fish said. "Just let me handle it."

Demo noted a tremor of doubt in his voice. He hadn't heard it before.

A loudspeaker from the cop car crackled. *"I need you gentlemen to put your hands up on the wall and kick your legs out and spread 'em. The individual inside the vehicle needs to come out now."*

The car pulled within twenty feet of the back of the SUV before it stopped. The interior lights were on and Demo's eyes recovered enough from the initial blast of the spotlight that he could make out a figure behind the wheel.

"Tell him I'm handicapped," the Big Fish said. "Tell him I'll have to stay right here."

"Damn," Molvar said. "It's Buck Holmes. He's fucking with us."

Demo blew out a deep breath and let his shoulders relax. He glanced over to see a smile form on the Big Fish's mouth.

"Very funny," Demo said to no one in particular.

The spotlight went out and the headlights on the sheriff's department SUV were doused as well. Holmes opened his door and climbed out.

"Howdy, boys," he said. His tone was more stern than jovial.

Holmes walked up alongside Demo's vehicle until he was at the Big Fish's open window. "You're lucky it was me on patrol tonight," he said. "Otherwise, you could all be in a world of hurt."

"We're grateful it was you," the Big Fish said. "Truly."

"What were you going to say if it wasn't?" Holmes asked. "There's no way in hell you could talk your way out of what you're doing."

"You're right," the Big Fish said. "It might have had to come to this."

As he said it, he raised his arm inside the car to reveal a blunt semiauto pistol in his grip. Demo was surprised.

"You'd shoot a cop?" he asked.

"Only if necessary," the Big Fish answered.

"*You'd shoot a cop for a library break-in?*" Demo said, feeling exasperated with the situation.

The Big Fish just shrugged as he lowered the weapon.

"You need to be more careful," Holmes said to them all, but clearly meaning the Big Fish.

"Molvar claimed he could pick the lock," the Big Fish said. "We wanted to make sure he could."

"If I'd had more time . . ." Molvar said, looking away.

"How much more time?" Demo asked. "A week?"

"Fuck off," Molvar said again.

"Look," Holmes said, "how many more days until the mission gets underway?"

"Two," the Big Fish said.

Holmes rubbed his jaw. "Monday, then," he said. "I can help, but we've got to be damned careful."

"How?" the Big Fish asked.

"We've got keys for all the county facilities at the office," Holmes said. "Just in case we have a call and we've got to get in. I can get a duplicate made for this door at the hardware store in Winchester. I'll let you know when I have it."

"That would be very helpful," the Big Fish said.

"I wish we would have known that," Demo added.

"I never thought about it until now," Holmes said. "I didn't know how you planned to get in."

"Neither did we until tonight," Demo said.

Holmes shook his head. "You've got to be more careful," he stressed. "This is a small town."

Demo nodded and Molvar said, "This place is normally a ghost town after midnight. You know that."

"I know that I caught you red-handed," Holmes said. "I'm not the only one who may have a reason to be out and about. The Stockman's down the street hasn't even closed yet."

The Big Fish said, "Point taken. We've come too far along to hijack ourselves now."

"That's what I'm saying," Holmes said. He turned and

walked toward his car. "I'll back down the alley and move along. Give me ten minutes or so before you drive away. I don't want anyone seeing us together."

"Got it," the Big Fish said.

The three men stood in silence while Holmes carefully backed his SUV down the alley and onto the street. He drove off with a curt wave of his hand.

"We caught a break," Demo said.

"Come get in the car," the Big Fish ordered. "Let's get out of here."

Demo felt the hairs on the back of his neck and arms prick up. He *hated* to respond to orders. Especially from this guy.

"Give me back my flashlight," Molvar said to him.

"Maybe I'll shove it down your throat," Demo growled. He meant it.

"Gentlemen, please," the Big Fish said from the SUV. "Can't you at least try to get along? At least until we've done this thing?"

Sunday, April 2

For the listener, who listens in the snow,
And, nothing himself, beholds
Nothing that is not there and the nothing
    that is.

—Wallace Stevens,

"The Snow Man"

CHAPTER FIFTEEN

I T WAS KNOWN around the tiny mountain town of Winchester as the "Marmot House," and Joe watched it emerge from the darkness at a distance through his spotting scope, waiting for the morning sun to spill across the steep arroyo in the foothills of the Bighorns. He'd left his house well before dawn and driven to and through Winchester to this location on a wooded hillside overlooking his target.

While he waited for the sun to come up, he sipped coffee from a thermos and listened to call-ins on the SALECS channel as other game wardens and law enforcement personnel checked in for Sunday duty. Other than that, there wasn't much happening out there. Daisy rested her big head on his lap.

The Marmot House was a dilapidated duplex halfway up the opposite slope four miles west of Winchester. Joe didn't know the history behind it other than it had been a wreck long before he ever showed up in the Twelve Sleep River Valley. It had once been painted yellow, but it was now mottled gray and the siding had been bleached by the high-altitude sun. There were two front doors and two porches.

The two-bedroom unit on the right was the reason for its name. Marmots—fat, stubby-legged, yellow-brown rodents that could weigh up to fifteen pounds—had long ago taken over the space. There were dozens of them inside, and they'd eaten through the interior walls, floors, and ceiling. Sometimes they could be seen peering out the broken windows and whistling at anyone who used the dirt road in front of the duplex. When they were very alarmed by visitors, the marmots scrambled to the roof of the duplex and whistled from there, hence their nickname "whistle pigs."

The left side of the Marmot House was occupied by Ogden Driskill and Leland Christensen. It was dark and lifeless, but Driskill's Silverado was parked out front. So was a detached snowmobile trailer with two machines and a large towing sled.

Which is why Joe was there.

As THE MORNING light infused the little canyon, Joe watched the duplex take shape through his scope. He could see no movement through the windows and no lights on inside the left unit. There was a large corrugated metal shed behind the duplex and tracks in the snow leading to it. Someone had been using the shed very recently, and Joe thought he knew why that was.

It was likely full of elk antlers.

JOE HAD ARRIVED early because he knew the best time to confront and engage tweakers was before they could get their wits about them. It could take a while. And who knew what they might blurt out before they were fully awake and lucid?

He was shocked, then, when the left front door blew open and Ogden Driskill stumbled outside. He was unsteady on his feet and Joe thought for a moment that he might pitch over. Driskill, though, returned to the house to kick the door closed and then he staggered to his pickup. The brake lights flashed and a puff of exhaust belched out from the tailpipe and Joe could hear it as it rumbled away.

Why was Driskill up so early? And where was he headed like his hair was on fire?

Joe quickly removed the spotting scope from its window mount and placed it on the seat, disturbing Daisy. He knew he might need to make a fast getaway so he wouldn't be discovered.

But instead of taking the road that crossed the floor of the arroyo and going up the slope toward where Joe was perched in the trees, Driskill turned left. That road also led to Winchester, but it was a back way.

Joe decided not to follow. If he did, they'd likely be the only two trucks on the mountain and on the road. There was no traffic to blend into, and even someone as dim as Driskill would soon notice that a green Game and Fish Department vehicle was tailing him.

Instead, Joe would stay at the location. He'd build his case: verifying that the snow machines on the trailer were the same make and model of the ones he'd seen the day before, and photographing the antler cache that was likely inside the shed.

And he'd do it quickly before Driskill returned.

JOE STARTED THE pickup and rolled down the road to the Marmot House. He parked thirty yards from the structure. It was a cool morning and the snow had a hard crust on it. He knew he'd likely leave tracks, but he hoped Driskill wouldn't be bright enough to notice them.

"Daisy, stay," he said.

He climbed out of the pickup with his gear bag and made every attempt to approach the duplex by stepping in boot tracks made the night before.

He photographed the two snow machines on the trailer. They were both Polaris models, and equally beaten-up. Their colors matched those he'd seen previously near Hazelton Road. Snow was still packed in their tracks.

The interior of the tow sled was scarred as if scratched by sharp objects. Antler tines could do that, he thought. A snowmobile helmet was strapped to the handlebars of one of the machines, a gold lightning bolt decal pasted on the side of it.

"Gotcha," he said aloud while he photographed everything.

KNOCKING SHARPLY ON the front door, he called out, "This is Joe Pickett, the game warden. Is anybody there?"

There was no response. He knocked and called out again. Silence.

He backed off the porch to make his way along the duplex to the tracks he'd seen leading to the shed. As he did, he walked along the face of the structure to the right.

Joe gasped and stepped back when three fat marmots suddenly thrust their faces out a broken window on the unit and squealed at him. The whistling was so high-pitched it hurt his ears. He was close enough to them that he could see their long yellow front teeth and their dead little eyes.

Soon, six or seven other marmot heads appeared from other broken windows or through holes in the exterior sheeting. Their shrill whistles blended into an awful cacophony.

"I thought you'd still be *hibernating*," he shouted at them.

Joe turned a hundred and eighty degrees and walked around the duplex the other way to the shed, fresh tracks in the snow be damned.

THE METAL SHED had large double doors on the front that were secured by a chain and a padlock. There were tire tracks, sled tracks, and boot tracks leading to the doors. He took shots of the disturbance to the surface of the snow, then he pulled on the lock, just in case, to see if it gave way. It didn't.

A single door on the side of the shed was also locked.

He circled the shed until he found a smudged window and he peered into it. The interior was illuminated by natural light that flowed down from a sheet of fiberglass on the roof.

Joe cupped his hands and raised them to his face to block out the light, then leaned into the glass until he could see inside. The filtered sun illuminated a four-foot-high tangled heap of elk antlers, their tines glinting. He could see the bloodied stump of some of the antlers that had likely been shed just the day before.

He'd found it. He had them.

The shed pile was hard to photograph through the window, but he managed to get several shots that clearly showed the evidence. It looked like Driskill and his buddies had been at it for a while, forcing the local herds into dark timber and collecting the results of the turmoil inside.

He took several dozen more shots of the shed, then carefully backed away so he could photograph it in its entirety.

Confronted with the evidence, would Driskill give away the others involved? Joe thought it likely.

And what else did Driskill know? What other crimes had he been involved in?

JOE ONCE AGAIN avoided the right unit when he made his way back to his vehicle. Instead, he glanced inside one of the windows of the left unit as he walked by and it stopped him cold.

A man's lace-up boot was on the floor, its scuffed toe pointing toward the ceiling. The boot was attached to a lower leg. The rest of the body was obscured behind a hallway wall. There was a slick of blood on the tile floor, and it had spread to a filthy carpet that had soaked it up into a two-foot-by-three-foot pool.

Quickly, he hit the on button of the digital recorder he always had with him and slipped it into his breast pocket.

He bounded up the porch and pounded again on the front door with his left hand. With his right, he unsnapped the security strap on his weapon and drew his .40 Glock from its holster.

"I'M COMING IN," he shouted. He knew he had probable cause for entering the residence without a warrant. The man inside might need immediate medical assistance.

There was no need to use his shoulder to break down the old door. It was unlocked.

Joe threw it open and flung himself inside, crouched in a shooter's stance. It took him a moment for the gloom to recede, and while it did he swept the front sight of his weapon around the room. He hoped no one was there waiting for him, and he wished he were a better shot.

Through the wall between the left and right units, he

could hear marmots scrambling and whistling, their claws scratching the walls and floors. The smell of rodent feces hung in the air. Despite the situation he was in, he wondered how Driskill could stand to live there.

The body belonged to Leland Christensen, and Christensen was dead. His throat was sliced from ear to ear, and the wound gaped. It was a brutal cut, so deep it went all the way through his neck muscles to the spine. Joe could see a wink of white bone, and he turned away, fighting a gag reflex.

He glanced around the residence. There were two mattresses on the floor of the single bedroom, both with peeled-back filthy sheets. Unwashed dishes and utensils were piled in the sink. Drug paraphernalia—pipes and lighters—were on the scarred kitchen table. Of course, there was a massive big-screen TV in the small living area.

Joe retreated, not wanting to leave any more traces of himself at the crime scene.

Even in his haste, he noticed that the blood on the floor wasn't fresh. It had already started to coagulate and separate. Meaning Christensen had been murdered hours before Joe arrived. Maybe even the previous night.

And Driskill hadn't fled the scene until that morning. What was *that* about?

ON THE FRONT porch, Joe fished his cell phone out of his breast pocket with a trembling hand. There was no cell

service in the arroyo. He'd need to get in his pickup and drive
to the top of the slope to locate a signal in order to call the
sheriff.

Although there was a roar of blood in his ears and the
marmots were whistling next door, he heard the rumble of an
oncoming vehicle and the pop of gravel from its tires.

Joe wheeled, expecting to see Driskill behind the wheel of
his Silverado. Instead, the grille of a black Ford Expedition
appeared from the timber where Joe had parked that morning. There were two figures inside.

Joe realized he was still gripping his weapon and what that
must look like as he stood there, so he slipped the Glock back
into its holster and waited.

THE EXPEDITION PULLED up and stopped next to Joe's pickup.
He could see Daisy rise from her sleep and stare through the
passenger window as two men got out.

The SUV had Utah plates and a location sticker in the
window that told Joe it was a rental.

The driver was small and compact, with short, neatly
trimmed brown hair and a boyish face. He pulled on an oversized thigh-length parka, but left it unzipped.

The passenger was a bear of a man with a shaved round
head, black chin hair with no mustache, and heavy-lidded
eyes. He wore a thick gray hoodie with USMC on the front and
a down vest over it.

"Good morning," the driver said to Joe. "Can I ask what you're doing here?"

"I could ask the same of you," Joe said.

They were feds. They reeked of it. While the driver looked more clean-cut and traditional, the passenger apparently wanted to pass himself off as a local redneck. He was probably experienced in undercover work and he wanted to try to look the part, Joe thought.

Joe introduced himself and said, "I'm here investigating a couple of shed hunters. Turns out, there's a dead man inside."

The two men exchanged a glance and Joe watched them carefully. He was glad he'd activated his recorder earlier. He knew from experience to *always* record conversations with federal officers, especially FBI agents. Because they never did.

"When you say dead man, can you elaborate a little?" the driver asked.

"A man was murdered. They cut his throat."

Again, the exchange of glances.

"And you just happened to show up?" the passenger asked.

"I told you already. I was investigating them for a state wildlife crime. I saw the body through the window and went in."

The driver said, "We appreciate you briefing us on the situation. You can stand down now and we'll take it from here."

Joe crossed his arms over his chest and stared at them in a squint.

"Why," he asked, "would the FBI be interested in a couple of shed-poaching tweakers?"

"Who said we were FBI?" the passenger asked. He had a slight smile on his face when he said it.

"Everything about you screams it," Joe said. "Utah plates, the straight-out-of-the-box outdoor clothing that is unzipped in case you need to draw a weapon, the over-the-top black four-wheel-drive luxury vehicle, and your attitude in general toward local law enforcement."

The driver glared at him, while the passenger grinned coldly.

"I'm Special Agent Fetterman," the passenger said. He chinned toward the driver. "Special Agent Scott."

"Pleased to meet you," Joe said.

"Do you want to see our credentials?"

"Not necessary."

"Then please step aside so we can observe the crime scene," Fetterman said.

"I'll do that," Joe agreed. "But you need to tell me how you just happened to show up here. What is it you're looking for?"

"We're not at liberty to say," Scott responded.

"Since when do the feds care about dead tweakers?" Joe asked them again.

"What he said," Fetterman added, nodding toward Scott. Then: "I like your dog. What's his name?"

"Her name is Daisy."

"I wish we could ride around all day with our dog with us in the car," Fetterman said. "That must be nice."

"What office are you from?" Joe asked. "You can at least tell me that. I know a few guys in the Cheyenne office."

Which was mostly untrue, Joe knew. He *used* to know

special agents out of the Cheyenne office, like Chuck Coon, but most of them had retired or quit. These two didn't look like Cheyenne types.

"We're based in Washington," Fetterman said. Joe was right. And it meant that whatever they were doing there came from FBI headquarters, not the Cheyenne field office.

He noted that Scott shot Fetterman a look when their base was revealed to Joe. Fetterman caught it and looked away.

Of the two, Fetterman was much more forthcoming, while Scott was buttoned up.

"Enough chatting," Scott said to Joe. "We'll have to ask you to move along so we can secure the scene. If you continue to stand there and block our access we'll charge you with obstruction and unlawful interference."

"I'm glad I got that on tape," Joe said, patting the recorder in his shirt pocket.

"You can't do that," Scott said, his face reddening.

"I just did," Joe said as he stepped aside. "This way we don't have a situation where it's your word against mine. You guys always have the advantage in those."

"Give me your recording device," Scott said, holding out his hand for it.

"Nope," Joe said. "It's perfectly legal for one party to record a conversation in Wyoming. Trust me on this."

Scott stood staring at Joe, as if contemplating his next move. Both Joe and Fetterman watched him. Joe heard Fetterman say in a low voice, "Let it go, Scott."

He was apparently persuasive, and Scott turned away and

strode toward the house without looking over at Joe. Fetterman followed.

"What's a shed poacher?" he asked Joe.

"Someone who harvests antlers before it's legal to do so," Joe said. "But these guys did much worse than that."

"Antlers?" Fetterman said, surprised. "You're here because of *antlers*? Like from a deer?"

"Elk," Joe said.

Scott was about to mount the porch steps when several marmots popped their heads out of the right unit and whistled at him. He jumped back and reached into his open coat and came out with his weapon and pointed it at the rodents in a shooter's stance. He was clearly shaken.

"Don't mind the marmots," Joe said. Fetterman grinned and looked away.

"You could have warned us," Scott said angrily as he holstered his weapon and stood up straight.

Joe shrugged. "I haven't called the sheriff about this," he told them. "I don't have cell service."

"We'll inform the locals," Scott said, dismissing Joe.

Fetterman nodded to Joe as he passed by on his way to the house.

"Tell me," Joe called to their backs, "does the fact that you're here have anything to do with the murder of a University of Wyoming professor?"

It was a shot in the dark and it was a miss. Both agents froze in their tracks for a few seconds, then continued toward the open door.

Fetterman paused on the top step, turned around with a puzzled look on his face, and said, "We have no idea what you're talking about."

"You don't?"

"No," Scott said. "And even if we did, we wouldn't tell you. You can move along now."

Joe took them at their word, and he felt a little foolish for taking the flier in the first place. Either both agents were very great actors, or they truly weren't aware of Wei's murder.

"We're done talking," Scott said as he shoulder-rolled toward the crime scene.

INSIDE THE CAB of his pickup, Joe asked Daisy, "So why are they here? What is going on?"

Daisy looked back at him with empathy. No answers, but empathy.

CHAPTER SIXTEEN

YOU'LL WANT TO put out an APB for Ogden Driskill," Joe said to Sheriff Tibbs once he received a strong cell signal on the top of the mountain and he was able to brief him. Joe had dialed 911 as a back-door way to connect with Tibbs via the dispatcher. "I saw him headed toward Winchester on the back road about an hour ago."

"Jesus," Tibbs said. Then: "Another one," he sighed.

"Yup," Joe said. "Do you need a vehicle description?"

"I'm sure we've got it in the system, but go ahead and give it to me."

Joe did. Afterward, Tibbs said, "What do you think it was? Some kind of drug deal gone bad? I thought those two were birds of a feather, you know?"

"I have no idea," Joe said. "It could have to do with their illegal shed-poaching side hustle, or maybe something else. And I can't verify that Driskill did it. All I can tell you is I saw him come out of the house this morning and drive away. He looked disoriented."

"That guy always looks disoriented," Tibbs said. "But you say the FBI is on it?"

"They're on the scene now."

Tibbs sighed again. "It would be nice if they gave a heads-up to the locals that they're around, you know? But I'm used to it: feebs bigfooting their way in. It's reason number five hundred and thirty-eight why I can't wait to retire."

"I get it," Joe said.

"I'll get Holmes and we'll head up there and introduce ourselves," Tibbs said. "Do you think they'll need Norwood?"

"You'll have to ask them," Joe said. "My guess is that they'd rather fly in one of their own forensics people."

"You're probably right. That way they can spend a lot more of our taxpayer money. Did they say why they were there in the first place?"

"Nope."

"Any ideas?"

Joe paused for a moment. "I really don't know. Maybe you can get something out of them. I couldn't." Then: "Once they're gone, I need access to the scene. Not the house, though. I need to get into the shed out back. They've got a bunch of illegal antlers in there."

"We'll get the warrant," Tibbs said. "Judge Hewitt is around, I believe."

"Thank you."

Knowing Judge Hewitt, Joe wouldn't be surprised if the

man met him at the scene with his shoulder holster on and a pair of bolt cutters to get into the shed. Hewitt despised poachers of any sort because he was a dedicated big-game trophy hunter himself.

"Sheriff," Joe said, "thanks for finally taking my call."

"I couldn't put you off forever, I guess," Tibbs said with resignation. "Calling 911 was a good trick, but it won't work again. I mean, look what happens when I talk to you. Another murder in my county and a killer on the loose."

"Have a great day," Joe said, and punched off.

A TEXT APPEARED a few seconds later on his phone from Marybeth.

> You need to call Lucy. She has something she wants to tell you about her friend Fong.

Joe tried Lucy's number, but it went straight to voicemail. He glanced at his watch and thought she was likely in church at the moment. At least he hoped that's where she was.

Since none of his daughters ever listened to messages, he texted her to please give him a call.

BECAUSE THE MAIN gated entrance to the Double Diamond Ranch was off the interstate between Winchester and Saddlestring, Joe called Clay Hutmacher from the highway.

"Are you around?" Joe said to the ranch foreman. "I told you I'd keep you in the loop regarding the investigation. I was also wondering if you had anything new for me."

"As it turns out," Hutmacher said, "my boss just flew in for a few days. He said he'd like to talk with you."

"Thompson?"

"In the flesh."

"I'll be there in fifteen minutes," Joe said.

As HE DISCONNECTED from Hutmacher, Joe heard a crackle from his radio and the dispatcher's familiar voice over the SALECS channel.

"The Twelve Sleep Sheriff's Department has issued an all-points-bulletin lookout for a 2008 silver Chevrolet Silverado pickup, license plate Wyoming 4-1616, last seen on County Road 34 eastbound en route to Winchester at 6:45 a.m. Subject driving is a single male named Ogden Driskill. Subject should be considered armed and dangerous."

THE TRADITIONAL TIMBER arch signifying the entrance to the Double D had recently been replaced with one made entirely of elk antlers forming an inverted U over the road. Joe drove under it and noted the security cameras hidden within the beams and tines that were no doubt broadcasting his arrival to whoever was monitoring the screens at the ranch head-quarters.

The mile-and-a-half road to the headquarters complex was graded and smooth and in better shape than ninety-five per-cent of all of the county roads Joe used every day. Hundreds of Black Angus cattle grazed on loose hay that had been spread over the top of the snow.

The headquarters was immaculate as well, with all of the buildings painted white with green trim and not a single er-rant vehicle or yapping dog in the huge courtyard. A heli-copter that Thompson had likely used to get there from the airport sat gleaming on a round concrete pad behind the main ranch house. The home, which was three stories high and gabled, had been there since the 1920s, and rather than knock it down and build a castle befitting a multimillionaire, Thompson and his new and much-younger third wife had overseen its restoration.

The biggest barn in the county stretched across the entire eastern edge of the compound. The Double D brand was painted in five-foot letters over the open barn doors.

As Joe pulled his truck up to a hitching rail, he saw activity inside the barn. Three or four employees, all wearing custom Carhartt coats embroidered with the Double D brand across the back, were washing a jacked-up Humvee.

Joe assumed from the scene that Thompson would soon set out on a tour of his ranch.

———

CLAY HUTMACHER EMERGED from the main house, clamped
on his hat, and waved from the covered porch for Joe to join
him. He was in Wranglers, boots, and a starched long-sleeved
shirt with yokes and snap buttons.

Joe parked against a hitching rail and told Daisy to stay.
He didn't want her to be alarmed to find a ranch yard without
any dogs, because it would be the first time in her life that
had happened.

"Dressing up for the boss, huh?" Joe said with a smile as
he shook hands with Clay.

"Part of the deal," Hutmacher responded.

Hutmacher looked the part and always had, Joe thought.
Slim build, broad shoulders, skinny bowed legs, thick silver
gunfighter's mustache, rodeo buckle, and eyes in a permanent
squint as if he were forever peering across the prairie.

"He's inside," Hutmacher said. "It was kind of odd because
he was asking about you about five minutes before you called.
He's generally pretty heavily scheduled, so this kind of
worked out."

"What does he want to talk about?" Joe asked.

Hutmacher shrugged. "It could be anything," he said.
"The man's mind works a million miles a minute. You'll see."

Joe looked at Hutmacher skeptically.

"He won't take too much of your time," Hutmacher whispered. "Because he's always in a hurry. You'll be out of here in
a few minutes."

"Can't wait," Joe said, following the foreman through the living room toward the back of the house.

BRANDY THOMPSON CAME down the wide stairs as Joe and Hutmacher passed below. Joe saw her and removed his hat and Hutmacher did the same.

"Good morning, gentlemen," she said with an affected twang.

Brandy was lithe and fit, with chestnut hair, a smattering of freckles, bright green eyes, and an outfit of cowgirl chic: tight bejeweled jeans that were tucked into purple boots, a tight white top, and a vest with a Navajo rug pattern. She was cradling a long-haired white cat.

"We're getting ready for our tour," she announced with a bit of a pout on her lips. Joe interpreted her statement as a way of saying, *Please hurry up with whatever you're here for.*

"We'll only be a few minutes," Hutmacher said to her.

"You must be the forest ranger," she said to Joe.

"Game warden. It's nice to see you again."

She squinted at that, trying to recall when she'd met him before, but not asking.

"Well, anyway, welcome to paradise," she said. "We love it here—in the summer. I wish there wasn't snow on the ground right now, but that's Wyoming in the spring, I guess."

Joe nodded.

"I heard there's another storm coming," she said. "I hope we can get back to Atlanta before it hits."

"I haven't looked at the weather forecast, but I wouldn't be surprised," Joe said.

"I don't know how you people do it," she said.

"Our winters keep the riffraff out," Joe said with a smile.

"Joe . . ." Hutmacher said, urging Joe to follow him.

Joe nodded goodbye to her and followed the foreman to a high-ceilinged office with original Western artwork on the walls and a huge glass-fronted gun cabinet filled with hunting rifles.

Michael Thompson sat behind a burled-wood desk with a varnished top. Bronze sculptures of mountain men on horseback were on pedestals behind him.

Thompson was conventionally handsome; dark tanned skin, blue eyes, longish silver hair, a perfect aquiline nose that hadn't always been so, and a downturned mouth that made him look serious and judgmental at the same time.

Joe had previously met both Michael and Brandy at a local fundraiser Marybeth had made him attend, but he doubted Thompson remembered him.

He didn't. Neither did Brandy.

"Michael Thompson, owner of the Double D," Thompson said, rising and jutting out his hand. Joe shook it.

"Joe Pickett," he said.

Thompson settled back into his chair and cocked a leg over the armrest. He wore caiman boots with tooled shafts.

"We need to talk about corner-crossing trespassers," Thompson said. "I've had it with those idiots. They're stealing from me, and you people are letting them get away with it."

The statement took Joe aback. Hutmacher was right—Thompson was unpredictable.

"What about corner crossing?" Joe asked.

"I want it stopped and I want the people who do it to be prosecuted to the full extent of the law. And as my local game warden, I expect you to do your job."

Joe remained still, but he could feel his blood rising. Thompson was the kind of landowner who really did think everyone worked for him.

"It's a complicated issue," Joe said.

"With a very simple solution," Thompson said. "Prosecute those who do it."

Wyoming, and most of the Mountain West, was made up of millions of square parcels of land that belonged to private landowners as well as different departments of the federal government and the state itself. The entire map looked like a checkerboard, and in some instances, like the Double D, squares of public land thrust their way into private land like a finger. Because of that reason, hunters, fishermen, hikers, and other recreationists had the right to access the parcels. Many of the public parcels touched only at the corners. Others were adjoined, creating huge swaths of public land.

"Corner crossers" were people who stepped from one parcel of public land to the next where the corners met without setting foot on private land. Since the proliferation of highly accurate GPS mapping software, the mystery of where public ended and private began had become accessible to anyone with a smartphone.

Some landowners, like Thompson, considered it trespassing, because the interlopers couldn't help but enter the airspace above their private corners while crossing.

Joe said, "The policy of our department is not to issue citations to people if they remain on public land and don't break any Game and Fish regulations."

"They're criminal trespassers," Thompson said. "Simple as that."

"Then the sheriff should be called," Joe said. "They can make that determination. As a game warden, I can't."

"Your sheriff is useless," Thompson said. Joe didn't argue.

"So you're useless to me as well," Thompson said.

"On this issue, I'm not much help," Joe agreed. "We'd all like to see the corner-crossing issue resolved. But until that happens—"

"Until that happens," Thompson said, "hardworking Americans like me buy multimillion-dollar ranches and find out that any redneck with a map on his phone can walk right onto them and kill trophy wildlife that we manage at our own expense. Does that sound fair to you?"

"It's an issue," Joe said. "But I can't solve it for you."

"Maybe Governor Allen can," Thompson said. "He seems sympathetic and he takes my calls. Unlike your last governor, who actually told me to, and I quote, 'fuck off.' What was his name?"

"Rulon," Joe said.

"That's right," Thompson said with disdain. "I heard he might run again. Let's hope *not*."

Joe didn't respond.

Thompson turned to Hutmacher, who hadn't said a word. He made his eyes wide, as if begging the foreman to share his exasperation. "What do we do in the meanwhile, Clay?"

"We do our best to keep 'em out," Hutmacher said to Thompson. "We spend as much time chasing trespassers off as we do ranching, it seems like."

"Then do better," Thompson said.

Joe saw his opening. He said, "Speaking of trespassers, maybe we can discuss the people who trespassed on your Bitcoin-mining facility. As you probably know, one of them was murdered and his body has yet to be found."

Thompson's eyes flashed, but he kept his mouth clamped shut for a few seconds, as if holding in what he was about to say. Then: "I'm fully aware of that situation. Clay kept me apprised. I'd appreciate it if you kept the whole thing under wraps."

Joe cocked his head and didn't respond.

"It's not the kind of PR I want or need right now," Thompson continued. "It's the kind of thing that could blow up online and damage my reputation and that of the Double D for quality hunting experiences designed for high-dollar clients. If they heard about this, they might think we can't manage our property or our big-game herds because anyone and their brother has access."

"You're not the only one who wants the whole thing to just go away," Joe said.

"Then maybe we're all talking sense," Thompson said. "Something you ought to consider."

"I found the body," Joe said. "Somebody shot at me."

"Which is very unfortunate," Thompson said. "I'm sorry that happened. But I can assure you my people weren't involved. Right, Clay?"

"No, sir," Hutmacher said. "Joe knows that."

"*It was trespassers*," Thompson said, jabbing his finger on the desktop for emphasis. "They got on my land and caused these problems. If they weren't in the wrong in the first place, none of this would have happened."

"I agree with you," Joe said. "That's not the point. This wasn't about big-game poaching. This was about your crypto-mining facility, I'm pretty sure. I don't see a UW professor driving hundreds of miles in his passenger car to poach an elk."

Thompson said, "The *point*, Pickett, is that I also can't let it be known that we've got millions of dollars' worth of computers for the taking sitting in remote locations on the Double D. If that gets out, keeping trespassers off of us will become a *full-time* job for my ranch staff." He nodded toward Hutmacher as he said it.

"Is that why you pulled all the computers out of there?" Joe asked. "So people wouldn't try to steal them?"

"Mostly," Thompson said, breaking eye contact with Joe. "The building operated without anyone knowing about it for seven months. That won't happen again if word gets out what I'm doing here."

Joe acknowledged that.

"That facility is completely legal, if that's what you were wondering," Thompson said to Joe.

"I get that."

"And we made a little money on it, I admit. But that can't happen if we have to take it off-line all the time to stay ahead of vandals and computer thieves. I'm also rethinking how deep I want to get into crypto. Have you seen the price for it lately?"

"Not at all," Joe said.

"It's not pretty," Thompson said.

There was a cough from the doorway and Joe turned. Brandy stood there with her cat and an expectant look on her face. She was ready for her tour, obviously, and she wanted to remind Thompson about it.

"We're done here," Thompson said to Joe as he pushed back in his chair and stood up. "But I want you to do something about those corner crossers. I'd hate for any of those rubes to get themselves hurt."

The threat was obvious.

As Thompson joined Brandy, Joe asked, "Have you ever heard of or worked with Professor Zhang Wei of the University of Wyoming?"

"Never heard of him," Thompson said. This time, he didn't avert his eyes.

"Do you have any idea why he was on your ranch?"

"None whatsoever. We have bad security, apparently."

Hutmacher looked down at his boots.

"Do you have any idea where his body is?" Joe asked. "There are lots of places to hide it on this property."

"We've wondered about that ourselves," Hutmacher said

to Joe. "That big snow covered up all the tracks in and out of the facility. Maybe when everything melts, we'll find him."

"And I hear there's another storm coming," Brandy said through a frozen smile. Then to her husband, *So I'd suggest we commence our tour.*

"You heard the lady," Thompson said as he came around his desk. He quickly shook Joe's hand as a way of saying, *Time to go.*

"I'll meet you at the Humvee," Hutmacher said to the Thompsons.

AFTER THE THOMPSONS had pulled on their coats and gone outside toward the barn, Hutmacher turned to Joe as they walked through the living room toward the door.

"Sorry about that," he said. "I didn't know he was going to ambush you."

"It comes with the territory," Joe said. "No harm done."

"I hope you know that I'm not going to start shooting trespassers," Hutmacher said. "Despite that my boss thinks it's a mighty fine tactic. I have to live here in this county, you know."

"I know," Joe said. Then: "Your boss—is he trustworthy?"

Hutmacher paused. He looked squarely at Joe and said, "Mostly. He's a tycoon, so he might throw a little shade at times. But he's basically honest."

"Do you believe him that he never heard of Wei?"

"I do."

Joe nodded. "But he shades the truth sometimes?"

"He does," Hutmacher said. "When it comes to business, he's a shark. He keeps his cards close to his vest and he doesn't mind throwing out a little misdirection, you know? Like about this little tour I'm about to give them. We're scouting other locations on the ranch where we have capped gas wells. He wants to move the building by the end of the month and get that mining operation back into business. He wasn't straight with you about that."

"That's his business, I guess," Joe said.

As they approached the door, Hutmacher said, "I don't feel right about him misleading you. I'll never do that and I hope you know it."

"I think I do," Joe said. "I appreciate that."

Hutmacher grinned and said, "Because who knows? With Clay Junior and Sheridan getting along so well, we might be relations one of these days."

"Who knows?" Joe echoed, feeling uneasy about sharing Clay Senior's excitement.

He fitted his hat on his head and walked to his pickup, while Hutmacher joined the Thompsons to go on their tour.

JOE'S PHONE BURRED as he drove away from the ranch headquarters. He drew it out and looked at the screen. It was Lucy.

"Hi, babe," he said.

"Hey, Dad. Do you have a few minutes?"

"For you, always," he said.

"It's about Fong."

"Yes?"

"I feel kind of bad about this, because I'm pretty sure she doesn't want me sharing what she had to say. But after dinner the other night, when she walked out, I thought you might want to know what bothered her so much."

"I do," Joe said. "Thanks for trusting me."

"Well, of *course* I trust my dad," Lucy said, as if it were the most obvious thing in the world. It warmed Joe's heart.

"You didn't say anything wrong," Lucy said. "It wasn't that."

"Good. So what was it?"

"It's a little . . . crazy," Lucy said. "Promise me this is between us."

"And your mom," Joe said. "You know how it works. There aren't any secrets between me and your mom."

"I get it."

"Well, what did she say?" he asked.

"Professor Wei might be a member of the Chinese Communist Party," Lucy said. "He might be a *spy*."

"*What?*"

CHAPTER SEVENTEEN

T HAT AFTERNOON, JOE circled through the too-small and too-full library parking lot for a place to park. Two rows of parking spaces were covered by a massive pile of plowed snow and therefore inaccessible. He gave up looking and he parked on the street.

Inside, he tipped his hat to Evelyn Hughes, the front desk librarian. "Is Marybeth in?"

"She's in her office. We have an all-staff meeting in half an hour."

"Okay."

"We're getting ready for the big announcement tomorrow," Hughes said, placing her hands together under her chin in a praying gesture to show how excited she was. Anything out of the ordinary made Evelyn excited, Joe knew.

"This won't take long," he said.

———

MARYBETH WAS TAPPING at her keyboard with her reading glasses on when Joe entered her office. He found her "hair-up and glasses" look quite attractive, and he told her so.

"Thank you," she said, deadpan.

"I talked to Lucy all the way into town," he said, taking a chair on the opposite side of her desk. "She told me some very interesting things."

Marybeth closed the laptop and swiveled in her chair toward him. When something involved one of their daughters, she always gave it her full attention.

"I've got some interesting news as well," she said. "Good news and bad news, actually. But you go first."

"I know you don't have much time," Joe said, "so I'll be quick.

"Lucy said she found Fong in her room in the dark last night and Fong was upset and crying. We know Lucy, so we know she did all she could to comfort her friend."

"She's good that way," Marybeth said with approval. She urged him to go on with a curt nod.

"Fong's parents are trying to get out of Hong Kong, I guess," Joe said. "They're pro-democracy activists and they're against the Chinese Communist takeover. They're trying to get to the United States and Fong is doing what she can to help them, but it's a tense situation."

"I feel for them," Marybeth said.

"Yup. I didn't know how bad it was. Anyway, at some

point in the last few days, Fong told her parents about Professor Wei—how he hadn't shown up for class. And, I guess, that I mentioned his name to them at dinner that night."

"Are you telling me Fong's parents know him?" Marybeth asked. "China is a big country."

"I'm just relaying what Lucy said. Apparently, Fong's parents are well connected within Hong Kong and they have inside knowledge about the CCP and their methods. So they might know *of* him without knowing him personally. Fong's parents are pretty sure Zhang Wei is a member of the party and that he was sent over here on behalf of the Chinese government."

"Sent here to do what?" Marybeth asked.

"Who knows?" Joe said. "If Fong knows, she didn't tell Lucy."

"That is crazy," Marybeth said. "A Chinese spy on the faculty of the University of Wyoming?"

"Apparently," Joe said.

Marybeth sat back. "You know, it might not be as insane as it sounds at first. I looked up the College of Engineering and Applied Science after you told me about finding the body. They're involved in a lot of projects that are high-tech and really out there. Atmospheric science, chemical engineering, computer science, robotics, petroleum engineering, things like that. They're considered really cutting edge. I'm sure they're doing things the CCP would value knowing about—and stealing."

"Go on," Joe said.

"I've been reading about it for a while now," she said. "It's really a thing. There are something like three hundred and seventy-five thousand Chinese undergraduates and hundreds of professors in the country. Obviously they're not all spying on us, but some of them are. Our universities are considered 'soft targets' for them, and we're not doing much to root them out. Your Professor Wei might have been one of them."

Joe shook his head in wonder. "Are there things you don't know much about?"

"Lots of things," she said with a smile. "But I'm a librarian. I have access to a lot of information."

"Why would Professor Wei drive nearly three hundred miles to check out a hidden Bitcoin-mining facility on a ranch?" he asked.

"I have no idea," she said. "Maybe the technology behind it is unique. The Chinese government has a weird relationship with cryptocurrency, too. Maybe it has something to do with that."

"Geronimo told me the Chinese government threw out all their crypto miners a few years ago," Joe said.

"This is getting intriguing," she said. "You didn't tell Fong it was Wei's body that you found, right?"

"Right. But I told Lucy and I asked her to keep it to herself."

"And it's still officially under wraps as far as you know?"

"As far as I know," Joe said.

"I did some research on Wei," Marybeth said. "He's single and he lives—lived—alone in Laramie. So he doesn't have a wife or a family to report him missing. The university knows, of course, but who knows how closely they monitor something like this? A professor being out of class a few days probably doesn't raise any alarm bells by itself."

Joe said, "It's driving me crazy. Everyone who knows anything about it wants to keep it secret. They might all have different reasons for that, but I'm starting to wonder if the answers aren't staring me right in the face and I just can't see them. I feel complicit in covering it up, even though I involved the sheriff and the governor's office."

"Governor Allen said something about national security, right?" she asked.

"It made no sense, but yes he did."

As he said it, Joe was reminded of his encounter earlier that day.

"Did I tell you I met a couple of FBI agents this morning? They were lurking around the Marmot House outside of Winchester."

"FBI? Did they say why they were here?"

"They made a point of *not* saying," Joe said. "When I asked them about Wei, they seemed not to have any idea what I was talking about. I think I would have been able to tell if they did."

"I have no good theories about what is going on," she said. "I need to think about this."

"Me too," Joe said. "And I need my team to come through somehow. Maybe between us we can start to connect the dots."

"Maybe," Marybeth said. "Have you heard anything from Nate?"

He shook his head. "Not yet. I know he planned to meet with Demo. I don't know how that went."

She eyed him closely. "Are you worried about him?"

"Yup, a little. I don't *think* he'd throw in with a bunch of crazies, but I can't completely rule it out, either. You know Nate."

"I do, and I'm a little worried, too." Then: "Especially if you suspect that all of these weird things going on are somehow connected."

"On that, I just don't know," Joe said. "I think if I keep poking around, I might discover the links—if there are any. That's all I know to do—just keep pushing."

"It's worked before," she said. "And it's also gotten you into a lot of trouble."

"True."

She glanced at her watch. It was time for her meeting to start. Joe could hear shuffling and murmuring outside her office door as the library staff gathered.

Joe asked, "What about your news?"

"Two things," she said quickly. "First, we've confirmed that Governor Allen will be here tomorrow to officially announce that he's running for governor again. He's planning to barnstorm across the state, just like I thought he would. Why he chose Saddlestring instead of Sheridan, Gillette, or other larger towns is beyond me."

Joe said, "Me too."

"The second thing," she said. "The bad news. I got a text from my mother. She's driving to Jackson and she wants to stop by tonight on her way through. She says she has gifts for the girls."

Joe moaned and let his head flop back.

"She's a clever one," Marybeth said. "She knows if she says she has gifts for her granddaughters I'm more likely to let her in the door."

Joe said, "Maybe we can leave a note and tell her to leave the packages on the front porch."

"She'll only be here for a few minutes," Marybeth said.

"That's still too long," Joe said.

"Maybe it won't be so bad," Marybeth said. "She's always at her most pleasant when she has a new man in her cross-hairs."

CHAPTER EIGHTEEN

NATE ROMANOWSKI ARRIVED at the riverside campground forty-five minutes early and backed his Jeep
into a pocket of naked aspen trees that flanked the
last campsite in the facility. There was still at least two feet of
snow within the shadows of the pines in the canyon. The
snow wasn't as deep on the road in, but he'd had to grind
through it in four-wheel drive to cut a fresh path. If nothing
else, he knew that no one had driven to the meeting place
ahead of him.

The campground was maintained by the U.S. Forest Service and it was manned in the summer by a volunteer tender
who lived in a small camper. The area was used by overnight
campers as well as fishing guides, who either put their boats
in or took them out at a rough concrete ramp. The facility was
completely unoccupied upon Nate's arrival, which is what he

had expected. The cinder-block restroom structure was still locked up, and a dirty snowdrift fanned down from its peaked roof like an ocean wave frozen in time.

Nate got out of his vehicle at the site and did a thorough three-hundred-and-sixty-degree pan. The canyon walls were steep here. A sniper could conceivably be up there looking down at him, but access to the top was limited at best. He didn't see a living thing except three bighorn sheep ewes picking their way across the scree on the western wall. They defied gravity the way they moved along the sheer rock cliff.

He swept the snow off a picnic table and benches and sat down with a pair of binoculars. From his vantage point, he could clearly see the entrance road he'd used into the campground from the southern part of the canyon. If anyone who was not Jason Demo arrived, Nate would know well before they got there. There was no other road into the campground or out of it.

The river was to his back. It was louder than in the summer because it was swelled with melting snowpack. Chunks of ice zipped along its surface and made graceful arcs in the current around half-submerged boulders in the river. A mature bald eagle sat on one of the boulders like a hood ornament, watching the river flow and flex its spring muscles.

Nate partially unzipped his parka and reached inside to grasp his .454 Casull. It was warm due to body heat. He knew he could grab it, pull it, cock it, and aim it in less than a second if need be. He'd done it before.

————

Jᴀsᴏɴ Dᴇᴍᴏ ᴀʀʀɪᴠᴇᴅ alone fifteen minutes after their designated meeting time. Nate watched the man behind the steering wheel through his glasses. There was no second vehicle behind him, and Demo wasn't on his phone or a radio while he approached.

That was a good sign.

Demo navigated his SUV in the tracks Nate had cut, and the man pulled into the campsite and nodded a greeting. Nate nodded back.

Demo got out and looked around. "Sorry I'm late," he said. "This place is a little hard to find."

"That's why I picked it," Nate said. "There's no cell phone signal and the canyon walls are too steep for clear radio reception."

"Tough to get a satellite image down here," Demo said. "You'd need a drone to get any video."

Nate nodded. He was impressed how quickly Demo had assessed the tactical challenges—and advantages—of the location.

"The Taliban chose places like this for meetings," Demo said. "It was tough to get usable intel on them when they were hunkered down in the bottom of a canyon. It was tough to hit 'em with smart bombs, too."

Nate chinned toward the bench on the other side of the picnic table. "Have a seat."

Demo didn't hesitate, but he remained on full alert as he approached.

"Are you packing?" Nate asked.

"Of course. You?"

"What do you think?"

"Should we place our weapons on the table?" Demo asked. Judging by the tight fit of his coat, Nate determined that Demo wore his weapon on his back right hip.

"No need," Nate said. "I can outdraw you."

Demo huffed a little chuckle as he stepped over the bench to sit down. "You probably can," he said.

"Keep your hands on the table where I can see them," Nate said.

Demo complied.

"So TALK TO me," Nate said, studying Demo's face carefully. "That's why I'm here."

Demo nodded. "Mind if I smoke?"

"No."

Demo's movements were careful and deliberate so as not to be confused as anything else. He fished his hand around in his upper coat pocket and drew out a pack of cigarettes. He shook the pack and offered one to Nate across the table.

"No thank you."

Demo placed one between his lips and lit it with a lighter. "Bad habit I picked up overseas," he said. "It seemed to me that if they gave us a smoke break I'd better use the opportunity to light up. I know it's a stupid reason."

"It is."

Demo grinned. He blew a cloud of smoke over his right shoulder.

"I'm happy you agreed to meet," Demo said, leaning forward and placing his hands on the tabletop. "We need more guys like us in the movement."

"You talked a good game when I met you," Nate said. "You seem like a man on a mission."

"That I am," Demo said. "And I won't waste words or try to convince you to get involved in anything you aren't passionate about. I admire you too much to bullshit you about what we believe and what we need to do to save our way of life."

"Good idea," Nate said. "Because that won't work."

"*Exactly*," Demo said.

The bald eagle shrieked and rose from the rock in the river over Nate's shoulders, its big wings flapping hard. Demo was startled by the bird and took his eyes off of Nate to view it.

When he did, Nate reached out with his left hand and pinned Demo's hands to the table. He stood up and drew his revolver with his right and whipped it backhanded through the air so the heavy barrel hit Demo's temple hard enough to make the man's head snap back and his cap fly off.

Nate scrambled over the table and landed on Demo with all of his weight, forcing him backward into the snow. Even though he was pinned beneath him, Nate could feel Demo's strength and coiled power. Demo was fit and strong and younger than Nate. Quick and decisive tactics were imperative.

He kneed Demo in the nose—*crunch*—while he yanked the hem of the man's coat up to reveal the Sig Sauer P220 ten-millimeter semiauto in its holster. He ripped it free and tossed it over his shoulder.

Then Nate crouched over Demo's upper body and pressed the muzzle of his weapon into the flesh between the man's eyes, which were wild with pain and surprise. Demo's nose was broken to the side and gouts of blood were coursing out of his nostrils.

With his free hand, Nate reached into Demo's coat pocket where he had stored his cigarettes. His fingers closed around something slim and metallic. He came out with a silver digital recorder. The power button was pressed down and a tiny green light indicated that it was operating. He'd noticed that Demo had activated it when he'd reached into his pocket for the cigarettes.

Nate held the device in front of Demo's eyes and turned it off. He tossed the recorder in the same direction he'd tossed the Sig Sauer.

"Do you also have your phone on you?" Nate asked.

Demo shook his head and chinned toward his SUV.

Nate leaned back on his haunches, but didn't move the gun. Then he reached down on the side of Demo's head and gripped the man's right ear.

"Now," he said, twisting the ear a quarter turn until Demo

winced, "it's time for our talk. If you aren't straight with me, I'll know it, and you can guess what happens next."

THEY RESUMED THEIR stations at the picnic table, only this time Demo pinched his nose to stanch the flow of blood and Nate held the muzzle of his cocked weapon on Demo's heart, his finger wrapped around the trigger.

"You know what a .454 round will do from two feet away, right?" Nate asked.

"It'll blow my heart right out of my back," Demo said.

"Correct. Who are you working for, the feds?" Nate asked. "Did they send you here to get me on tape agreeing to join the Sovereign Nation?"

Demo looked away and didn't respond. Nate granted him the time because whatever the man said next would determine his fate and they both knew it.

Finally, Demo said, "Not really the feds. I'm undercover, but not for any specific agency. My job is to convince you to join up and to get you to say something incriminating on tape that can be used in an indictment. This operation has been in the works for a while."

"Who is running it?" Nate asked.

Demo shrugged. "I only know him as the Big Fish."

"How did he approach you?"

Demo said, "I have a bandana in my back pocket. I want to get it out and hold it against my nose to stop the bleeding."

Nate nodded, *Go ahead.*

With the compress in place, Demo said, "I wasn't lying to you at all about being a special operator. Or about becoming real disillusioned with our country when I finally got back. All of that is real."

"I know that," Nate said.

"After I left the service, I just wanted to live a good life with my wife and my two daughters in Montana. I wanted to hunt and fish and most of all to be left the hell alone."

"I understand."

"They'll never leave you alone, though," Demo said. "They come at you from every direction. They want you to bend the knee, you know? They won't be happy until everyone votes their way, thinks their way, drives an electric car, gives up their guns, and sends their kids to be indoctrinated in government schools. They won't give up until everybody hates our country as much as they do."

"That doesn't answer my question," Nate said.

Demo nodded. When he spoke, his voice was partially muffled by the compress. Nate was impressed that the man seemed to harbor no ill will toward him despite his broken nose and bloody ear, which was an indication of his training and his professionalism.

Demo said, "The Big Fish is—or was—one of the insiders. Deep state, you know? The guys who run things out of Washington, no matter who the president is? He's one of them and he's still connected."

"How did he approach you?" Nate asked.

"I'll take you back to last summer," Demo said. "I was actually mowing my lawn in Livingston, and thinking how great that beer was going to taste later when I was grilling burgers in my backyard. He shows up and parks across the street and just grins at me like, you know, 'the jig is up.' I knew the second I saw him that he was going to impact my world for the worse."

Demo paused and said, "Which he has done."

Nate urged Demo to go on by nudging his weapon forward an inch.

"He told me he needed to talk to me, but he didn't want to do it in front of my family," Demo said. "I appreciated that at the time, and I still do. As far as my wife is concerned, I'm on assignment. She doesn't like it, but she's used to it.

"Anyway, I agreed to meet the Big Fish that evening at a dive bar. That's when he laid the whole thing out for me. Either I cooperate with him, or he makes my life a living hell. Meaning federal prison time, ten to twenty, maybe more. He said he could also bring down all my buddies from the unit along with me. He showed me a list of their names and addresses all over the country. They have families, too. So when the Big Fish laid it all out to me and showed me what he had, I didn't feel like I had a choice. I still don't. I couldn't be responsible for what was likely to happen to them, you know? We'll always be brothers."

"What did he have on you?" Nate asked.

"Everything he needed," Demo said. "He had access to all of our personnel records and covert operations from overseas, which meant either he or his friends were as deep into the deep state as you can get. He knew about our deployments, our off-the-book wet work—*everything*."

Nate urged him to go on. The story was starting to sound depressing and familiar.

Demo said, "I heard a little about the situation you found yourself in back when you were an operator. Your superior was running a back-channel operation aside from your mission and he got you involved with it. That changed everything you thought about the cause, your loyalties, everything."

Nate nodded. In fact, his superior had run a falcon- and arms-smuggling operation benefiting Middle Eastern royalty and hangers-on, including future international terrorists within al-Qaeda. Nate had suspected what they were doing was illicit, but he hadn't acted on those suspicions. He'd been so used to operating in the shadows for so long that he could no longer even see the lines he shouldn't cross.

When it had all become clear, he was in too deep to turn on the superior without being disappeared himself. His boss, and his boss's boss, had too much on him. Instead, he'd methodically eliminated those who threatened him. Afterward, he'd gone off the grid for years and forged his own path in Wyoming.

It took a deal between the former governor of Wyoming, Spencer Rulon, and the feds to finally put an end to their pursuit of him. And a high body count. But Nate had never been under the illusion that it was truly over. He was convinced of that now.

"As far as what I got involved with," Demo said, "I won't go on and on. It was wrong. I know that now. I should have known it at the time, but when you're asked to do things—you do them."

Nate nodded. "What?"

"Basically, we were getting intel from Afghani warlords in exchange for looking the other way as they shipped tons of unprocessed heroin to Mexican cartels. Most of that heroin made its way here, eventually. It was the brainchild of our CO. At the time, we all assumed it was part of a bigger operation endorsed by the CIA. Turns out, it wasn't. Our CO got a healthy cut of the revenue, and he now lives on a giant ranch in Costa Rica, from what I understand."

"Ah," Nate said. "And the Big Fish had all of your names. So why did he target you in particular?"

"I asked myself that," Demo said. "And I eventually came up with an answer. The reason he targeted *me* was because he wanted *you*. I guess he looked at the psych profiles of our unit and figured that a Montana guy with libertarian leanings might get along with a Wyoming outlaw falconer with some of the same views. My job is to reel you in."

Nate sat back and squinted at Demo. Then: "Why?"

"He's got a burr under his saddle for Nate Romanowski," Demo said. "It's something personal, is my guess. He's never said, just like he's never told me his real name."

"Describe him to me," Nate said.

"Burly white guy, arrogant as hell, early sixties, buzz cut. He's had some serious injuries because he can hardly get around without a cane or a walker."

Nate sat up. "Drives a big RV?"

"How'd you know?" Demo asked.

Nate didn't respond to the question. Instead, he asked, "How many people has he recruited for the Sovereign Nation?"

"Too many, in my opinion," Demo said. "This is what I can't figure out. He doesn't really seem to care about the character or quality of the people who've signed up. He just wants as many warm bodies as he can get. They're all loose cannons and reprobates, except for one woman. He's got tweakers and drug dealers and white trash and not much else. They've got guns and attitude, but they're not the kind of people you want to depend on. I know how important it is to be able to trust the guy next to you. I was in that situation for years. I don't think I can trust *any* of these losers. I just don't get it."

"I do," Nate said, surprising Demo. "So what is the Big Fish planning? What does he want to get me involved in?"

Demo sighed and then winced at the pain from his broken nose.

"It's a big one," Demo said. "He wants to kick off the arrival of the Sovereign Nation movement with a bang."

"Walk me through it," Nate said.

"If I do, there's no turning back," Demo said. "For you and for me."

Nate urged him to continue once again with a wag of his weapon.

DEMO OUTLINED THE plan and the date and the place it was supposed to happen. Nate listened and nodded along.

When Demo concluded, Nate said, "Tell him I'm in."

Demo's eyes got wide. He said, "If he finds out everything I just told you . . ."

"He won't hear it from me," Nate said, getting up and holstering his weapon.

He found Demo's Sig Sauer in the snow behind the picnic table and handed it back to him. Then he retrieved the digital recorder.

"You're giving these back to me?" Demo asked. "Aren't you worried I'll double-cross you?"

"No. That would put you in a worse position than you already are," Nate said. "Plus, I could tell you were honest the minute you drove up to my place."

Nate gestured to the digital recorder. "Turn it on when I tell you," Nate said. "Let's make a tape."

Demo was confused. He said, "Won't it be incriminating? This is what he wants."

"Then we'll give it to him," Nate said with a smile he knew looked cruel to others. Then he drew his cell phone from his pocket and punched up the video app.

Nate raised the phone until his face filled the screen and he turned it on.

"This is Nate Romanowski. It's two fifty-five p.m. on Sunday, April 2."

He turned the camera across the table. "This is Jason Demo. We're recording this for posterity at a picnic table on the bank of the Twelve Sleep River in Wyoming. We're making two recordings. The second one is an April Fool's joke. When I say the word *yarak*, it means that every sentence spoken after that is false. Any record of this conversation from then on is a lie."

Nate eyed Demo, paused for a few seconds while Demo placed his thumb on the record button of his digital device.

"*Yarak*," Nate said.

CHAPTER NINETEEN

THAT EVENING, SHERIDAN Pickett swung into a booth across from Clay Junior at the Stockman's Bar. She could tell from the moment she saw him that he was out of sorts, so she tried to lighten his mood. She reached across the table and squeezed his hand.

"I'm sorry I couldn't make it last night," she said. "We had a meeting that went on for a while, and by the time we were done I was tired."

"So you said," Clay Junior pouted. He looked everywhere around the bar but at her.

She said, "Really, I'm not kidding. My parents were there and my bosses were, too. I couldn't just get up and leave."

"Is that right?"

"That's right. I texted you, remember?"

"Yeah, I know. But sitting here by myself waiting was, you know."

"I said I was sorry," she said. "I'm here now, right?"

Finally, he thawed a little. She could tell by his semi-glassy eyes that he'd already had a beer, or several. She also sensed that he wanted to have a bigger argument with her, that he'd been gearing up for one, and now he was a little . . . disappointed.

Sheridan had met him as soon as she could after work. She'd showered, done her hair and makeup, dressed in a purple top she knew he liked, and arrived with a smile on her face. He'd texted her that he'd like to meet her so they could have a drink before they grabbed some dinner somewhere, and she'd readily agreed.

The Stockman's was ancient and legendary, she knew. With its knotty pine interior, mirrored backbar, scuffed floors, high-backed booths, pool table, and black-and-white rodeo photos on the walls, it looked like something out of the 1940s. It was also Clay Junior's favorite place, which she found quite odd. The Stockman's was an old people's bar.

She surmised that Clay Junior considered himself an old person already, which, she thought, didn't bode well.

"Well," he said finally, reaching out to grasp her hand, "I guess you realized that you missed me and you just couldn't resist."

"Something like that," she said.

Clay Junior signaled the owner for two more beers.

"I'd like red wine instead," Sheridan said to Margaret Weber, the new owner of the bar. Weber acknowledged the order and filled two beer mugs and two wineglasses and brought them over.

"It's your lucky day," Weber said. "Happy hour is over in five minutes."

"I knew that," Clay Junior said to her with a grin. "Margaret, you know Sheridan, don't you?"

Weber wiped her hand on her jeans from spilled beer and extended it to Sheridan. "Are you Joe and Marybeth's daughter?"

"I am."

"It's a pleasure to meet you. I've seen you in here before."

"It's Clay's favorite bar."

"Margaret has worked here for twenty years," Clay Junior said. "She just bought the place."

"Thirty years," Weber corrected. "Thirty long years of putting up with local yahoos like Clay Junior." When she said it, she winked at Sheridan.

"Oh, he's all right," Sheridan said in response.

Weber was slim and fit and she wore her dark hair cut short in a pixie cut. She had bright green eyes and it was obvious that the men at the bar enjoyed looking at her. She'd purchased the Stockman's from longtime owner Buck Timberman, who now sat on the closest barstool to the wall and stared at his glass of light beer as if he were seeking some kind of answer to whatever he was pondering.

"So," Clay Junior asked Sheridan when Weber returned to her place behind the bar, "are you breaking up with me?"

The question startled her. "Why do you say that?"

"It just seems like you don't want to be with me sometimes."

She shook her head. "Do you mean last night?"

He nodded. "It seemed like you wanted me to leave you alone."

"Well," she said, sipping her wine, "you're wrong. I'm not breaking up with you. I just didn't want to interrupt the meeting I was in. It was a pretty serious discussion, and if you'll recall I didn't know you were going to stop by."

She hoped he wouldn't ask what it was about and he didn't. Clay Junior was only interested in things that involved him, she realized.

"But, Clay, I do have to say that this is all moving a little fast," she continued. "When you talked about having kids the other night, it threw me."

"Sorry," he said. "I get a little ahead of myself at times."

"Yes, you do."

He drank half of one glass in a single pull and set the mug down. "It's just that I really like you, Sherry."

"I like you, too," she said. "I just don't want to rush into anything right now. Let's take our time, is all I'm saying. We're still getting to know each other."

"Oh come on," Clay Junior said. "We grew up together."

"We grew up in the same town," Sheridan said. "You wouldn't give me the time of day in high school, and now we're adults. We've been in the *vicinity* of each other, but this is all new."

"Is there someone else?" he asked her suddenly. "Because there are lots of girls out there who . . ."

He didn't finish his thought, which to Sheridan was a very

good decision. That he would even go there annoyed her and she pulled her hand back from his.

"Never mind," he said. "I didn't mean . . ."

"I know what you meant," she said.

"Really, Sherry, I should have kept my mouth shut."

She said, "You're not used to it when a girl doesn't fall all over herself for you. I get it. But what we have is a pretty good thing, I think. I'm just not ready to move as fast as you are at the moment, okay?"

He nodded his head and looked sheepish.

"I've had a few beers already," he said.

"I can tell. Let's put this discussion on hold for a while."

"That's probably a good idea," he said. Then, looking up, he announced: "Hey—I bought a new AR today."

"Oh, you did?" she asked. She wasn't nearly as excited about semiautomatic rifles as Clay Junior and probably everybody else in the Stockman's Bar, Saddlestring, and the state of Wyoming. "Don't you already have one?"

"I do," he said. "But you know a man can't have too many guns. Didn't you hear what the president said the other day? They're going to come for our guns, you know."

"They'll have a tough job of that here," she said.

"Damned right," he said. "They call them 'assault rifles,' which is ridiculous. It's the same rifle we carry in all of our trucks on the ranch, only it looks scarier, I guess. It's not a machine gun! I know the difference, you know. But if they're going to try to take them away, I'm going to keep buying until I can't.

"Plus, I ordered a couple of thirty-round magazines. I've got to load up before they outlaw our way of life," he said.

While he talked, Sheridan felt a puff of cold air on the back of her neck as someone opened the door and entered the bar from the street. Two men walked by, headed for the rear of the building. One was a giant of a man with a shaved head and a tuft of whiskers beneath his lower lip. The other was small and athletic and he wore an oversized parka.

She overheard the small man as he told Weber, "We're going to take the last booth in the back and we'd appreciate a little privacy."

"Do you want something to drink?" she asked him.

"Fetterman?" the small man asked his colleague.

"Couple of beers," Fetterman responded.

The small man opened his coat and dug his wallet out of his jeans and handed Weber a credit card to hold on to.

"We'll run a tab," he told her.

Before he closed his coat again, Sheridan saw that he had a pistol and holster clipped to his belt.

She watched them move through the long narrow room and slide into the last booth. They did so tentatively, with the small man looking around the place and studying some of the old rodeo photographs along the way. She guessed that he was new to the Stockman's, and new to Saddlestring as well. They were also overdressed when it came to winter clothing, like they'd expected arctic conditions.

"And have you tried to buy any ammo lately?" Clay Junior asked her.

"I have not," she said.

"It's just plain ridiculous," he said. "The shelves are bare in every sporting goods store and at the hardware store. People show up before they open their doors in the morning to see if a new shipment has come in. It's nuts . . ."

A moment later, she felt another puff of cold air.

A big man with a full white beard and a large belly strode by their booth. As he did, he nodded at the two men who had preceded him and he made his way directly to them.

"The usual," he said to Weber as he passed by. "They're buying."

"Yes, they are," Weber said. "They opened a tab."

The bearded man joined the first two and he vanished from Sheridan's view when he sat down in their booth.

"Yeah, our president is the greatest gun salesman in history," Clay Junior continued. "The more he talks about taking them away, the more he sells. I wouldn't be surprised if he had shares in all the gun manufacturing companies. Him or his son—"

"Excuse me for a minute," Sheridan said.

Sheridan took her wine to the bar and sat on a stool. From her new vantage point, she could see the tops of the heads of the three men. The bearded man sat with his back to her and the first two sat together directly across from him. It was too far away to hear anything they said, but it was obvious they were in a tense conversation.

When Weber approached her, Sheridan said, "Do you know who those men are who just came in?"

Weber didn't immediately stare over at them, for which Sheridan was grateful.

"I don't know the little guy," Weber said. "It's the first time I've seen him in here. But I met the big one the other night when he came in by himself. I think his name is Dan, or Dave, or something like that."

"Fetterman?" Sheridan said.

"I think so, but don't quote me on it. I didn't pay that much attention."

Weber lowered her voice as she filled the men's beer mugs. "He sat on the stool you're sitting on now and he was trying to put the make on me."

"I would suppose that happens a lot," Sheridan said.

"I limit it to one try per customer," Weber said. "Unless I don't. Ask your friend Clay Junior if you don't believe me."

"I won't and I do," Sheridan said.

"Anyway, he was kind of hinting around that he was quite an important guy. You know the type. He was acting all mysterious about why he was here and hinting that it was kind of a confidential assignment or something. When I asked him what he was talking about, he said he couldn't tell me 'at the moment.' Meaning that if I went out with him, he might."

She topped off the three beer mugs and shrugged. "I wasn't interested enough to pursue it."

"Did he say where he was from?" Sheridan asked.

"I think he said Virginia. One of those states back east that I don't care a hoot about," she said.

"What about the third guy? The guy who just came in?"

Weber snorted and said, "I sure as hell know Cade Molvar. I've had to throw him out of here a bunch of times, and I won't extend him credit anymore because he always 'forgets' to pay."

When Weber said "forgets," she made air quotes with her fingers.

"Why do you ask?" Weber said to Sheridan.

"Just curious."

Weber placed the three mugs of beer on a tray and left to deliver them to the men in the back.

While she was gone, Sheridan leaned forward and looked behind the bar near the cash register. Weber had placed the small man's credit card on a flat surface above the cash drawer.

She drew her phone out of her pocket and quickly accessed the photo app screen and zoomed in on the card and snapped a shot. When she looked at the image, it showed a platinum American Express card issued to Thomas J. Scott. She lowered the phone before Weber came back, and rejoined Clay Junior in the booth.

"You want to know what I finally found online?" he asked her as if she'd never left. "Two thousand .223 rounds made by some Russian company. I snapped them up, even though I've never heard of the company and I sure as hell don't trust the Russians to make great ammo. But what choice do I have?"

"You don't have a choice," she said sympathetically.

While Clay Junior went on, Sheridan lowered her phone

to her lap and googled the name Thomas J. Scott. It wasn't an exotic name, so scores of results came up. The top three were from news stories in the past two years, one from Michigan, one from Mississippi, and one from Virginia. In each, FBI Special Agent Thomas J. Scott testified in different criminal trials. In Michigan, he was testifying in a case involving accused militia members in a plot to kidnap a state official. In Minnesota, he testified against a man accused of being an "insurrectionist." The Virginia trial involved three parents who were charged with "domestic terrorism" against school board officials.

She swiped out of the screen so she could read the stories in full later.

"Will you excuse me again?" she said to Clay Junior.

He sighed and sat back with a *Here you go again* look.

"I need to use the restroom," she said.

"I'll be right here when you decide to come back," he said.

SHE KNEW IT wasn't unusual for a woman her age to clutch her phone in her hand as she walked to the bathroom, which she did.

Sheridan didn't raise it when she passed the three men in the booth, but she faced it toward them surreptitiously and got a quick shaky video of them in deep discussion. When the one called Fetterman looked over at her she feared she'd been caught for a moment, but she realized he was looking over her figure from top to bottom. And she could feel his eyes on the back of her jeans as she pushed her way into the women's restroom.

Inside, she sent both the photo of the credit card and the three-second video to her parents' phones.

She captioned the message, **Are these your FBI agents with Cade Molvar?**

Then she returned to the booth with her own local yahoo.

CHAPTER TWENTY

JOE FELT HIS phone vibrate in his pocket with an incoming message, and he heard Marybeth's phone chime from somewhere in the kitchen, but he didn't look at his screen immediately.

Instead, he stood back and folded his arms across his chest and waited for his mother-in-law, Missy, to leave.

She'd arrived two minutes before when her black Hummer H2 with Teton County plates parked in their driveway. Joe and Marybeth had watched through the living room window as the headlights doused and a squat man with a buzz cut emerged from behind the wheel and opened the door in the back for Missy. She swung out of the vehicle with an armful of brightly wrapped presents, which the man quickly took from her. He'd followed her up the walkway until she rapped on the outside door.

"This is Bruno, my driver," she'd announced as a greeting.

"Do you mind if he uses your bathroom? It's been a long drive and it took us a while to find this place. Could you be any more off the beaten path?"

"Hello, Mom," Marybeth had said, deadpan.

JOE NOW OBSERVED as Marybeth and Missy faced each other from a few feet away, neither apparently sure what to do next. After a pause, Missy beamed and threw open her arms in a *Come to me* gesture. Marybeth went to her for a quick and awkward hug.

"It's been so long," Missy said, stepping back and looking around. "It's a whole new house!"

To Bruno, Missy said, "Their last one burned down, but it was a dump anyhow. This one is much nicer. Now, put down those gifts."

He nodded and carefully lowered them to the cushions of the couch. Bruno was dark and powerfully built, and he moved with the stiffness of a weight lifter, Joe thought.

"The bathroom?" Missy asked Marybeth for him.

"Down the hall to the left," she said.

Bruno nodded and slid past Marybeth.

"I have a driver now," Missy said. "Since I got LASIK surgery, I can't drive at night anymore. Too many crazy headlights out there!"

That wasn't the only work she'd had done, Joe noted. Although Missy was practically ageless—a Barbie doll in amber—her face was tighter than the last time he'd seen her.

The skin around her eyes looked like alabaster and her forehead appeared immovable. She was dressed in New West chic—tight black slacks, tooled-shaft boots, a short leather jacket over a white top, a large silver and turquoise necklace with a matching bracelet. As always, her dark hair was perfect.

"I brought gifts for the girls," she said. "Are they around?"

Joe sensed his wife's exasperation when she said, "Mom, our daughters aren't in the house anymore. I'll make sure they get them, though."

Missy did her best to display a pout. "It's hard to keep up with them when we don't talk for so long."

Joe could see Marybeth's mouth harden at that. But she kept her cool.

"Well," Missy said, "this is certainly a much nicer place than you had before. You must be going up in the world since you got rich from that high-tech mogul."

"So you heard," Marybeth said. "It turned out not to be as lucrative as everyone assumed. But what we got certainly helped."

Joe felt a pang of guilt. He always did whenever their finances were discussed.

"One thing I've learned over the years," Missy said to Marybeth, "is that maintaining a high quality of life is always a struggle, always a constant quest. One can't sit idly by and just *hope* it all turns out for the best."

Then, on cue, she turned her head and said, "Oh, hello, Joe. I didn't see you there."

"Hello, Missy. I haven't seen you since you were canoodling with Governor Allen."

Missy's grin didn't break, but her eyes betrayed a fraction of surprise. "He's a very close friend," she said. "His wife left him and you know about Marcus's condition. Colter and I are kindred spirits."

Joe nodded.

"Marybeth," she said while quickly turning away, "we must have a glass of wine together and catch up. Just one."

"Just one," Marybeth echoed.

"If you don't have good wine, I think I have some out in the car," she said.

"I have wine," Marybeth said through gritted teeth.

"I'll help," said Joe.

IN THE KITCHEN, Marybeth exchanged a glance with Joe that revealed her mixed feelings. He nodded again.

"She has a way . . ." Marybeth said in a whisper. "Every time. No matter how old I get or how our circumstances change, she has a way of putting us down. You especially."

"I'm used to it," Joe said as he poured bourbon into an ice-filled tumbler.

"How she found out about Steve-2's gift to us, I have no idea."

"She's like a truffle pig," Joe said. "She's an expert at sniffing out piles of money. Even if it's someone else's money."

He paused a moment, then said, "*Especially* if it's someone else's money."

Marybeth filled two glasses with less wine than she usually poured for herself. "One glass, that's it," she said.

"I'll drink to that," Joe said.

BACK IN THE living room, Missy detailed what was in each of the gifts she'd brought for her granddaughters.

For Sheridan, Missy had purchased a genuine Turkish cotton bathrobe that cost well over five hundred dollars. "I *hope* I remembered to remove the price tag," she said.

April would receive cashmere pajamas that cost roughly the same amount. For Lucy, there were silk sheets, pillowcases, and a sleep scarf.

Joe thought the gifts were impractical and that they showcased Missy's unique outlook and style. She always gave gifts *she'd* want, not what her granddaughters asked for. Most of her gifts for them didn't align at all with their personalities, although Lucy had once enjoyed wearing designer labels.

Sheridan, as far as Joe could remember, had never worn a bathrobe around the house. She preferred sweat clothes and slippers. April despised pajamas and slept in an oversized T-shirt. Lucy was likely to think that silk sheets were gauche and likely would embarrass her friends, so she'd donate them to a homeless shelter.

"That's very nice of you," Marybeth said.

"I wish they were here," Missy said. "I'd love to see their faces when they open their gifts. Especially Lucy. Lucy has always appreciated the finer things."

"She'll be the only sophomore in Laramie with silk pillowcases," Joe said. "That's for sure."

"I hope she doesn't mind that I spent twice the amount on her than I did the older girls," Missy said. Then to Marybeth: "Promise me you won't tell her."

Which meant *Tell her as soon as you can*, Joe knew.

"So how is Marcus doing?" Marybeth asked.

"With the pancreatic cancer?"

"Yes. What else?"

"The doctors say he has a few weeks at best," Missy said. "I've kept him alive two years longer than they said was possible, you know. Now we're in the process of saying goodbye and getting his affairs in order. That's why I need to be back in Jackson tonight."

Joe had to grudgingly give Missy credit for prolonging Marcus Hand's life. The woman had scoured the world for experimental drugs and exotic treatments and had overseen his medical care despite the fact that most of what she'd done was illegal. She hadn't let him pass away until she gave her permission to do so.

"Give him our best," Marybeth said. "We're praying for him."

Missy looked pensive for a moment. "You'd be surprised how many people say that. I wish it helped more than it does."

Despite her assurances, Marybeth drank the rest of her

glass in a long pull and rose to go get some more. She didn't offer Missy another splash.

Joe sat in his chair in silence, waiting for his wife to return.

"So you were in Cheyenne," Missy said to him.

"I was."

"Ignore the rumors."

"I didn't hear any rumors. I saw you myself," Joe said. "You and the governor."

"I don't know what you saw," she said. "But talking about it is not helpful in any way."

"Folks will find out soon enough, right?"

She took a sip of wine, but her eyes never left his. "He's a fine man," she said. "An important man. He's got a future ahead of him."

"Is that why you're financing his campaign again?" Joe asked.

"*What?*" she asked coolly.

"He's got a war chest even bigger than when he ran before," Joe said. "It must be costing you and Marcus quite a lot—if Marcus even knows about it."

"You think you know things, but you do not," she sniffed. "I'm most certainly not funding his run this time around. I already got him there, if you'll recall."

"I recall."

He also recalled that Missy had whispered in the new governor's ear that Joe should be fired. Her scheme was for Marybeth and the girls to move in with her because Joe could no longer provide a home for them or a decent income. The plot had been blown up when ex-governor Spencer Rulon intervened and served as Joe's pro bono employment attorney.

"Besides," Missy said, "he doesn't need my money this time around. If you knew anything about the way the world works, you'd know that incumbency attracts all kinds of new dollars."

"From who? From where?" Joe asked.

"From all over," she said. "I mean, *all over.*"

Joe shook his head, not understanding her meaning. That's when Marybeth returned to the room. But instead of a full wineglass, she held her phone.

"Joe, have you seen this from Sheridan?" she asked.

"No."

"Seen what?" Missy asked. Then: "Marybeth, take a photo of Sheridan's gift and send it to her. Maybe she'll want to come here and open it."

"Mom," Marybeth said with a sigh, "it's time to go. Marcus needs you."

"Just like that?" Missy said. "Just like that, you say it's time for me to go?"

"Marcus is waiting and dying and Bruno is out in your car and your granddaughters don't live here anymore. So just . . . *go.*"

Missy placed her glass down hard on the end table. Not hard enough to break it, but hard enough to make a statement.

"Maybe I should just take these presents back with me," she said.

"Fine," Marybeth said. "Take them. That'll show your granddaughters."

Missy stood and appeared to be getting ready to say something back, but she thought better of it. She nodded to Marybeth, ignored Joe, and said, "I'll let you know when Marcus dies. It'll be a very small and private celebration of his life, as per his wishes.

"You might want to see if you can make the time to be there," she said acidly.

Before closing the door behind her, Missy turned and said, "I'm leaving the gifts. My granddaughters deserve *something* nice in their lives."

When the taillights of the Hummer receded into the timber and Missy was gone, Marybeth said, "I don't feel very proud of myself right now. I mean, she is my mother."

"I admired your restraint," Joe said, placing his hands on the top of her shoulders and touching her forehead with his.

"She just brings out the worst in me, Joe."

"She's good at that with both of us," he said. "I just checked the bathroom to make sure Bruno didn't plant a listening device. That's how much I trust her."

"Somewhere deep down inside of her, I know she means well," Marybeth said. "But those gifts are ridiculous. She really doesn't know our daughters at all because she's never really tried."

Joe said, "Tell that to April when she's swanning around in her cashmere pajamas."

They both laughed at the image because it was so discordant.

Then Marybeth brought her phone up and showed Joe the message and the video they'd both received from Sheridan. He watched it three times and frowned.

"It's them all right, Scott and Fetterman. But what are they doing with Cade Molvar?"

Marybeth shrugged. "There's something going on that we obviously don't know about. First those agents show up at the Marmot House, now they're talking to Molvar. It doesn't make sense."

Joe pulled out his own phone and texted Good detective work to Sheridan.

Thank you, she replied.

Joe: Are they still there?

Sheridan: They just left.

Joe: Together?

Sheridan: Molvar first, then the feds.

"I think I need to talk to Molvar," Joe said to Marybeth.

"Stay away from the Keystoners, Joe," she said. "They're dangerous."

"I don't think I'd get anywhere with Scott or Fetterman."

She pursed her lips. "If you do go talk to Molvar, don't go by yourself."

"I think Molvar would be less likely to talk if I showed up with Sheriff Tibbs or any of his guys."

"I was thinking of Nate and Geronimo," she said.

He nodded slowly, mulling it over. Then: "I wonder what Missy meant when she said Allen was getting money *from all over*?"

"When did she say that?"

"When you were in the kitchen swilling wine," Joe said. He grinned to indicate he was kidding.

"Did she mean he has a lot of donors—which I find hard to believe—or did she mean the money is coming from somewhere outside the state?" she asked.

"Your mother can be obscure," Joe said. "She wouldn't say for sure."

"She might not know where it's coming from and she's blowing smoke at you. Maybe she's funding his campaign again, but she doesn't want us to know it."

"That's possible," Joe said. "One thing our conversation revealed to me is that she's really close with him. I mean, *really close.* I think she realizes she has enough money of her own finally. Especially when Marcus goes and leaves her everything. Now she wants to be close to power, and she thinks Colter Allen is going places."

"What places?"

Joe raised his eyebrows. "I don't know, of course. But I believe Allen and Missy might be delusional enough to think a conservative western governor may have a shot at the White House. Or maybe interior secretary, at least."

Marybeth shook her head. "That woman" was all she said.

Joe had nothing to add to that.

———

When a set of bright headlights swept across the dining room window, Marybeth said, "Oh no. She's back."

Joe approached the glass and looked out. "It's Nate's rig. Geronimo is with him."

"It's like they heard us talking," Marybeth said.

"Yup."

Joe stepped out of the house onto the porch and lifted his arm in front of his eyes against the piercing headlights just as Nate killed them. It was cool and the air had the distinctive metallic taste that indicated another spring storm was coming.

He looked up at the sky for clouds, but it was clear and filled with a wash of hard stars. The snowstorm might be building, but it wasn't there yet.

Nate climbed out of his vehicle and approached Joe in the dark. Geronimo did the same. Starlight glinted off the triple barrels of Geronimo's shotgun that he held down at his side.

"Greetings, gentlemen," Joe said.

"We need to talk," Nate responded.

"About what?"

"I had a conversation with Jason Demo," Nate said. "Big things are afoot."

Geronimo whistled and said, "You-all are even crazier up here in Wyoming than I thought."

Monday, April 3

Come see the north wind's masonry.
Out of an unseen quarry evermore
Furnished with tile, the fierce artificer
Curves his white bastions with projected roof
Round every windward stake, or tree, or door.
—RALPH WALDO EMERSON,
"The Snow-Storm"

It is not power that corrupts but fear. Fear of
losing power corrupts those who wield it and
fear of the scourge of power corrupts those who
are subject to it.
—AUNG SAN SUU KYI,
"Freedom from Fear"

CHAPTER TWENTY-ONE

J OE FILLED HIS coffee cup for the second time at four-thirty in the morning and stepped outside to survey the sky. He had barely slept after listening to Nate's story, so rather than toss around in bed and disturb Marybeth, he'd gotten up and padded out of the bedroom.

"Can't sleep?" she'd asked him.

"Nope."

"Neither can I," she said. "I'm sick with worry."

"That makes two of us," he'd said.

OUTSIDE, IT WAS still clear, but the metallic taste in the air was stronger. A significant storm was building in the north-west, but it hadn't yet shown its face. His intuition was confirmed when he returned to the kitchen and pulled up the weather forecast on his phone.

A massive storm was likely. Twenty-four inches of snow in the mountains, hurricane-like winds, a plunge in temperature. There was a possibility of a classic spring "apocalyptic blizzard" in the Rockies, with the brunt of it in the northern Bighorn Mountains within the next twenty-four to forty-eight hours.

Just what they needed, he thought bitterly.

DESPITE THE HOUR, an incoming text chimed on his phone. It was from Rick Ewig.

Call me, was all that it said.

Joe called.

"I didn't mean this *minute*, for Christ's sake," Ewig said. "What are you doing up so early?"

"We game wardens are always on duty. Twenty-four seven," Joe said. "You should know that."

Ewig chuckled and said, "I need you to help out on a big poaching-ring case in Rock Springs. We're about to lower the boom on four locals who've been slaughtering moose and elk in Sweetwater County."

"I've heard something about that," Joe said. The case had been ongoing for over three years, but he was instantly suspicious. Why the sudden urgency?

"I can't leave right now."

Ewig hesitated. "Joe, this isn't a request."

"I get that," Joe said. "But I can't leave for at least two days. I need to be here right now. Big things are afoot," he said, echoing Nate from the night before.

"Look," Ewig said, "the governor has a real bug up his ass about this case. Up until last night, I didn't even know he cared about it. But his office called and tore me a new one, said I needed to get every game warden I could spare over there to bust it up. He specifically requested you."

Joe nodded and said nothing for a moment.

"Joe?"

"I'm here. I'm just wondering why the governor who tried to fire me now suddenly realizes how wonderful my detecting skills are. Don't you find that interesting, Rick?"

"The poaching ring has been spotted on his ranch," Ewig said. "Maybe that's why he's so hot to get these guys. Either that, or he needs a big win right now as the campaign ramps up. I don't know for sure, but I know what an order is."

"Have you considered that maybe he wants me gone from here for a few days?" Joe asked. "There's fifty other game wardens in the state and a lot of them are closer to Rock Springs than I am."

"You're making this real damned difficult," Ewig said. "This is getting close to out-and-out insubordination."

"What happened to you, Rick?" Joe asked. "You were a game warden once. You used to have our backs out here."

"Things change," Ewig said angrily. "You'll see, if you ever sit behind my desk."

"I won't," Joe said. "I can't put politics first. I've got a job to do."

"Don't throw that at me," Ewig said. "You're not so high

and mighty." Then: "Joe, I'm not only ordering you to go, I'm begging you. I've only got a few months left to retire to collect my full pension. I can't get fired now because I've got a rogue employee who won't follow an executive branch directive."

"And I'm sorry about that," Joe said. "But right now I'm up to my eyeballs in a situation. We've got two murders, and one I'm supposed to ignore. I'm closing in on the bad guys running a shed-poaching ring right under my nose. And I got some information last night that has me reeling."

"Joe . . ."

"Rick, are you aware of an FBI operation going on up here right now?"

Ewig said, "FBI operation? No."

"The governor's office didn't brief you on that when you chatted?" Joe asked.

"No."

Joe believed him. "Two days," Joe said. "After that, if I'm still kicking, I'll go to Rock Springs. Tell the governor whatever you want, even though the honest approach would be best in my mind. But that's the way it is, Rick."

Ewig moaned. "Maybe I can put him off for two days. But *only* two days. And I can't promise he won't tell me to fire you on the spot."

"I'll take that deal," Joe said, punching off.

He realized that his hand holding the phone was trembling. It was either anger, fear, age, or too much coffee.

All four, Joe thought.

———

HE WAS ON the highway north to Winchester and the Marmot House an hour before the sun came up. Daisy was distressed that he'd left her behind and Joe missed having her along with him. Replacing Daisy on the passenger seat was his shotgun loaded with double-ought buckshot.

While he drove, he listened to the mutual-aid channel on his radio for call-ins and dispatches. Ogden Driskill had still not been located. Joe's guess was that Driskill was still in the area. Where else would he go?

Joe placed a call to Sheriff Tibbs's phone. He wasn't surprised that the man didn't pick up, so he left a message.

"Sheriff, Joe Pickett. I'm on my way up to the Marmot House to check out those antlers in the shed. I've got no reason to go into the house or disturb the crime scene. I don't know if you've got a guy up there or not, but you might want to let him know I'm coming."

He punched off.

Joe's next call was to Judge Hewitt, who lived alone in a massive home on the grounds of the exclusive Eagle Mountain Club on the outskirts of Saddlestring.

He wasn't surprised when the judge picked up on the first ring. The man was an early riser, and he still had stamina as well as a burning motivation to get to work every day in his courtroom to sentence criminals to prison. Every morning, no matter what the weather, Judge Hewitt took a long walk around the golf course at the club.

"Judge, this is Joe Pickett."

"I know that. I can read the screen. A little early in the day to call, isn't it?"

Hewitt was out of breath and obviously in the act of walking.

"Judge, I need a favor."

"Of course you do," Hewitt said without enthusiasm.

Joe outlined the case and said he knew where to locate the cache of antlers to seize them. Hewitt was instantly furious, but not with Joe.

"I *hate* shed hunters," Hewitt spat. "I wish our legislators would get off of their asses and strengthen our laws so that it really hurts these scumbags if they break it. Those shed-hunting bastards run around in the woods stressing out big game right after a hard winter. And you say these miscreants actually drive herds into heavy timber to knock off their antlers before the season opens? That's despicable."

"Yup," Joe said. "I saw it happen. That's why I need a search warrant for the premises."

"Granted," Hewitt said. "Come by my office first thing this morning to pick it up."

"Actually, I'm on my way to the shed right now."

"So you want the warrant to be retroactive?" Hewitt said with skepticism.

"I'd appreciate that," Joe said.

"Don't make a habit of it, Joe."

"I won't," he said. "This is a special circumstance."

"I'll send it to your phone," Hewitt said. Then: "Actually,

I'll ask Betty to do it. I'm hopeless when it comes to technology."

"That would be great. Thank you."

"Don't call again this early unless it's an emergency," Hewitt said. "And get those bastards. I want to see them standing in front of my bench."

JOE TURNED OFF his headlights and activated his sneak lights on the wooded two-track overlooking the Marmot House. He crept down the switchback road. The sneak lights were located under his front bumper and they threw a soft glow directly on the ground in front of the vehicle so he could proceed in the dark without being observed. He parked and turned them off when he found an opening in the timber where he could get a clear view of the Marmot House on the opposite hillside.

If either the sheriff's department or the FBI had stationed an officer at or near the house, he couldn't see them.

As the morning lightened up enough to see details, Joe saw that a notice had been tacked to the front door and yellow crime scene tape had been stretched across the threshold. Other than those items, the Marmot House looked dark and empty. He *assumed* that Leland Christensen's body had been removed and the interior processed by a crime scene unit, but there was no way to tell for sure from where he was located.

He started the pickup and slowly rolled down the hillside to cross the small stream at the bottom. Snowmelt had swelled the spring creek, so it was as high as his axles when he drove across it.

Joe parked adjacent to the shed in the back. The chain and padlock on the double doors looked undisturbed since the last time he'd been there.

Joe got out and found a set of bolt cutters in his equipment box in the back of his pickup. He opened and closed the cutters a few times to make sure the tool worked, then started for the front of the shed.

He snapped open a link in the chain and the padlock dropped to the snow. Pulling the chain through the steel door handles, he tossed it aside.

Joe opened the doors a few inches, then put his shoulder to the right one. It slid to the side on an internal track.

He could immediately smell the musty odor of elk and blood inside. The stack of antlers was piled as high as his hat. He searched the inside wall for a light switch, but didn't find one. As before, the only light emanated from the clouded side window and the light green fiberglass sheet on the roof.

Joe returned to his truck for his flashlight and clicked it on. He swept the beam over the stack of antlers. Most of them were from bull elk, but there were buck deer antlers as well and a few moose paddles. Hundreds of pounds' worth.

He could see the bloody stumps on the base of some of the sheds, and guessed that they had been the ones knocked off recently in the heavy timber.

Joe circled the pile, using the beam to probe inside it. When the light reflected on something green and slick, he paused. When he moved the beam farther to the right inside the tines, he saw a small label on the material and he realized he was looking at the back of a man's coat.

Breathing heavily as his heart whumped, Joe went to the rear of the stack to find the twin soles of snow boots, heels up, splayed out on the floor of the shed in a V. It was a body, all right. The body of a man had been dragged into the shed and covered up with antlers.

JOE DOCUMENTED WHAT he'd discovered by snapping several photos of the scene with a trembling hand. He tried to step carefully around the boot prints on the dirt floor. Then he snatched a full six-point shed from the top of the pile and drove it tines-first into the dirt floor. He used the curl of the horns to rest his flashlight so that the beam lit up the back of the stack. He bent down and grasped the ankles of the victim and pulled back using all of his strength. The victim was frozen solid. It was difficult to slide the body out because the points of so many antlers tugged at the clothing as he pulled.

Finally, he slid the body out away from the pile and retrieved his flashlight. The dead man was facedown and his arms were pinned to his sides. Joe grunted as he rolled him over.

Staring up at him with frozen dead eyes was Professor Zhang Wei. Joe recognized him from his driver's license photo and the fact that the top part of his head had been sliced off cleanly just above his eyebrows.

"There you are," Joe whispered aloud.

———

HE DIDN'T WANT to tamper with the crime scene any further, and his mind was reeling. Were Driskill and Christensen murderers? Had they stumbled onto Wei while poaching sheds and fed him into the minipod fan? It was a possibility he'd not previously considered, although it now seemed to fit what he knew. Had Christensen threatened to blow the lid off of the murder by confessing or bragging? And had Driskill killed his buddy over it?

Since there was no cell phone signal in the draw, Joe couldn't call either the sheriff or the crime scene tech immediately. In their absence, he took a series of additional photos of the scene and the body from every angle he could think of.

As Joe backed out of the darkened shed into the morning light, he sensed a presence on his left and he turned quickly around.

Deputy Buck Holmes had pulled his SUV behind Joe's pickup and was climbing out of the vehicle. Joe hadn't heard the man arrive. Holmes clamped on a cap with a sheriff's department logo and glared at Joe with his best cop stare as he did it. Holmes wore a black tactical body armor vest.

"I'm glad you're here," Joe said. "I guess the sheriff got my message after all."

"Something like that," Holmes said.

"We've got another body inside. It's the professor."

Holmes didn't react to Joe's words, which Joe found odd.

Instead, he approached him in a deliberate pace until he was six feet away.

"Maybe you didn't hear me," Joe started to say when Holmes quickly pulled his yellow Taser 7 CQ from his gear belt. He tased Joe point-blank in the chest, in the gap between the zippers of his coat.

The twin probes stuck into Joe's pectoral muscles through his uniform shirt and the instant electrical charge exploded through his body. He knew that this particular weapon had a five-second cycle and produced fifty thousand volts. Joe tried to swipe at the wires that connected to the Taser, but his arms and legs were locked up as if he'd been paralyzed. Joe felt like his head could explode and send his hat flying into the sky. The pain was excruciating, and it surged through every muscle.

Joe teetered in place like a statue unmoored from its pedestal, then fell hard to his side. His limbs were locked up and it was impossible to raise his arm to block the impact. He wound up with a mouthful of snow. The last image he had of Holmes was of the man following him down with the muzzle of the Taser to keep the electricity flowing. Morning sun glinted off the thin wires that stretched from the weapon to the probes.

Joe grunted as Holmes climbed on top of him and pinned him to the ground with his knees. He could feel the deputy remove his Glock from its holster and a canister of bear spray from the other side of his belt. Then his tingling arms were jerked back and he could hear the ratcheting of handcuffs cinched tight around his wrists.

The pain from the Taser strike subsided slowly, and it took a few moments before he could feel his arms and legs again. The jolt of electricity had made him suddenly exhausted and nauseous. His tongue seemed too thick for his mouth and his nostrils were filled with an acrid burning smell as if he'd been grilled on the inside.

Holmes grasped Joe by the collar and hauled him up into a sitting position. Then he squatted down on his haunches directly across from him.

"Hurts, don't it?" he asked. "We had to get tased at the academy. I know what it feels like. Did you piss yourself?" he asked, narrowing his eyes to look at Joe's dry crotch.

Joe had trouble focusing at first. "Why?" he asked. "Why did you do that?" His voice was slurred.

"You left me no choice," Holmes said. Then, almost sadly, "Why don't you ever just stay in your lane, Joe? That's what all of us always wonder about you. Once you get ahold of something, you're like a fucking dog with a bone, aren't you?"

As his head cleared, Joe was able to meet Holmes's eyes. They were as dead-looking as the dead eyes he'd just seen in the shed.

"I'm investigating a shed-poaching case," Joe said. "I've got a warrant. The body of Professor Wei is inside."

Holmes shook his head, as if amazed at Joe's stupidity. "Do you think I don't know that?" he asked.

It hit Joe hard. Even though he'd heard about Holmes's

flirtation with the Sovereign Nation from Nate the night before, Joe didn't know how deep the deputy was in the ideology and movement until that second. He'd assumed Holmes was overreacting to his presence at the crime scene, that he'd been sent there by Sheriff Tibbs after Joe's call to him that morning. That Holmes was doing his job with too much zeal.

"So that was you on the snowmobile with Driskill and Christensen," Joe said. "You've thrown in with them."

"I haven't thrown in with anyone," Holmes said. "I'm my own man and I know what I know. They're trying to turn this nation into just another shithole country. We've got to stop them. You can't pick all of your brothers who believe the same thing and fight on your side. Some of them are idiots."

"Like Driskill and Christensen," Joe said.

"Like Driskill and Christensen," Holmes echoed. "They leave me a lot of shit to clean up, you know?"

"Like the body of Professor Wei?" Joe asked.

Holmes looked to the sky for a second, then lowered his eyes to Joe again. "There was no good reason for that Chicom to be where he was," Holmes said. "He got what was coming to him for trespassing on private land. And after he got a good look at us . . ."

"You fed him into the fan," Joe said.

Holmes leaned in. "It's strange how things turn out. I was worried about someone finding the body before we could dispose of it. Then it turns out that my official orders are not to even talk about it. So that worked out okay, I'd say."

"Who was the fourth guy on the snowmobile?" Joe asked.

"Cade Molvar," Holmes said. "I borrowed his sled and he wanted to come along."

Joe was confused. "You guys didn't know anything about Wei before you found him that day? Is that what you're saying?"

"I didn't know the guy from Adam," Holmes said. "Driskill and Christensen were tweaking at the time and they were all paranoid about getting caught hunting sheds. I'm not sure they even knew what they were doing. But when that fuckin' guy started pointing at us and yammering, we went after him. He must have tripped or something, and the next thing we knew he was stuck in that fan face-first. We just helped him along. It was a hell of a thing, you know?"

"Did you kill Christensen, too?" Joe asked.

Holmes said, "Collateral damage. Leland had a hard time keeping his mouth shut. He'd have ratted us all out at some point. He had a traitorous heart."

"So you're all working for the Big Fish?" Joe asked. "The Sovereign Nation?"

That surprised Holmes, and he gave Joe the side-eye. Then: "I don't work for anyone but myself and my beliefs. That others feel the same way is something I just accept. If the Big Fish wants to throw a little cash my way, who am I to complain? You know how much they pay you in law enforcement. Every little bit helps."

"So now what?" Joe said. "What do you plan to do with me?"

"That's what I'm trying to decide, Dudley Do-Right."

Joe said, "You're a cop. You're on track to become the sheriff, if Tibbs has his way."

"Yeah, so?"

Joe grimaced and said, "You took an oath. You pledged to serve and protect."

"That's what I'm doing," Holmes said. "I'm doing my best to serve and protect the good people of this country from forces that want to dominate us and eliminate our way of life. They want to bleed us dry while they drive around in their electric cars and fly to climate change conferences on private jets."

"None of the people you killed—or are about to—are the people you describe," Joe said. "Has that occurred to you?"

Holmes glared at Joe in silence. He was obviously contemplating what Joe had just said, and he was hesitant about what would happen next.

Joe pressed: "Buck, think about it. You're pissed off at a group of people, I get that. I've heard this all before. You have reasons to be angry. But is this the right way to go about it? You're a cop. You're supposed to be one of the good guys."

"I *am* one of the good guys," Holmes said with finality. He'd made up his mind.

Joe briefly closed his eyes. It was hard wrapping his mind around the fact that very soon he was going to die. Holmes would never have told him as much as he had if there were any other conclusion.

And there he was. He could almost see himself from above as if he'd floated away from his body and looked down.

He was sitting in the snow, handcuffed and humiliated near the mouth of an open door with a mountain of poached shed antlers and a dead body inside. All just a few yards away from the Marmot House.

He thought first of Marybeth, then of his daughters. He didn't feel terror, but heartbreak. He'd let them all down in the end, something he'd spent his life trying not to do.

"Here," Holmes said, grasping Joe's collar again, "let me help you get to your knees."

Holmes stood and tugged Joe forward.

"I don't want to die on my knees," Joe said. His voice sounded remarkably calm, even to him.

"I can't stand you up and have you try to run off," Holmes said. He didn't help Joe get to his feet.

"On your knees is a compromise," Holmes said.

"It's an execution," Joe said.

"It's not personal."

The deputy drew his service weapon and circled around Joe until he was directly behind him.

Joe closed his eyes again, and whispered, "Dear God, please make it quick." Then: "I love you, girls."

The gunshot was deafening, and the full weight of Holmes's body slammed down onto Joe's shoulder and nearly sent him sprawling in the snow again.

Joe opened his eyes, wondering why he was still lucid. Holmes lay beside him with a hole in his chest so large that Joe could see a meaty part of his exploded heart. The round that had hit him had blown through Holmes's body armor as if it were tissue paper. Snow around him took on a bright pink hue.

Joe wheeled around and looked over his shoulder. Nate and Geronimo Jones stepped out of a grove of skeletal aspen. Nate held his still-smoking .454 in his hand. Geronimo wielded his triple-barrel shotgun, but it didn't appear that he'd fired, for which Joe was grateful. The distance was such that he'd likely have been hit by the shotgun blast as well as Holmes.

"Oh great," Joe heard Geronimo say to Nate, "now we shot a cop."

"We're just getting started," Nate replied.

Joe sat back and took a deep breath. He said to Nate, "You saved my life."

"It's worth saving," Nate replied.

"Thank you."

"Where's the key to the cuffs?" Nate asked.

"Look in his pocket."

"I'll get it," Geronimo said, sticking his big paw into Holmes's uniform pants pocket and coming out with a ring of keys.

"How did you know I'd be here?" Joe asked Nate.

"You told us, remember?"

CHAPTER TWENTY-TWO

B UT AT THE Pickett home the night before, it hadn't
been Joe who had done most of the talking. It had
been Nate. And the longer he'd talked, the more frequently Joe, Marybeth, and Geronimo had looked at each
other and shaken their heads, trying to wrap their minds
around what he was saying.

"It's all a big, complicated, stupid, elaborate *trap*," Nate had
told them. "Normal patriotic agents and operators go to work
every day to solve crimes and fight against the enemies of our
country so they can feel good about what they do and to feed
their families. I used to be one of them, and so was Jason Demo.

"But not these guys," Nate said. "These guys *burn* with
privilege and ideology. They've gotten used to doing whatever
the hell they want to do because they've never, *ever* been held
accountable for it."

"Two systems of justice in the United States," Geronimo

stated. "One for us and one for them. It's an old story for some of us, but now it's not just about race anymore. Now it's about who really runs the country."

Nate said, "These men crossed the line so long ago they forgot what their job is supposed to be."

"I'm having a struggle with this," Marybeth said. "You're saying that the Sovereign Nation was made up by the FBI? That it doesn't even really exist?"

Nate said, "There are always nutcases out there on the fringes. But as an organized movement of bona fide extremists? Hell, no. The Sovereign Nation as a movement exists only in the heads of spooks in D.C. to label as their enemies. It's something they want to promote so they can go after people like Demo. People like me. We're their number one target because we used to be on the inside until we rejected them. They set up plots to suck us in. Then they point at us and call us domestic terrorists."

Joe was well aware how long certain forces within the government had targeted Nate Romanowski. He thought that had been settled years before, but apparently not.

At one time, Joe had rolled his eyes and scoffed when Nate spooled out conspiracy theories. Much like Geronimo did now.

But one by one, Nate's theories had played out. Joe no longer doubted him.

NATE HAD GONE on to recap the long conversation he'd had with Jason Demo at the campground. Joe had listened carefully even though he was troubled by the coercive nature of it, and knowing that nothing Nate had gotten out of Demo would stand a chance in court. Not that Nate cared about legalities.

"They targeted Demo for specific reasons," Nate had said. "They knew they had him by the short hairs. And they knew that a guy like Demo, with his beliefs and background, could get to me. Once they had him firmly in place, they could start recruiting others to make it seem more like a movement."

"You almost had me fooled," Geronimo had said to Nate. "I thought you were buying what he was selling."

"It's not like I didn't like some of what I was hearing," Nate replied. "Demo knew what buttons to push."

Geronimo moaned in mock pain.

"What about the Keystoners?" Marybeth asked. "What about Cade Molvar? Are they on board with this fake Sovereign Nation group?"

"Yes," Nate said, "to different degrees, from what I understand. Demo thinks more than half of the Keystoners are all in. But here's where things get interesting."

Nate leaned forward and lowered his voice. "Cade Molvar is playing both sides. He's the leader of the Keystoners *and* he's an FBI informant."

Joe and Marybeth exchanged glances at that.

"That's why he was meeting with Scott and Fetterman," Joe said. "We've got video of them at the Stockman's Bar."

"I would guess that at least half of the Keystoners are also on the payroll," Nate said. "The individuals might not know that the guy next to them is getting paid by the feds because they think it's only them. But that's how they operate. We've seen it before. They infiltrate a loose collection of losers and get them organized to some degree. Then they steer that group to do something illegal and outrageous so they can bust them in a big, high-profile takedown. Only later do we find out that most of these losers would never have done it in the first place."

"Is Sheriff Tibbs working with the feds?" Joe had asked. "If he is, it might explain why he's been slow-walking the two murder cases. Maybe he's been asked to sit on the sidelines until the feds can spring their trap?"

"It's not the sheriff," Nate said. "He's just lazy and counting the hours until he can retire with a full pension. The one we need to look out for is Buck Holmes. Demo described Holmes as a true believer in the Sovereign Nation cause. He probably didn't even need to get paid. And he might not even know who is *actually* behind it all. He probably thinks the Big Fish is a rich guy operating on his own."

At that point, Joe had sat back and rubbed his eyes. He was used to Nate and his penchant for spinning out a conspiracy theory in his own time and in his own way. It took Nate two hours to describe a two-hour movie. But he was getting anxious to hear the rest of the story.

"So who is it?" Joe asked. "Who is running the operation? It's not Fetterman or Scott—they just got here."

Nate shook his head. "No, those two are here for support."

"So who is it?" Joe asked again.

"You know him," Nate teased.

"Come on, Nate," Joe said impatiently.

"He drives a thirty-nine-foot Entegra Reatta RV," Nate said. "And he's parked in a Forest Service campground as we speak."

Joe had been shocked. "Jeremiah Sandburg? Sandburg is back? He's not even with the FBI anymore."

FBI Special Agent Jeremiah Sandburg had shown up in Saddlestring several years before as part of an investigation into the Sinaloa cartel and specifically a violent offshoot known as the Wolf Pack. Joe had encountered Sandburg and his partner and he'd found the two arrogant and unprofessional and definitely operating with an agenda of their own. Sandburg had tried to entice Joe to lie to him so he could arrest him on federal charges, but Joe had been ready for it and avoided the scheme.

Because of the actions of the two rogue agents, a solid game warden from the next district named Katelyn Hamm had been killed. Additionally, their interference had resulted in a massacre on the courthouse steps by two cartel gunmen. Sandburg's partner had been killed, and Sandburg had been seriously wounded.

The agent had blamed Nate for the debacle and the fact that their case had been blown out of the water. Sandburg had vowed to Nate that he'd get revenge. And now it appeared that he was fulfilling his pledge.

"He's part of the cabal," Nate said. "He's always been part of the cabal. Guys like him don't really quit or retire. And for him, this is personal.

"Who better to run an operation like this than an old retired guy who can barely walk?" Nate asked. "Sandburg is a voluntary cutout. If he somehow got caught, it would be harder than hell to connect him with the men who are still active and running things in D.C."

"And he's always had it out for you," Joe said to Nate.

"And you're a close second on his hit list," Nate said back.

"We have to stop him," Marybeth said, alarmed. "We have to stop them all."

"And we have to do it ourselves," Joe said with a grimace. "We can't count on local, state, or federal law enforcement. They're either involved with this scheme or they've been ordered to stand down."

"This is crazy as fuck," Geronimo said, draining a tumbler of Joe's best bourbon. "I don't know how I got myself into this. You people are nuts up here. What's going on is *insane*."

"You don't know the half of it yet," Nate said to Geronimo with a cruel smile. "Wait until you find out what they plan to do."

"When?" Geronimo asked, wide-eyed.

"In less than twenty-four hours," Nate said to him.

Marybeth gasped and placed her hand over her mouth. "Less than twenty-four hours?" she said. "The governor is going to officially kick off his reelection campaign at my library."

Nate turned to her and raised his eyebrows, indicating that she'd stumbled upon the answer to her own question.

"*No*," Marybeth said.

"Yes," Nate responded.

Joe went cold.

"What in the hell are you talking about?" Geronimo asked the table.

"They're going to kidnap or kill Governor Colter Allen and place the blame on the Sovereign Nation," Nate said. "They're counting on me to be with them."

He paused for a moment and let it sink in. "There was something Demo told me that struck a chord. He said it was almost as if the Big Fish just wanted as many warm bodies as he could get to join the Sovereign Nation—that the character or quality of the men didn't matter. That didn't make any sense to me until I realized what was going on here. The deep state wants to publicize a bunch of losers and they want to make sure my name is included."

Geronimo laughed so hard it shook the table. It was a crazy laugh, as if he had no other way to respond.

"They've been orchestrating it from the beginning," Nate said. "Now it's about to happen. This will help prove to everybody that organized right-wing extremists are out here threatening the country. It's a bonus added if I get swept up in it and go back to federal prison."

"But what if something goes wrong?" Geronimo asked. "What if your governor is hurt or killed? Or innocent people get caught up in the crossfire?"

"Oh well," Nate said. "That would be a small price to pay."

"Insane," Geronimo said again.

"We'll need your help and your special skills," Nate said to Geronimo. "Can I count on you?"

"Of course," Geronimo said with weary resignation. "It's me to the rescue. Again. How could I pass up a chance to get arrested or killed in a state I've spent all of three days in? And for reasons I don't yet understand?"

"Thank you," Nate said. He turned to Joe and Marybeth. "We need a plan. We've got to hit them hard and fast tomorrow before they have a chance to know that we're onto them. If we give them any time to coordinate, it's over."

Joe nodded. He explained why the first thing he needed to do in the morning was to visit the Marmot House.

CHAPTER TWENTY-THREE

T HE FIRST BIG wet snowflake of the approaching storm hit Joe's windshield with a smack and left a starburst of tiny droplets. A half minute later, several more self-immolated on the glass.

Joe leaned forward as he drove toward Saddlestring and looked up at the sky. Two massive black storm clouds punched up like fists over the top of the mountains to the north. They looked ominous and slow-moving and they were dense enough to darken the morning light by several degrees.

He was still vastly unnerved by how close he'd been to death back at the Marmot House, and his stomach roiled. The twin jolts from the Taser had turned his muscles into mush and he was slowly regaining control of his limbs. The sound of Nate's gun hung with him, as did the impact of Holmes's weight as the man fell on him. Joe entertained a wild notion for a moment that Holmes *had* pulled the trigger, and that everything that had happened since was imaginary.

He disabused himself of that notion when he glanced at his rearview mirror and saw Nate and Geronimo in Geronimo's SUV close behind him. He could see their faces clearly, and their expressions of seriousness both encouraged and scared him.

Both falconers stared forward with blank, stoic determination. Joe was familiar with the look from the falcons he'd observed on the hunt and from Nate himself. Nate and Geronimo were entering *yarak*—a deadly and all-consuming fugue state that would narrow their focus to the situation at hand and inevitably result in an explosion of violence. *Yarak* was unique to predatory raptors and the master falconers who lived and hunted with them.

Joe did a quick self-inventory of his own mental state. It would take time for the adrenaline surge and pure terror he'd felt to abate. His hands still trembled on the wheel of his truck, and his mouth was dry.

He'd need to get over it if he was to pull off his part of the plan.

Joe's shotgun was propped on the passenger seat beside him. He'd wiped snow off his .40 Glock and canister of bear spray that had been tossed away by Holmes and he'd returned both to their holsters on his belt. Over his uniform shirt and jacket he wore a tactical vest with GAME WARDEN stenciled across the back and over the right breast. The vest was lined with ceramic plates of body armor. The vest was stiff because the only time he had ever put it on was when the department had sent it to him the year before.

He kept the radio on but turned down low, and he'd not checked in with dispatch that morning. Joe didn't want anyone to know that he was in the field or what his exact location was, especially anyone from the Twelve Sleep County Sheriff's Department. The last time he'd tipped the sheriff as to his whereabouts and intentions, Buck Holmes had shown up to blow his head off. Joe knew he couldn't trust them.

Who else within the department aligned with the goals and beliefs of the Sovereign Nation, and therefore considered Joe to be an impediment?

He activated his phone and called Marybeth. He could tell from the background noise when he connected that she was in her minivan and on the move.

"Are you still sure you want to do this?" he asked her. "The situation just got a whole lot more complicated."

"Meaning what?" she asked.

"Buck Holmes showed up at the Marmot House this morning. He was going to take me out, but Nate and Geronimo saved my skin."

Marybeth gasped. "Are you all right?"

"Yup."

"Are you sure?"

"Yup," he lied. "I found the body of Professor Wei inside the outbuilding. That's where they hid him."

"*My God*. You were right."

"Buck confessed that he was involved. He was also involved with Leland's murder at the Marmot House. So you see why I'm asking whether or not you still want to do this," Joe said. "The whole situation has exploded. It's all got to go down even faster than we talked about last night."

"If we go back home now it might leave loose ends," Marybeth said. Then: "No, I'm sticking to the plan. Sheridan is right here with me and we're headed out of town into the national forest. We're going to carry on."

Joe heard his wife lower the phone and ask Sheridan, "We're still doing this, aren't we?"

And Sheridan replying, "You bet we are."

Joe took a deep breath. He was conflicted. He said, "Things might really get out of control. If they do I'm going to call you and ask you to abort. Will you at least agree to do that if I ask?"

Marybeth hesitated, then said, "Yes."

"Have you heard anything from Governor Allen's team? Will this storm screw up his schedule?"

"I talked to his campaign manager a few minutes ago and he's coming, come hell or high water," Marybeth said. "That's a quote. If need be, they'll land the state plane in Billings and drive down. But he's *not* going to cancel. According to his people, canceling would be bad optics. Allen wants to make his announcement in the heart of Rulon country."

Joe looked again at the black storm clouds. If the governor landed within the next hour, he might miss the brunt of the blizzard.

"Keep in touch," Joe said. "Text me your progress."

"I'll ask Sheridan to do that, since I'm driving," Marybeth said.

"Good. Stay safe. I love you both."

He said it knowing he'd already said goodbye to them earlier that morning.

JOE EXITED ONTO an emergency pullout on the northern outskirts of Saddlestring. Nate and Geronimo followed and parked next to Joe's pickup.

Nate's passenger window and Joe's driver's-side window whirled down at the same time.

Nate asked, "Any chatter on the radio about Buck Holmes?"

"Not yet," Joe said. "I'm thinking that he was operating on his own and the department doesn't know where he went this morning. They haven't put anything out on the radio, so I'm guessing they're not that alarmed."

"Allen?" Nate asked.

"He's still coming. I talked to Marybeth and they're moving. I asked her to reconsider, but of course she didn't."

"That sounds like her," Nate said. "So everything is still a go, then?"

"Yup."

Nate nodded, then turned to Geronimo at the wheel. "You ready?" he asked him.

"Ready as I'll ever be," Geronimo said. "Let's get this thing done so we can install that crypto miner and start *making some money.*"

Joe had forgotten about the minipod.

Nate said to Joe, "You won't hear from us until my part is done. I don't plan to even take my phone inside."

"Gotcha," Joe said.

A wave of fresh snow swept across the highway and engulfed them for half a minute. When it cleared, Joe said, "This storm is going to make things more difficult."

"Maybe. Or we can figure out how to use it to our advantage. People slow down during a big storm. They lose focus. But we can't," Nate concluded.

Joe agreed. He exchanged looks with both Nate and Geronimo, but didn't say anything more. There was nothing to be said. If everything worked the way they'd planned it, they'd see each other again soon. If it didn't, this was goodbye.

Nate's window rose. It was streaked with snowmelt from the last flurry.

Joe pushed the button on his armrest and his window closed as well.

Then Geronimo drove away with a brusque wave of his big hand. They were going to the southern end of Saddlestring, past the incorporated town limits.

Joe planned two stops. He checked his watch, then eased the transmission into gear.

CHAPTER TWENTY-FOUR

J ASON DEMO PACED in the front room of Cade Molvar's
log home in the rolling foothills south of Saddlestring.
The man lived on fifteen acres covered with sagebrush
and scrub. A thick wall of willows on the western property
line bordered a brackish tributary of the Twelve Sleep River.

As he paced, Demo kept his focus on the meadow between
the house and a hole in the wall of river cottonwoods to the
east. That's where the entrance road was located. It was the
only road to and from Molvar's compound, and a half-dozen
vehicles that had already arrived that morning were parked
haphazardly out front.

An untrammeled blanket of snow still covered the sagebrush of the meadow. The high-altitude sunshine since the
first spring storm had transformed the accumulation and had
melted it down into an ice quilt. Bony fingers of sagebrush
reached up through it in places. At the moment, swirling

clouds of large white flakes rolled through the trees and filtered down on the clearing. Demo wondered if this new storm would make it a perfect white sheet once again.

The house was large and shambling, two stories with four bedrooms, three baths, and a crudely finished basement entertainment room cluttered with sleeping bags and clothing from when Keystoners held all-night meetings. A built-in bookcase in the great room had no books in it, but the shelves were stocked with drugs, guns, and explosives. Remnants of Molvar's ex-wife remained in most of the rooms although she'd been gone for years, Demo noted. Prints of American Indian children with big eyes, doilies on the end tables, and tiles with vapid inspirational quotes spoke to her decorating tastes.

Molvar's home was the unofficial headquarters of the Keystoners and they'd assembled that morning to arm up, go over last-minute details, and start to change the political and cultural direction of the state of Wyoming and the Mountain West. At least, that's what Molvar had declared once everyone had arrived.

Now Cade Molvar came out of the kitchen and walked among the men with preternatural calm. He winced when he noticed how his visitors had tracked snow and mud all over the floor, but he said nothing about it. Molvar had a coffee mug in his right hand and he sipped from it as he moved throughout the room. He wore a shoulder holster over his thick flannel shirt and the grip of a semiauto jutted out from it. In Molvar's left hand was his cell phone, no doubt so he could be in constant communication with the Big Fish, who wasn't there.

ON MOLVAR'S HEELS was Ogden Driskill, who, to Demo, had never looked worse. Driskill was skittish and fidgety, and his eyes were pinpricks in shallow dark bowls. The man was on the run from the local cops and Molvar had offered him sanctuary.

Molvar strolled over next to Demo and stood shoulder to shoulder with him. Without looking over, he asked, "What's up with you?"

"Nothing's up," Demo answered.

"Watching you is like watching a fart on a hot skillet," Molvar said. "You're all nerves. I thought you'd been through this kind of high-intensity shit many times when you were a special operator."

Demo detected a note of sarcasm in the words *special operator*, but it wasn't blatant enough that Molvar could be called out on it.

"I have, many times," Demo said. "But I was with professionals. They had my back and I had theirs. We were all well trained and we knew our roles. We were brothers-in-arms."

Demo chinned toward a group of four men at a table under the kitchen window, then at Driskill. "I mean, *look* at these guys."

Driskill wheeled to stare at the four Keystoners in the

kitchen. He didn't seem to realize he had been included in the group of losers Demo had pointed out.

"I see warriors," Molvar said, challenging Demo. "What do you see?"

The four men at the table sat in chairs across from each other. They had a certain look about them, Demo thought, blue-collar gone to hell. They all wore beards of different lengths and brimmed trucker caps with logos on the front. They had rough hands and thick clothing, and they looked like what they were: out-of-work pipe fitters, welders, tool pushers. Men who were proficient with hand tools and firearms, men whose dignity had been taken from them and who filled their empty souls with weed, meth, alcohol, and resentment.

On the table between them were pistols, handcuffs, flashbang grenades, a tangle of holsters and tactical gear, walkie-talkies, and boxes of ammunition. The room smelled of Hoppe's gun oil and pungent marijuana smoke that clung to their clothing, even at fifteen feet away. Two of the men had just returned from smoking outside and their eyes were red and glassy.

Demo didn't know any of the four men well, and none of them had made any effort to get to know him, either. Molvar had never brought them to all-hands meetings with the Big Fish. Demo knew them by their handles rather than their actual names.

Adam "Ant" sat in one chair methodically loading a

thirty-round rifle magazine with gleaming .223 cartridges. He'd been one of the smokers.

Across the table from Ant was Brandon, known as "Weedy."

Daniel, "the Bear," was obviously high on something, and his glassy eyes looked like twin mirrors. He'd laced one of his two Sorel pack boots, but had apparently forgotten to complete that task with the other. His big fists hung down at his sides at the table.

Across from the Bear was Barry, known as "Buddy" the elf. Buddy's specialties, Demo had heard, were motorcycles and explosives.

"Look at them," Demo said to Molvar. "Do I really need to say more?"

Defensively, Molvar said, "They're lost and they're angry. But they've got motivation to do this. Men with nothing to lose are dangerous men.

"By the way," Molvar said, "Where is *your* guy? I see you keep looking out the window. Are you sure he's coming?"

"Oh, he's coming," Demo said. "He's good to his word."

Molvar snorted. "I don't know what it is with you and the Big Fish, why you want him with us so bad. You guys love this Romanowski character. I think he's all hype."

"He's not all hype."

"I just don't like it," Molvar said. "You keep complaining about my guys here, but at least they showed up. Romanowski doesn't know a thing about what we're going to do, or what our plan is. He could fuck everything up, if you ask me."

"Why isn't the Big Fish here?"

Molvar looked at him with scorn. "You know why. If the shit hits the fan, we need to go mobile fast. The Big Fish is not that. Plus, we need him to oversee the whole operation from the outside. He's gonna monitor police frequencies and social media posts so he can relay intel and let us know what's going on."

"Do we know anything about the governor's security detail?" Demo asked.

"*One* guy," Molvar said with a shake of his head. "He travels with one guy—an ex-trooper. We should be able to neutralize the cop pretty quick."

Demo took in a long breath, then said, "Are we sure Allen is the right target? I can't help thinking there are others out there who would be better. No one outside the state has ever even heard of Colter Allen. And those who have don't think of him as a wild-eyed libtard, like about ten other governors I can think of."

"I thought we discussed this," Molvar said with obvious irritation.

"We didn't discuss anything. The Big Fish gave us our assignment and we went with it. It's not like we had a big debate on our highest-value target."

"You must not have paid any attention," Molvar said. "The Big Fish explained everything very clearly. We have no shot at a high-ranking federal official, or an out-of-state politician. Those people have real security around them and we might never get close. This is our state, our backyard. We know what we're doing here.

"No, Allen is a good target," he continued. "He's a du-plicitous snake, even though he likes to pretend he's just an old stand-up rancher. Don't forget that he just stood there like a statue and let the feds screw us by shutting down our pipe-lines and our energy industry. Allen is the reason all of us are out of work. He could have done something.

"He's not a fighter," Molvar said. "He's got no balls or backbone. He sat on his ass as the feds bankrupted our state and put us all out on the street. He's a pussy and he deserves whatever he gets. This will send a message loud and clear to our betters in D.C., and that message is: *Stop fucking with us.*"

Demo looked away and sighed.

"What—are you getting cold feet?" Molvar asked.

"No, I'm in."

"Good," Molvar said. "Or else you'd wind up like Driskill's buddy."

"That dumb fuck," Driskill said. "Leland brought it on himself."

Molvar nodded his agreement.

"Who's that?" Driskill asked, pointing toward the living room window.

Demo looked over. The snowfall had increased in intensity in just the last few minutes and it had turned the wall of cot-tonwoods into a gray smudge in the distance.

Out of the smudge, a figure appeared. He was tall and he walked straight for Molvar's house. As he got closer, Demo could see it was Nate Romanowski.

"I told you he'd come through," Demo said.

"Lucky us," Molvar said. Then he narrowed his eyes and said to Demo: "Your job is to keep a close eye on him. Don't let him screw anything up. And if he does, shoot the son of a bitch on the spot. I'm holding you personally responsible for him."

CHAPTER TWENTY-FIVE

O N HIS WAY to Saddlestring and the Twelve Sleep County Building, while pewter-colored storm clouds drew a dark curtain across the face of the Bighorn Mountains, Joe's rearview mirrors lit up with a kaleidoscope of flashing lights. He glanced up and winced when he saw the grille of a Wyoming Highway Patrol cruiser closing in on his pickup with remarkable speed.

He groaned out loud and slammed the heel of his hand into the dashboard several times as the cruiser filled his mirrors and whooped its siren for him to pull over. Joe's stomach instantly knotted up and he checked his speed. He'd been going twenty-five miles an hour over the speed limit. He'd been caught.

Although Joe was law enforcement himself, he still got the familiar feeling of dread from his youth when he was being pulled over. Not that he was worried about the violation.

What he fretted about today was the possibility of a long delay.

Joe tapped on his brakes to indicate that he'd pull over, then he eased to the shoulder and parked snugly between two delineator posts. The cruiser stayed right on his tail as he did so.

He could only pray that the trooper would be reasonable. That wasn't always the case, and Joe had encountered too many patrolmen over the years who loved nothing more than hassling a game warden. Although they were both state employees, too many troopers thought game wardens had glamour jobs and that they spent their days fishing, hunting, and napping.

Joe looked into the mirror. He didn't instantly recognize the trooper, who was young, square-jawed, and clean-shaven. There was someone in the back of the cruiser Joe couldn't make out.

Why would a trooper with a prisoner in custody take the time to pull over a pickup for speeding? It didn't jibe, and Joe realized what kind of situation he could suddenly be in:

- There were two dead bodies at the Marmot House, and Joe had been the last person to be at that location;
- The Sovereign Nation group was arming up and about to deploy;
- Governor Allen's airplane was due to arrive within the hour;
- And Marybeth and Sheridan were en route to engage in a confrontation that could go horribly wrong.

Joe considered what the trooper would see when he approached his pickup and looked inside—a loaded shotgun within reach on the passenger seat and the .40 Glock on his hip.

Before Joe rolled down his window, he activated the dashcam and spun the lens ninety degrees to the left so that there would be video of his interaction with the trooper through the driver's-side window. Then he carefully placed his hands on the top of the steering wheel, where they could be seen clearly. He made himself still and vowed not to make any sudden moves.

He watched through the side mirror as the trooper turned in his seat to converse with his passenger. After an exchange, the trooper nodded and opened his door. The patrolman fitted his hat on his head as he approached Joe from the driver's side. Curiously, Joe noted, the trooper didn't place his hand on the grip of his weapon as he neared, which was protocol.

"Hello, Officer," Joe said through the open window. "I know I was speeding. I hope you can write me up for it and I can get on my way."

"Yes, you were speeding," the trooper said. "Are you Joe Pickett?"

"I am."

Joe turned his head and studied the trooper's face as the man filled his window. Now that he could see the man close-up, there was something vaguely familiar about him. Joe couldn't recall when he'd seen him before.

"I'm Aaron Holt," the trooper said as he held out his hand to Joe. "We met a few years back at the capitol.

"It's okay if you don't remember," Holt said. "You had a lot on your plate that day. I was a fly on the wall when you had your meeting with Governor Rulon and Governor Allen."

"Now I remember," Joe said. And he did. Holt had been in plainclothes at the time, and obviously providing security for the new governor. It was at that meeting in which Rulon had negotiated a deal on behalf of both Joe and Nate where the new governor agreed to drop the charges on both of them and set them free. It was either that, Rulon had said, or he would reveal information on the new governor that Allen never wanted to see the light of day. It had been a desperate win for Joe, all thanks to Rulon.

"My passenger would like a word with you if you have a minute," Holt said.

Joe narrowed his eyes. "Your passenger? I thought you had someone in custody."

Holt grinned at that. "I wish he was. If he was my prisoner, I wouldn't have to do everything he told me to do, like chase a game warden down the highway with my lights and siren on."

"Governor Rulon?" Joe asked.

"Who else?" Holt said.

JOE FOLLOWED HOLT back to the cruiser.

"Yeah," Holt said over his shoulder, "Allen busted me back to patrol after that meeting. I'm lucky he didn't fire me for knowing what I'd heard about him that day. But I don't mind going back into my uniform. They didn't cut my pay and I've got a family to feed."

"Is this going to take long?" Joe asked.

Holt shrugged, then opened the back door for Joe to slide in.

"Hello, Range Rider," Rulon said while extending his hand. "Have a seat in my office."

"Hello, Governor," Joe said. Holt closed the door and turned his back and leaned against the cruiser.

RULON LOOKED BETTER, Joe thought, than the last time he'd seen him. He was still ruddy and he'd lost a few pounds. He looked younger and healthier and he still oozed a particular kind of charisma that drew others to him, including Joe.

"There's a little-known provision in state regs that allows for ex-governors to request security from time to time," Rulon said. "I asked for Holt in particular. He's a good man, very loyal. But he's not a brownnoser, which is the kind of syco-phant Allen surrounds himself with. In fact, he reminds me of you, Joe."

"Thanks," Joe said. He knew his face was flushing.

As he always had, Rulon got straight to the point. "I was hoping to run into you today. I was searching for your number on my phone when I looked up and saw the green Game and Fish pickup go by. Providence, I'd say."

"What were you going to talk to me about?" Joe said.

"Allen is announcing his reelection campaign today in

Saddlestring," Rulon said. "I'm here to rain on his parade, and you're going to help me."

Joe winced. He had no idea what Rulon was talking about.

"He's scheduled to talk at your wife's library this afternoon," Rulon said. "I'm sure you know about that."

"I do."

"We can't let him run again," Rulon said. "He'll be even more of a disaster than he was in his first term. That's why I've got to be here to sink his boat before he even gets it launched. It's for the good of the state."

"You know I don't do politics," Joe said.

"I do, and I've always admired that about you, even when it drove me nuts at times. You can be so obtuse. But this isn't about politics or campaigns. This is about saving the state and maybe even the country from harm."

Rulon paused and leaned close to Joe. "Allen is in bed with some very bad people, Joe. They're rooting for a second term so they can wreak holy hell because he owes them so much."

"Do you mean Missy?"

Rulon threw back his head and laughed. "Oh, her, too. Your wonderful mother-in-law."

"So you're running again?" Joe asked.

"I will if I have to," Rulon said. "I'm not passionate about it, and I wish somebody else—somebody good—would step up and throw their hat into the ring. I don't care whether they're R or D—just someone honest and trustworthy who puts the people first. Allen doesn't, you know. He talks a good game and he says what his consultants tell him to say, but beneath the surface he's amoral. He's a malignant narcissist of the highest order.

"No, I'm not one of those politicians who has to be always running for something. I have a good life, a great law practice, and I don't have to put up with lobbyists or the stinking feds anymore. But this is too important."

"What are you referring to?" Joe asked.

"I don't have time to lay it all out for you right now," Rulon said. "But trust me on this. Allen will win if he runs because every Wyoming governor has won reelection in my lifetime. So we have to stop him now. I think he'll withdraw if I have a little chat with him."

Joe nodded, but he didn't understand.

"I need you to hold him in one place before his announcement," Rulon said. "I'll only need a few minutes with the son of a bitch. This is actually a favor to him, Joe. If I can talk with him before his announcement, he'll have the chance to do the right thing. If I can't visit with him beforehand, I'll have to publicly blow him out of the water *after* he speaks. That would be nasty and messy as hell for both of us."

"Hold him in place?"

"Hold him in place," Rulon said. "Now, go. Allen's plane will touch down very soon."

"I know," Joe said.

"I'm kind of surprised he's flying in this weather," Rulon said, looking over Joe's shoulder at the darkening sky. "Probably the bravest thing he's ever done."

"You're not going to tell me what's going on, are you?" Joe said.

"Not now," Rulon said. "No time. Just trust me on this. You trust me, don't you, Joe?"

As he asked, Rulon's eyebrows raised mischievously.

"Sure," Joe said.

"Good man," Rulon said, placing his hand on Joe's shoulder and pushing him toward the door. "I hope to say hello to your lovely wife later. You're a lucky man, Joe Pickett."

"I agree," Joe said. The door opened as he reached down for the handle. Holt ushered him out.

"I guess I've got my marching orders," Joe said to Holt as he put on his hat.

"Welcome to my world," Holt said. Then: "Stay under the speed limit on your way to town. The next trooper who picks you up might not be so friendly."

JOE PARKED IN the alleyway behind the county building rather than in the front lot. The back door led into the storeroom used by the sheriff's department, then into the department itself. By using that entrance, Joe could evade the lobby, the metal detector, and the front counter, where the receptionist might be under instructions to delay him or keep him out.

He used a key he'd been given years before and was supposed to have returned, but never did. When the door closed behind him, he was in complete darkness except for a single red light from a smoke detector on the ceiling. He ran his hand along the interior concrete-block wall until he located a light switch.

As the fluorescent bulbs hummed and blinked to life, Joe found himself standing among tall shelves packed with office supplies, storage boxes, and plastic containers filled with who-knows-what. He could hear stirring coming from the individuals in the department beyond the interior door to the room.

So he wouldn't alarm the occupants any more than necessary, Joe propped his shotgun in the corner of the storage room to retrieve later, then pushed his way into the central office.

Sheriff Tibbs, standing in the middle of the departmental lobby in full dress uniform, read aloud from a sheet of paper in his hand to Deputies Bass and Steck, who leaned casually against their cubicle walls on either side of him. He was obviously briefing them on the schedule for the day.

"At ten forty-five, the state plane will land at the airport—"

Tibbs didn't finish his sentence when he saw Joe, and he stood with his mouth agape. Then: "What in the hell are you doing here? And why did you come through our back door?"

Bass and Steck had followed Tibbs's gaze and turned to Joe. They were also clothed in their dress uniforms, which Joe had never seen before. Steck instinctively placed his right hand on the grip of his service weapon.

"No need for that," Joe said to Steck, who relaxed and dropped his hand to his side.

Joe said, "I'm glad I got here before you all left for the airport to meet the governor."

"Damn it," Tibbs said, "I asked you what you're doing here coming through an unauthorized entrance."

"About that," Joe said, looking directly at Tibbs, "I couldn't take the chance of getting further delayed. Since you won't take my calls, I needed to tell you this in person."

"You're not taking Joe's calls?" Steck asked Tibbs. "Why the hell not?"

Tibbs ignored the question. Instead, he asked Joe, "So what is it that's so damned important that you have to break into our department to tell us?"

"There's a plot to kidnap or kill Governor Allen and I need your help to stop it."

"What the fuck?" Bass asked, screwing up his face. "Here in town?"

"At the library," Joe said. "The local branch of the Sovereign Nation plans to do it, with a little help from the FBI."

"What is this bullshit?" Tibbs said to Joe. "You've really gone off the deep end this time."

"I know it sounds crazy," Joe said. "But we know it's happening. We've heard it straight from the mouth of someone directly involved."

"They're going to hit him at the library?" Steck asked.

"That's the plan unless we can stop it."

"How many people are we talking about?" Tibbs asked.

"A half-dozen, at least," Joe said. "That includes someone you're real familiar with."

"Who?" Tibbs asked.

"Think about it for a second," Joe said. "Who do you all know who's sympathetic to the Sovereign Nation around here?"

The three officers looked at each other for a moment.

"Cade Molvar?" Steck asked.

"Yes, Cade Molvar," Joe said. "But who else? Who closer?"

Tibbs's eyes hooded. "Buck," he said. "Buck's into that conspiracy crap."

Joe nodded. "And where is Buck today?"

"Nobody's heard from him," Tibbs said. "We've been trying to reach him all morning. He won't pick up on his phone or respond on the radio."

Joe nodded again. "He's part of it."

"Is that why he's not here?" Bass asked.

"Yup," Joe said.

"Do you have any proof of what you're saying?" Tibbs asked. "It sounds half-cocked to me."

Joe realized he'd painted himself into a dangerous corner. If he told them everything he knew about the whereabouts of Buck Holmes and what had happened that morning, it was very likely the officers would detain him on the spot, and they'd be right to do so.

"The Marmot House is where they planned everything," Joe said. "That place doesn't have cell service or radio reception."

"He's at the Marmot House?" Steck asked.

Joe nodded again. He hadn't lied, but he'd certainly with-held information.

"So what do we do now?" Bass asked Sheriff Tibbs.

Tibbs glowered at Joe, then looked down at the polished tops of his own boots. He seemed to have frozen while standing.

"Boss?" Steck asked Tibbs.

Nothing. Tibbs looked both pained and confused.

"You should all come with me to the airport," Joe said. "We need to keep the governor on his plane for his own safety. We can't let him go to the library."

"We were supposed to escort him there," Bass said. "That's why we're all dressed up."

"And you look very spiffy," Joe said. "But now you've got another objective: saving the governor's life."

"I like how that sounds," Bass said, puffing up his chest.

"I wish I liked the son of a bitch," Steck grumbled as he reached for his jacket on the back of his desk chair. Bass saw him and turned on his heel for his coat.

"*Hold it*," Tibbs said to them. "We have no way to verify that what he's telling us is true."

"You're right," Joe said. "You just have to trust me."

"C'mon, boss," Steck said. "It's Joe telling us. And since we were headed that way anyway . . ."

"Hold it, I said," Tibbs barked. Both of his deputies froze.

Joe thought he could read what was going on. Tibbs wasn't in on the plot, but he was gripped with a kind of bureaucratic inertia that prevented him from making a decision. Joe had seen it before firsthand, and it infuriated him. In a tense situation or standoff, law enforcement officers often had everything possible going for them—numbers, firepower, equipment, armor, communications, and training. What they didn't have in some of these kinds of crises was leadership. And Joe was seeing it in real time.

"Look," Joe said to Tibbs, "I know you're reluctant to believe me and take action. I get it. I've been a thorn in your side. But after you leave here and take your retirement, do you want your legacy to be that you were in command on the day that the governor of Wyoming was kidnapped or killed? Do you want that hanging over your head for the rest of your life?"

It was an appeal to his self-interest.

"Well, no," Tibbs said. Then he looked up and said to his deputies, "You two go to the airport, but it probably doesn't make strategic sense for all of us to be in one place if something really does go down. I'll stay here and monitor the situation."

He jabbed his finger at them. "When you get there, you need to be in communication with me and you need to follow my orders. Do not listen to anyone else. Not Joe Pickett. Not anybody else. Got that?"

"Got it, boss," Steck said as he pulled on his jacket. Then he looked at Joe and rolled his eyes.

"Got it, boss," Bass said as well.

"I'll meet you out front," Joe said to Bass and Steck. Then he strode toward the storeroom door for his shotgun. He could feel Tibbs's eyes burning holes in his back as he did so.

JOE LED THE three-vehicle convoy toward the edge of town, followed by Steck and Bass in their department SUVs. There was no need for lights or sirens because there were very few cars on the streets. Locals, Joe guessed, were already bunkered in their homes awaiting the blizzard that could hit at any minute. The only parking lot that was full was at the grocery store up on the hill. Residents were stocking up.

Deputy Steck called him on his cell phone. "I'm not using the radio because I don't want anyone hearing this," he said.

"Smart."

"I'm glad Tibbs stayed back."

"Me too."

"You know why he did that, don't you?"

Joe nodded. "This way, if everything doesn't go down exactly like I said, he comes out smelling like a rose."

"Exactly," Steck said. "He's not the only one counting the days until he's out of here."

"Gotcha."

"Buck doesn't surprise me," Steck said. "I've always thought he was a sneaky son of a bitch. Holier-than-thou, if you know what I mean. He seems like he's always hiding something."

So am I, Joe thought but didn't say.

Steck said, "So if what you say is true, what do we do once we alert the governor? We're gonna need serious backup if we go after the Sovereign Nation guys—or they come to us."

"Yup," Joe said. "It's handled."

"What do you mean, it's handled?" Steck asked.

"I *hope* it's handled. My buddy Nate Romanowski is with them now."

"Sweet Jesus," Steck said. "That guy scares me."

"He scares everyone."

"Where are you going?" Steck asked as Joe took a right off Main. "Aren't we going to the airport?"

"We've got to make a quick stop at the Holiday Inn first," Joe said. "I'll need your assistance. I'll brief you when we get there."

Joe checked to make sure Bass was still with them. He was.

"SO WHAT ARE we doing?" Bass asked as they walked quickly from the parking lot toward the front lobby doors of the hotel.

"Remember when I told you the Sovereign Nation was getting an assist from the FBI?" Joe said. "What I should have said was that we've got a couple of out-of-staters impersonating FBI agents. We've got to neutralize them now so they don't screw things up for us later."

"Are they armed?" Steck asked Joe.

"Yup. So be careful and smart. We don't want them drawing on us."

"Are we gonna bust their doors down?" Steck said.

"I've got a better idea."

Joe paused before entering the building and addressed both deputies. "They're going to claim they're feds," he said. "They might even have fake badges on them. Don't listen to a word they tell you."

Steck said to Bass, "Whatever you do, don't tell Tibbs what we're doing. He'll call us off."

Bass clapped his hands and exclaimed, "This is getting fun."

THE LONE FRONT desk clerk was an ex-con in his thirties with slicked-back blond hair, light green eyes, and a nose ring. Joe had arrested the man several years before for hunting wild turkeys out of season. When the clerk looked up and saw who was coming through the door, his eyes got big. Then he quickly turned his head toward the door behind the desk as if he were considering his escape.

"Feeling guilty about something?" Joe asked him.

"No, sir. I'm clean and sober now." Beads of sweat dotted his forehead.

"I'm sure you are," Joe said as he approached the counter and leaned across it. He laid his shotgun on the glass, eye level to the clerk. The deputies flanked him. "We need to know a couple of room numbers. The guests are Thomas J. Scott and a guy named Fetterman. I don't know his first name."

The clerk took a long breath. "I'm not supposed to—"

Joe didn't let him finish when he turned to Steck and said, "Deputy, arrest him for not cooperating."

Steck played along. He scowled at the clerk and started to reach for the handcuffs on his belt.

"Fetterman is in 321 and Scott is in 324," the clerk said in a rush.

"Don't worry," Joe said. "I'm not going to ask you for room keys. Just tell me if anyone else is staying on the floor."

"There were," the clerk said, "but they already checked out. There isn't much traffic here in April, you know."

Joe thanked him and turned for the elevator and pushed the button. Before the doors opened, he said to the clerk, "Don't call them before we get there and don't do anything if you hear an alarm. Okay?"

"Okay," the clerk replied. He was obviously relieved that Joe and the deputies were done with him.

"AN ALARM?" STECK said once the elevator doors closed and the car rose.

"We've got to get them to come out of their rooms at the same time," Joe said. "If we bust in on one guy the other might hear it and grab his gun. We don't want that situation. We want to take them cleanly with nobody getting hurt."

WHEN BASS WAS positioned next to room 321 on the hinge side of the door and Steck was at 324, Joe whispered, "Ready?"

Both officers had drawn their weapons and avoided passing in front of the peepholes in the room doors. Bass mouthed *Yes* and Steck nodded quickly and repeatedly like a bull rider in the chute saying, "Open the gate!"

Then Joe reached up and pulled the fire alarm on the wall next to the elevator.

The interior hall lights strobed rapidly and a shrill *whoop-whoop-whoop* alarm sounded so loudly it made Joe wince.

An equally loud recorded message kicked on.

"An emergency fire alarm has been activated throughout the building. At this time, all guests and employees are instructed to immediately go to the stairwells at the end of each hallway and proceed to the hotel lobby for further instructions. Do not pack up your personal items and do not use the elevators. Stay low and don't breathe in smoke. Remain calm. There is no reason for panic."

After a beat, the message began again.

Before it was over, the door to 324 opened and Special Agent Scott peered out with an annoyed expression on his face. He was dressed in a shirt, tie, and slacks and he was in his socks. His hair was still wet from the shower. His look of annoyance turned to surprise when he saw Joe raise his shotgun, and then to fear when the muzzle of Steck's weapon pressed into the flesh behind his ear.

"Facedown on the floor with your hands above your head," Steck shouted.

At that moment, Fetterman entered the hallway wearing only boxer briefs and black socks. Joe was reminded of a white whale.

When Fetterman saw Scott dropping to his knees with an armed deputy behind him, he sprang into action. He turned on his heel and his knees bent as if he intended to launch himself back into his room through the air. Bass blocked him and pointed his weapon at Fetterman from two feet away. The deputy was braced in a shooter's stance and he was pointing his gun at Fetterman's big forehead.

"On your knees," Bass hollered, his eyes crazy and wide. Joe could see Bass's finger whiten on the trigger. "Get on your fucking knees with your hands behind your fucking head."

Joe felt a bolt of terror shoot through him. "Tom, be cool," he yelled.

Fetterman groaned and lowered to his bare knees. He reluctantly raised his hands and placed them on the top of his long thinning hair.

"We're special agents of the FBI," Scott pleaded in fury. "You assholes don't have any idea what you're doing here."

"Yeah, right," Steck said with a sneer. "And I'm Buffalo Bill."

THEY LEFT THE two men in Scott's room, both handcuffed and sitting back-to-back on the floor with a roll of duct tape wrapped around their heads and covering their mouths. Joe located their phones and weapons and placed them in a hotel pillowcase to take with him.

Scott glared at him with pure hatred. Fetterman stared at the wall in front of him as if he were stunned by what had just happened.

Joe lifted the bag and said to the two furious agents, "Stay calm. You won't be tied up all that long. I'll get your things back to you eventually."

IN THE ELEVATOR on the way down, both Steck and Bass were giddy. They were proud of themselves and how they'd handled the situation, and they were thrilled they'd completed the takedown without any casualties. Joe was simply grateful.

"My guy looked like a fucking *hippo*," Bass laughed. "Did you see the size of him? He could have snapped me in two if he wanted."

"I thought you were gonna shoot him in the face," Steck giggled.

"I don't want this feeling to go away," Bass said, hugging himself. "When it does I want to inject it into my veins."

"Save some for me, brother," Steck said.

WHEN THEY STEPPED outside, Joe noted that the storm had raced down the face of the mountains and was marching toward Saddlestring from the northwest in a boiling wall of white. He also saw the outline of the governor's plane, a black dot against the storm clouds, as it descended through the sky.

"Good timing," he said.

On the way to their vehicles, Steck carefully inspected the wallet badge that he'd found in Scott's room.

"Damn, this looks authentic," he said. "I wonder where they got it made?"

Leaving that question unanswered, Joe said, "On to the airport."

CHAPTER TWENTY-SIX

NATE SHOOK THE snow off his coat and nodded his greetings at the men inside Cade Molvar's home as he entered. To a man, they glared at him without a word, except for Jason Demo, who looked away.

Don't act so guilty, Nate thought.

It was obvious that he wasn't welcome but that he was being tolerated.

Nate quickly sized up the situation. Four Keystoners sat at the kitchen table, one on each side. Demo and Molvar stood shoulder to shoulder in the middle of the room with Ogden Driskill hovering nearby. There were weapons everywhere—on the table, on the counters, on the bookshelves, in holsters and slings.

Then a surprise: Clay Hutmacher Jr. sauntered into the living area from the kitchen. He was also covered with snow and had obviously just arrived via the back door. He had an AR-15-style semiautomatic rifle with a thirty-round magazine slung over his shoulder.

The men at the table greeted him and he greeted them back. Clay Junior, Nate noted, was very familiar with the home and the people inside.

"You're Nate Romanowski," Clay Junior said with an embarrassed grin. "I've heard all about you from Sheridan, and you were at dinner the other night."

Nate pointedly didn't respond. Instead, he thought, *Eight men, five bullets in my revolver.*

"Are we still on?" Nate asked Molvar.

Molvar raised the cell phone in his hand and said, "I just talked with the Big Fish. Allen's plane is landing. We're still on."

"After we've got Allen, where are we going to take him?"

"The Marmot House," Molvar said with a wink to Ogden Driskill. "Then an old line shack up in the mountains."

"Unless he resists," Driskill said while drawing a finger across his throat.

"When do we move out?"

"I'll find out," Molvar said as he crossed the room into a bedroom and shut the door.

"Hey, Nate," Demo said, finally looking over. There was fear in his eyes.

"Hey," Nate said.

As he approached Clay Junior, Nate noticed that one of the Keystoners at the table, the one they called Buddy the Elf, had not taken his eyes off him since he'd arrived. Was the man suspicious of him? Did he know something?

Nate didn't engage Buddy, but he made sure he was aware of him in his peripheral vision. If the little man made a sudden move, Nate was prepared to wheel on him.

Clay Junior was taken aback when Nate approached him and bumped his chest with his own. It wasn't a friendly greeting, and Clay Junior reacted with surprise.

"*Get out*," Nate said in a whisper through clenched teeth. He spoke out of earshot of the others in the room.

"What?"

"Go home. Take your rifle and go home now. You're not supposed to be here."

Clay Junior frowned at Nate and shook his head. "This is something I believe in," he said.

"Then unbelieve it. Does Sheridan know?"

"Of course not. I told her about my new AR, but—"

"*Go*," Nate growled.

Apparently, something in Nate's eyes convinced Clay Junior to listen. Or maybe it was the mention of Sheridan. Either way, he took a step back.

"Don't make a show of leaving," Nate hissed. "Just walk out the door you came in. Leave like you're going outside to piss or something."

Clay Junior nodded. Nate watched him closely until he went outside through the back door. The boy looked dejected, Nate thought, which was fine with him.

OUTSIDE, FROM BEHIND a four-foot stack of split firewood on the side of the house, Geronimo watched in silence as the young man with the AR-15 emerged from the back door and walked slowly to his truck. He never even glanced in Geronimo's direction. He seemed consumed with his own thoughts.

The snow had moved in quickly. First, Geronimo could no longer see the outline of the mountains. Then it was the foothills. It was coming down so hard that all sounds had been hushed and the wall of trees to the east had become a gray brushstroke.

An inch of snow had already built up on the top of the firewood stack, and Geronimo could feel a cold finger of snowmelt inch down his spine from where it had dissolved on his face and neck.

He was no stranger to snow, having grown up in Detroit. Where he lived with Jacinda, in a beautiful home outside of Denver, they'd gone through some rough weather.

But the blizzards he'd experienced in his life were all from the inside looking out. He'd never sat outside while heavy, wet snow clung to his clothing and head. It was a ridiculous situation to find himself in, and he vowed to never let Nate forget about it. *Never.*

His triple-barrel shotgun was sheathed in a fat scabbard inside his long coat. He wanted to keep it dry and he didn't want to risk plugging up the muzzles with packed snow.

How long was he supposed to stay there? he'd asked Nate.

The response was "As long as it takes."

Geronimo knew that one of two things was about to happen. Either Nate would step outside and wave him in, or he'd never see the falconer alive again.

MOLVAR CAME OUT of the bedroom with a puzzled look on his face.

"He didn't pick up," he said. "Maybe this storm has fucked up our cell service."

That, Nate thought, *or he's thrown you all under the bus.*

"We don't need his okay," Buddy said. "We know what we're supposed to do and when we're supposed to do it. I say we get moving."

"Fucking right," Weedy said. "If we sit around here much longer we might get stuck trying to get out."

The rest all seemed to agree.

Nate observed Molvar closely, wondering what he'd decide to do. Was his plan to accompany the group into town and slip away before the fireworks, or to let himself be caught with them so he could be quietly released later? Was he in on it with Jeremiah Sandburg, or were both of them operating on separate tracks?

Driskill said, "Lock and load, gentlemen. Lock and load."

Molvar didn't object. To Nate, the man seemed to be swept up in the consensus. He probably couldn't stop it now if he tried.

Nate took a couple of slow side steps so that his back was

to the wall and all of the men in the room were in front of him. He reached into his parka and drew out his .454 Casull and held it at his side.

"Nobody's going anywhere," Nate said.

"*What?*" It was Buddy. He was incredulous. "I told you assholes we couldn't trust this guy."

Nate said, "I need all of you to disarm if you're carrying. Do it slowly. Then sit down in the middle of the floor. Don't any of you reprobates decide to play hero. If you do, all of you are going to die right here, right now."

As he spoke, Nate noticed that Demo had moved away from Molvar and Driskill. He hadn't yet showed his hand.

"Listen to what he says," Demo said. "You don't know him like I do."

"This is fucked up," Buddy said. "There's only *one* of him."

"There only needs to be one of me," Nate said.

Ant, Weedy, and the Bear all looked to Molvar for some kind of guidance. Molvar didn't offer any.

"Tell 'em," Nate said to Molvar. "Tell them how you've been working with the feds all along. Tell them how you were going to offer them up as cannon fodder."

Molvar stared lasers at Nate.

"Bullshit," Driskill said, shaking his head. "Cade wouldn't do something like that."

"The hell he wouldn't," Demo said.

Nate caught a sudden flash of movement beneath the table and Buddy jumped to his feet with a small silver semiauto pistol in his hand. His first shot was wild and it went into the floor as he inadvertently pulled the trigger while raising the gun to aim at Nate. The second shot was in the ceiling because Nate, in one smooth motion, had cocked his weapon, raised it, and blown half of Buddy's head off.

BOOM.

Buddy's lifeless body dropped out of view behind the table. The wall in back of him was painted with red.

The room erupted, with Keystoners grabbing at weapons, Molvar diving onto the floor, Demo darting into the spare bedroom, and Driskill hurling himself toward the kitchen.

Weedy stood up from the table with a .44 Bulldog revolver in hand and Nate blew his heart out.

BOOM.

With wild bloodshot eyes, Ant furiously worked the slide of a twelve-gauge shotgun. Nate's first shot clipped the top of his shoulder, but didn't knock him down. His second shot hit Ant between the eyes.

BOOM. BOOM.

The Bear upended the table and fled toward the back door with Driskill. He held his hands up as he ran as if they would ward off bullets. Nate couldn't get a clean shot at him.

Nate glanced down to see Molvar crawling away across the floor toward the open bedroom door.

"Freeze," Nate said, to no avail. He aimed at the back of Molvar's right knee.

BOOM.

The man screamed and writhed and rolled to his back. He reached for his shattered knee with both hands and howled.

"I said freeze," Nate said, ejecting the spent cartridges to the floor and quickly reloading.

OUTSIDE, GERONIMO SAW a fist-sized hole appear in the siding in the front of the house, accompanied by a muffled gunshot. He ducked behind the woodpile and yanked his shotgun out of its sheath.

Then another shot. And another. And another. And another. *Five*. Nate had emptied his gun.

When he peeked over the top of the woodpile, he saw the back door fly open and two men run out. Each had a pistol in his hand.

"Go, go, go," the skinny tweaker yelled to the huge man in front of him. As he did so, his eyes locked with Geronimo's and he snapped off two quick shots that sailed somewhere near the distant wall of trees.

Geronimo stood and swung his shotgun and unloaded two barrels. Both men flew backward into the snow as if kicked by a mule.

A movement flashed in his peripheral vision and he jerked the muzzle to his left and pulled the shotgun tight against his shoulder. He had one more shell before reloading . . .

Nate stood in the open back door, aiming his revolver at Geronimo with two hands. When he saw who it was, Geronimo lowered his shotgun. Nate did the same with his revolver.

They stood and stared at each other in the hushed silence

of the hard snowfall. It had all happened so fast. Multiple gunshots echoed in Geronimo's ears and he could feel his heart pounding in his chest.

"What the hell just happened?" Geronimo asked.

"Well, *that* didn't go exactly according to plan," Nate said.

CHAPTER TWENTY-SEVEN

AT THE SAME time, Jeremiah Sandburg piloted his behemoth RV out of the Forest Service campground and down the narrow access road. It was snowing so hard that his windshield wipers could barely keep up with it.

The access road was more of a tunnel, with high walls of plowed snow from the last storm bordering both sides. It was quickly filling in with new snow. He needed to proceed two miles through the trees and meadows to get to the county road, which was plowed, wider, more packed down. From there, he'd have clear sailing for the fourteen miles out of the mountains to the interstate highway.

Then he'd turn east on I-90 and just keep going.

On the passenger seat next to him was his phone. The screen showed four missed calls from Cade Molvar. Sandburg would discard the phone in pieces along his trek, which was eighteen hundred miles over twenty-eight hours to his home in Reston, Virginia.

IT WAS SUCH a whiteout, with the snow not only falling from the clouds but swirling like smoke from gusts of wind, that he had to concentrate on his driving and stay between the walls on the sides of the road. Twice, he'd wandered a few feet to either side and scraped against the hard-packed snow.

Getting to the county road would feel like a release, he thought. Just like getting out of this godforsaken county and state would feel like a release.

As he approached the mouth of the junction, there appeared to be something dark blocking it.

It was a minivan, and it was parked lengthwise across the road.

"Fuck," he said. "What a place to get stuck."

Then he noticed two figures, one on either side of the van. It was two women. The one on the right was a younger version of the woman on the left. Each brandished weapons.

The older woman had a shotgun, and she held it out away from her body so that he'd notice it. The younger woman worked the lever of a Winchester rifle while she glared at him.

Sandburg had a decision to make, and he made it.

He jammed the accelerator to the floor and the RV's mighty engine roared as the vehicle shot forward. His intent was to build up enough speed so that he could swerve off of the road and plow through the deep snow toward the county road. He hoped his momentum would carry him through until he burst free.

Sandburg wrenched the wheel to the right. A wave of snow flew up and covered the glass. He hoped he wouldn't collide with the back of the van, but there was nothing he could do about it because he couldn't see clearly. He wished he wasn't pulling the Bronco behind his RV because it acted as an anchor in deep snow.

Then the RV bogged down and lurched to a stop. He could feel and hear the tires spinning behind him. But instead of propelling him out of the deep snow, they dug the RV in farther and it listed slightly to the right.

He threw his elbow over his seat so he could see better out the back and he tried to reverse out of the quagmire. The wheels spun and threw twin plumes of snow along the side of the RV, but it didn't move. Instead, the big motor home sunk in deeper.

He cursed again and lurched for the weapon he kept in the console. He had guns stashed all over the RV. But as he did so he heard a tapping on the driver's-side window.

Sandburg looked over and saw the muzzle of the Winchester a half inch from the glass.

The younger woman mouthed something he couldn't hear.

He squared himself in the seat and powered down the window.

"You need to come with us," she said.

CHAPTER TWENTY-EIGHT

JOE, STECK, AND Bass arrived at the Saddlestring Municipal Airport just as the governor's plane taxied toward the terminal from the single runway. The state plane was one of two twin-engine Cessna Citation Encores. Although the new governor had dubbed it *Air Allen* and his name was painted on the tail, Joe still thought of the aircraft as *Rulon One.*

They swung into the circular drive and Joe left his pickup running while he jumped out and pushed through the double doors to the lobby. Rusty Rogers, who had been the single gate agent at the facility for as long as Joe could remember, looked up from where he sat behind the counter and quickly closed his laptop.

"No watching porn when the governor comes in," Joe said.

"It's not porn," Rogers sniffed. "It's a documentary about penguins."

"I need you to open the side gate," Joe said. "We're here to escort Governor Allen to the library."

"I wish you'd escort him across state lines and leave him there," Rogers said. Then: "Okay, okay."

Rogers triggered the motorized chain-link gate on the side of the building and Joe thanked him.

THE THREE VEHICLES pulled up next to the Cessna on the tarmac and Joe got out just as the door on the plane opened and a set of stairs unfolded to rest on the snow-covered asphalt. The pilot, in his white shirt and tie, filled the opening. He pulled on his jacket as he said, "It was pretty hairy flying over those mountains today."

"I bet it was," Joe said.

"But we made it."

"We're here for the governor."

"So I gathered," the pilot said.

The state plane held eleven passengers, but Joe could only see three people through the side windows: Governor Allen; his mother-in-law, Missy; and a state trooper in plainclothes. Both Allen and Missy looked annoyed to see him.

Before ascending the stairs, Joe turned to Bass and Steck.

"I need to talk to him alone," Joe said. "Would you guys please be kind enough to let the pilot and the governor's security guy sit in your vehicles and keep warm? And please, don't let anyone near this plane or let anyone else off of it."

Both deputies nodded. Steck pointed at the trooper inside the aircraft and grinned. "I know Anderson. We went to the academy together. He can stay with me."

Joe took the first few steps up into the plane before pausing. He turned around and said, "There's another car coming, so please let the passenger come inside."

"And who would that be?" Bass asked.

"Ex-governor Rulon."

"I always liked that guy," Steck said. "Some people said he was a little crazy, but maybe that's why I liked him. He's the only Dem I've ever voted for."

Joe nodded and climbed the rest of the steps. Warm air emanated from the open doorway and he ducked inside.

Allen and Missy sat at a Formica table covered with what looked like briefing papers or copies of Allen's announcement speech. Anderson sat in one of the plush leather passenger seats across from them. Missy's eyebrows were arched with scorn, as if daring Joe to say something stupid.

Allen demanded, "What in the hell is going on?"

Joe tipped his hat brim at Allen and said, "You're not going into town."

"Bullshit," Allen said, his face reddening. "In case you've forgotten, I'm the governor of this state and you work for me. I'll go wherever the hell I want."

"Nope," Joe said. He looked at both Trooper Anderson and the state pilot. The copilot still sat in the cockpit. "I'm here to make sure the governor stays on the plane. You guys can take a break if you want to."

"No," Allen bellowed to them. "All three of you will stay right here."

The pilot and Trooper Anderson looked at Allen and then to each other.

"We'll go up front," the pilot said. They shuffled into the cockpit and the trooper leaned against the open doorframe.

"This better be good," Allen said to Joe with menace.

"Joe has a way of ruining everything he touches," Missy said to Allen. "Including my daughter's career path. And now he's here to ruin something new."

Joe winked at her.

"Well?" the governor asked. "What are we waiting for?"

"A guest," Joe said. "Governor Rulon is on his way. He needs a word with you."

Allen's face blanched and his mouth went slack.

"What is it, Colter?" Missy asked him.

"I'm not going to stand for this," Allen sputtered. He shouted toward the front of the plane, "Start up the jet. We're leaving now."

To Joe, Allen said, "Get the hell off of my plane."

Joe shook his head. He'd been surprised by Allen's reaction, and hadn't expected the man to want to run. Whatever Rulon had on Allen must be powerful, Joe thought.

Joe bent over and peered out the window. Rulon's car was pulling through the gate near the terminal and was headed for the state plane. Allen saw it, too.

"Go," he shouted at the pilot. "Go."

The pilot glanced at Joe with a pained expression, then

turned in his seat and buckled his seat belt. The copilot did the same.

"I said, get off of my plane," Allen shouted at Joe. As he did, he pulled the front of his jacket open to reveal the butt of a holstered pistol. It was a threat.

Joe turned and leaned out the door. Then, instead of leaving, he drew his Glock and shot four rounds into the left engine before it could be powered up. For good measure, he shot it two more times.

The pilot looked over at him, his face aghast.

"Sorry about that," Joe said as he holstered the Glock.

"My God, Joe," Missy cried. "What have you done?"

Rulon's cruiser pulled alongside the aircraft and the man bounded out of it for the stairs.

"You've damaged a lot of state vehicles," Rulon said to Joe as he climbed the steps. "Is this the first time you've disabled a state plane?"

"Yup," Joe said. Then he stepped aside so Rulon could enter.

"Hello, Colter," Rulon said as he blew in. "It's been a while."

Allen's face was ashen. Missy looked to him for some kind of explanation, but Allen ignored her.

"This was always my favorite plane," Rulon said. "I always used to tell everyone that if I ever died in a fiery crash, it would be in the *other* Citation. I always felt safe in this one."

Rulon looked around at the interior. "Still the same," he said.

"Spencer, what do you want?" Allen asked. "I've got a schedule to keep."

"Oh, you're not keeping it," Rulon said as he rooted through cabinets near the bulkhead with familiarity.

"Wonderful, it's still here," Rulon said, pulling out a half-full bottle of Blanton's bourbon from where he'd hidden it years before behind a pile of personal flotation devices.

"Want a snort?" he asked Allen. "You might need one."

"I'll take one on the rocks with a splash," Missy said. She didn't see Allen shoot daggers at her, but Joe did.

Rulon grabbed two glasses from the pantry and made drinks, then he sat at the table across from Allen and Missy.

"Joe, would you please close the door?" Rulon asked. "It's getting cold in here."

Joe did as he was told.

"You're going to make an announcement today," Rulon said to Allen, "but it won't be the one you were prepared to make. Instead, you're going to let everyone know that you've chosen *not* to seek reelection."

"Colter, what's this about?" Missy asked him.

"I have no idea," Allen said. "He's bluffing. Rulon always was a blowhard."

Then to Rulon: "Are you going to run against me?"

"I haven't made up my mind," Rulon said. "I have to have long talks with my family and blah-blah-blah. But I wouldn't rule it out. You know that if I run, I'll win. And whether I do or not, the people of this state will turn against you once they hear what I have to say. You might even go to prison."

Rulon chuckled and took a sip of his bourbon. It was a signal for Joe.

"Governor," Joe said, "how long have you known about the plot against you that's not going to happen today?"

Joe saw Allen blink involuntarily. It was a tell. Then his expression went back to normal a half second later.

"A plot against me?"

"That's why you added Saddlestring to your list of stop-overs," Joe said. "I couldn't figure that out until now."

Rulon leaned across the table and wagged his finger. "This is your chance to come clean, Colter."

Allen took a deep breath and looked away. As he did, Joe moved to the table and reached across it, grabbing Allen's pistol before the governor could react.

"You won't be needing this," Joe said.

"Colter," Missy said harshly, "what in the hell is he talking about?"

When Allen didn't respond once again, Rulon said to her, "Colter is compromised. He's a puppet of the Chinese Communist Party. They've got him by the short hairs."

"*What?*" Missy said. She was clearly shocked. So was Joe.

"Who do you think has financed his campaign?" Rulon asked. "Who else would pay just about any amount to own an American governor? Especially one who oversees a state with vast mineral wealth and a whole lot of missiles in the ground?"

"You're insane," Allen said to Rulon.

"How do you know this?" Missy asked Rulon.

"I know it because before I left office, they came to me," Rulon said. "They sent a UW professor to my office to lay the groundwork. At first, their offer had to do with financing coal and oil projects that would benefit the economy of Wyoming because our own federal government cut us out in the name of climate change. I heard the guy out, and I almost agreed to do it. But something about him hit me wrong. He seemed particularly interested in what some of our entrepreneurs were doing with Bitcoin mining using natural gas. He said the technology behind it was interesting.

"Then I thought: Why was a professor authorized to speak on behalf of the Chinese government? The answer was clear. He was a fucking *spy*. So I threw him out on his ear."

Rulon continued. "I learned later at a national governor's association conference that the CCP is attempting to infiltrate any institution they can: universities, high-tech firms, aerospace companies, even local governments. The governor's office of a U.S. state would be quite a prize for them."

"The man who approached you," Joe asked Rulon, "was his name Professor Zhang Wei?"

"That's him," Rulon said. "I reported him and his offer to the FBI and from what I know nothing ever came of it. No surprise there. It seems the FBI has other priorities these days."

"Wei was murdered on the Double D Ranch," Joe said. "I think he was there to check out their minipod. He just happened to run into three bad locals who were stealing sheds from the ranch at the time. One or all of those guys confronted him and he wound up getting his head chewed up in the fan. They also took a couple of shots at me. We'll probably never find out who was directly responsible."

Rulon wheeled on Allen. "Wei and the CCP bided their time, didn't they? They waited until they had a governor in office who was desperate, didn't they? And you betrayed this state for their support."

Allen opened his mouth to speak, but no words came out. He clamped it shut again.

Joe reeled from the revelations, but it made sense when he thought about it. Steve-2 said he had dirt on Allen, but he hadn't revealed what it was at the time. No doubt the CEO of a high-tech social media firm had been the target of the CCP, just like Wyoming's governor.

"That's why you didn't want me to investigate, isn't it?" Joe said to Allen. "When you found out the victim's name, you panicked and tried to cover it up because a real investigation of the murder might eventually tie him to you."

"Bingo," Rulon said. Then to Allen, "I suspected the CCP owned you when you sat by and let the feds put our energy sector out of business without a fight. Who benefits from that? The people who make the batteries in China.

"Plus, I saw how much money you were spending on the campaign. I sure as hell knew no legitimate donor would give you that much. Not even Missy here."

Joe noticed that while Rulon spoke, Missy had inched away from Allen on the bench seat. Now she glared at the man with contempt.

Joe said to Rulon, "I'm still not getting it all. What does Wei have to do with the plot to kidnap or kill Allen? How does that connect?"

"It doesn't," Rulon said. "Right, Colter?"

Allen looked away.

"Even with the Chinese behind him," Rulon said, "Colter still wasn't certain the voters would be swayed in his direction. So when the rogue feds approached him about going after local lunatics in Wyoming, Colter saw his opportunity to round up some of his enemies and come out looking like a hero."

It took Joe a moment before he got it. When he did, he closed his eyes and took a deep breath.

"How did you figure this out?" Joe asked Rulon.

"Simple," Rulon said. "The same agents of the FBI came to me before I left office with a wild-eyed scheme to round up what they called 'DVEs,' or domestic violent extremists. It was a new classification they'd just come up with. They said they were trying to identify members of the Sovereign Nation in our state. We did our own due diligence and confirmed that the Sovereign Nation only existed in the twisted minds of bureaucrats in the fever swamp. So I told them to piss up a rope. Like the CCP, the same people waited for a more compliant governor."

Someone rapped on the door of the airplane.

"Who is it?" Joe asked the pilot, who was peering through his window outside.

"Two cars of people," the pilot said. "A couple of scary-looking dudes in one car and a pair of ladies in the other."

Joe bent down to see. A crowd had formed at the base of the stairs to the plane. It was snowing so hard that he could barely make everyone out. Nate and Geronimo stood on either side of Cade Molvar, who they propped up between them. Molvar appeared to be injured. Marybeth and Sheridan stood behind Jeremiah Sandburg and urged him up the stairs.

"The gang's all here," Joe said as he opened the door.

A FEW MINUTES later, Molvar and Sandburg sat in the two rear passenger seats next to Colter Allen's table. Both were disheveled and their clothing was wet with melting snow. Molvar grimaced and held a bloody right palm up against the side of his head. Sandburg glared straight ahead with obvious disdain for everyone who had crowded onto the plane.

Missy had now moved so far away from Colter Allen that she was about to slide off the bench, Joe noted. She had subtly moved closer to the accusers and away from the accused.

Joe asked Deputies Steck and Bass to alert Sheriff Tibbs to get the jail ready at the county building for three suspects.

"After they're in custody," Joe said, "you'll need to check out the Marmot House. There are three bodies up there: Professor Wei, Leland Christensen, and Buck Holmes."

"Sweet Jesus," Steck said.

"GOOD WORK," JOE said to Marybeth and Sheridan. "I'm proud of you." Sheridan beamed.

Then to Nate, "Are the plotters all in the wind?"

"Something like that," Nate said. Geronimo shook his head as if he still couldn't grasp it himself.

Joe felt his eyes go wide. *"All of them?"* he said.

"Except for Demo and Molvar here," Nate responded. "Demo's on his way back to his family in Montana."

Again, Joe said, *"All of the Keystoners?"*

"I let one of them get away before the fireworks started," Nate said. He turned to Sheridan. "We need to talk about your boyfriend."

Sheridan's mouth dropped. "Clay Junior was there?"

Nate nodded.

"My God," she said. "He never told me."

Nate said to Joe, "It took a little ear-twisting to get Molvar to talk."

"I see that."

Governor Rulon listened intently as Nate revealed what he'd learned from Molvar.

"The idea was for the Keystoners to storm the library when Allen was making his announcement," he said. "Then the gov here would whip out his pistol and order them to stand down. Molvar planned to throw down his weapons and give up, and urge his guys to do the same thing. Allen was going to keep them all covered and in one place until Fetterman and Scott showed up to take over and to arrest them all in front of the cameras."

Rulon clucked his tongue and chortled. He said, "Colter, did you think this act of bravery would make you more popular with the voters? Was that your intention? Did you think the voters would rally around you when they saw how tough you were?"

Allen stared at the top of the table.

"What a sad little man you are," Rulon said to him.

By then, Missy had gotten to her feet and had joined Marybeth and Sheridan.

"AND YOU," RULON said to Sandburg, "you were orchestrating it all from the comfort of your recreational vehicle. You should be ashamed of yourself. Your job is to catch and arrest bad guys—not create them. The Sovereign Nation is a myth, no matter how much cash you pay losers to join it."

Sandburg smirked and looked at his hands.

Rulon said, "When I reported Wei to the FBI back then, I'm sure it ended up on the desk of someone like you— someone who thought their own personal political agenda was much more important than something that happened out here. So rather than follow it up and possibly avoid the situation that we just saw happen here, the report went into some file and was never acted upon.

"You think that when this is all over, you'll just return to D.C. and hang out with your buddies, don't you?" Rulon said. "Because that's how it works these days, isn't it? You think that if you can round up enough DVEs that it will justify anything you do. Isn't that right, Agent Sandburg?"

Sandburg grinned and said, "I don't know what you're talking about. I'm retired now. I was touring the country in my RV and somehow got caught up in all of this."

"Tell that to Judge Hewitt," Rulon said. "But I doubt it'll get you very far."

For the first time, Sandburg looked concerned.

"That's right," Rulon said. "You're not going back to your beltway bubble. You're staying right here in Wyoming.

"No, you're guilty of too many crimes to count, Mr. Sandburg. Entrapment, conspiracy, fraud, inciting a riot—I'll prosecute you myself if need be. And you'll be spending quite a bit of time getting to know the layout of our state penitentiary in Rawlins."

Sandburg suddenly looked stricken. "You can't do that."

"Watch me. You'll be the only coastal elite in the prison population," Rulon said. "That'll make you feel real special."

SHERIFF TIBBS ARRIVED a few minutes later, and Joe watched him interact with his deputies on the snowy tarmac. His response to what they told him made Tibbs cover his face with his hands.

"Off you go to jail," Rulon said to Molvar and Sandburg. Then: "Colter, you stay here."

Allen was whipped. He looked warily at Rulon.

"We'll take my car to the library," Rulon said. "You can work on your statement on the way there. I'd suggest not lying, if you can manage that. Just explain that at this point in your life you feel that you can better serve the people of Wyoming from the private sector, instead of in the governor's office. Tell them you miss your cows and you want to be back with them. They'll understand.

"And if you don't do it right," Rulon said, "I'll be standing right there next to you, ready to jump up and recap everything we discussed on this airplane."

"If you don't," Missy hissed to Rulon, "*I will.*" Then, jabbing her finger at Allen: "You betrayed me, Colter."

Joe fought a grin from spreading across his face.

MISSY LEFT THE plane with her cell phone pressed to her ear. She didn't glance at anyone inside while she placed a call. And she didn't greet her granddaughter Sheridan.

"Bruno?" she said. "I need you in Saddlestring immediately. As in right now."

GOVERNORS ALLEN AND Rulon followed. Allen's shoulders slumped and he appeared to have gotten a decade older than when Joe first saw him sitting with Missy behind the Citation table.

Trooper Holt bounded out of his cruiser and opened the door for Allen, then did the same for Rulon. Rulon waved a curt goodbye to Joe, followed by a knowing wink.

WHILE TIBBS, STECK, and Bass led Molvar and Sandburg down the aircraft stairs to the waiting cruisers, Sheridan said, "Why don't we all fly to Aruba or the Bahamas right now and get away from this snow? I mean, when will we ever have another opportunity to take our own private jet?"

"I like it," Marybeth said, smiling at her daughter. "I've got some vacation time coming. We can go after the announcement is made at the library."

"I'm sure your staff can handle that without you," Geronimo said. "Let me call Jacinda. She'll get a kick out of this and the timing is great. She probably won't be able to travel yet with Pearl, but it's worth a shot."

"Folks?" the pilot said from the cockpit. He said it again until he had everyone's attention. Joe winced, knowing what was coming.

"We aren't flying anywhere," the pilot said. "Our left engine is shot up. We'll be on the ground until we can get it repaired."

Sheridan moaned, followed by Geronimo.

Nate placed his hand on Joe's shoulder. "It was you, wasn't it?"

"Yup."

"*Dad*," Sheridan said.

"Off to the Stockman's we go," Joe said as cheerily as he could. To the pilots and the security trooper left behind by Governor Allen, he said, "Come on along. I'm buying."

He linked arms with Marybeth and turned for the open door.

ACKNOWLEDGMENTS

THE AUTHOR WOULD like to thank the people who provided help, expertise, and information for this novel.

Hank Tanner of Automation Electronics in Casper shared his knowledge and design of Bitcoin minipods and how they work. Saratoga game warden Levi Wood provided background and insights to illegal shed hunters and their methods.

Special kudos to my first readers, Laurie Box, Molly Box, Becky Reif, and Roxanne Woods.

A tip of the hat to Molly Box and Prairie Sage Creative for cjbox.net, merchandise design, and social media assistance.

Congratulations to Doug Wick, Lucy Fisher, John Dowdle, Drew Dowdle, Michael Dorman, and Julianna Guill for bringing Joe and Marybeth to life on television.

It's a sincere pleasure to work with professionals at Putnam, including the legendary Neil Nyren, Mark Tavani, Ivan Held, Alexis Welby, Ashley McClay, and Katie Grinch.

And thanks once again to our agent and friend, Ann Rittenberg.

ABOUT THE AUTHOR

C.J. BOX is the author of over 30 novels including the Joe
Pickett series. He has won the Edgar, Anthony, Macavity,
Gumshoe and Barry Awards, as well as numerous other
US and international awards for literature. Two television
series based on his novels are in production (*Big Sky* on
ABC and Disney+ and *Joe Pickett* on Paramount+). He is
an Executive Producer for both series. He and his wife
Laurie live on their ranch in Wyoming.

Follow C.J. Box at cjbox.net